MYS
KIL

Gift

906 ✕

High Rhymes
AND
Misdemeanors

High Rhymes
AND
Misdemeanors

A Poetic Death Mystery

Diana Killian

POCKET BOOKS

New York   London   Toronto   Sydney   Singapore

An *Original* Publication of POCKET BOOKS

 POCKET BOOKS, a division of Simon & Schuster, Inc.
1230 Avenue of the Americas, New York, NY 10020

ISBN: 0-7394-3813-1

POCKET and colophon are registered trademarks of
Simon & Schuster, Inc.

Front cover illustration by Ben Perini

Printed in the U.S.A.

To Mom and Dad,
for supporting us in all our dreams.

High
Rhymes
AND
Misdemeanors

Prologue

*I*t was six o'clock in the evening. The thunder had retreated into the distance, but the rain continued to drum down on the roof in a ceaseless tattoo. Not the gentle April showers of home, this, but a dirty deluge that turned the narrow streets of Missolonghi to a stagnant swamp. A shutter banged in a gust of wind that whispered through the window casement and sent the candle on the writing table guttering. In its dying light the words written on the unfinished letter already seemed faded and old: *My Dearest Augusta* . . .

A small flat wooden box rested on the table beside the letter.

Outside in the hall, the servants were weeping. The man in the bed did not hear them. Sleep had turned to coma, easing the lines of pain and exhaustion on the chiseled face.

It was still a beautiful face, a famous face, though a

long way from home and those who knew him best. His chestnut curls were damp. Sweat beaded his cold, pale face. The feverish murmurs had stopped now. The sensitive sardonic mouth was silent. The brilliant, expressive eyes had closed for the last time.

In the streets below, the dogs began to howl.

The stream chattered merrily over the rocks, undeterred by the motionless form of the man lying facedown in the shallow water.

It seemed to Grace that she had been standing there for an eternity, not moving, not even breathing, trying to focus and telling herself it was a trick of the light.

But though the tall copper beeches cast long, sinister shadows, turning grass and water black, this was no illusion of the lingering English twilight. Nor was this a figment of her own active imagination. There really was a body lying in Grace Hollister's path.

As the realization slowly sank in, it seemed to Grace that all the world hushed and paused, waiting, waiting . . . Only the burble of the stream and Grace's own harsh breathing met her ears, and unexpectedly a feeling of light-headedness crept over her.

Impatiently she blinked back the weakness, forcing herself to focus on impersonal details. The body was male; a tall, graceful body ungracefully sprawled in the rocks and mud. It—he—wore Levis and a white shirt. His thick pale hair ruffled in the breeze revealing a sickening dark patch on the back of his skull.

Grace's stomach rose in protest. She recognized him; it was Mr. Fox, a fellow guest at the inn where Grace was staying. Only that evening Grace had observed him in the dining room—or rather, observed the two young waitresses observing him. Mr. Fox with his copy of *Punch*, and his odd, not quite handsome face.

The lax, long-fingered hands moved delicately, feeling nothing as the stream rippled through them. Beneath the water Grace could see the second hand of his watch still methodically ticking away.

Only seconds had passed since Grace came upon the scene in the woods; it took far longer to describe than live those unreal, intense moments before she stumbled forward, clutching at the inert, sodden mass, dragging the body back out of the water and stones and mud.

Though he was a tall man and a dead weight, and Grace was only a medium-sized woman in average shape, adrenaline gave her extra strength. She hauled with all her might; the body of Mr. Fox slithered forward, the stream releasing him with a squelch.

Grace rocked back on her haunches, landing in the mud. Panting, sweating, she crawled over to the drowned man, rolling him onto his back. His head lolled, face white and wet in the gloom.

He looked dead, no doubt about it. He wasn't breathing, and there was no telling how long he had been underwater. Grace hadn't spotted Mr. Fox during her twilight ramble through the woods; he could have been soaking there since dinner.

So much for my nice, restful vacation in jolly old England, Grace thought, ripping open the dripping shirt and pressing her ear to a broad and clammy chest. Sparse golden hair tickled her cheek. There was no sound beneath her ear. At least nothing Grace could hear over her own thundering pulse. She stared and stared but could detect no rise and fall of his chest.

Pushing away the thought that it was already too late, Grace tipped back Mr. Fox's heavy head. Face close to his, she listened intently.

Nothing.

Not a flicker.

Feeling the wet silk of his hair beneath her fingers, Grace stared down at the death mask of a face wiped clean of all intelligence, all emotion, all life. It was a strange face: high-boned and clever, a reckless slash of black brows, a wide, mocking mouth. It was a strange moment; Grace knew she would never forget it. Never forget Mr. Fox.

Accepting this, accepting that it was too late, still Grace went through the motions, pinching shut the man's nostrils, taking a deep breath and covering his slack mouth with her own.

As Grace exhaled strongly she felt a faint resistance. This was so different from practice with dummies in a noisy gymnasium.

Between snatches of air, Grace breathed forcefully into Mr. Fox's unresponsive lungs four times. Then she paused, feeling for the pulse in his throat with uncertain fingers.

It had grown too dark to see; dusk's slow retreat falling back beneath the night which swallowed the green woods and fells, the mountains and dales of the Lake District. Feverishly Grace labored under the black tracery of leaves blotting out the first faint stars.

Still nothing? Not even a twitch?

Grace shifted around on her knees. Mr. Fox was all long, strong bone and muscle, no excess flesh as she felt cautiously over his rib cage, brushing over a hard, flat abdomen, finding the place where ribs met breastbone.

To pick the wrong place meant risking injury to the ribs and chest wall. *Like it matters at this point,* a pessimistic little voice whispered in Grace's ear. She shrugged off the voice of doom. Surely a strong man like Mr. Fox wouldn't give up his life so easily.

She placed the heel of one hand on Mr. Fox's chest, the other hand on top. Locking elbows, Grace began compressing, at first tentatively, then more strongly. She counted, her voice sounding loud and fierce in the darkness.

"One and two and three and four and five."

How many minutes did it take before the effects of drowning were irreversible? She couldn't remember. It didn't matter. She had no idea how long Mr. Fox had been in the water.

Down and up, down and up. Finding her rhythm Grace leaned into Mr. Fox's body and relaxed. It was like squeezing a giant, sodden sponge. Grace worked over the body till her arms began to ache.

And then, just as she was giving up hope, Grace was startled to hear a great rattling cough. The corpse became a man again, suddenly giving up the stream water he had swallowed.

Grace had never heard a more beautiful sound.

Mr. Fox's chest heaved beneath her palms, and she heard him gulp in huge lungfuls of the night air. Amazed at herself, at what she had just accomplished, Grace rested on her heels, her teeth chattering with reaction while Mr. Fox coughed and spluttered and continued to catch at gusts of air like a landed fish.

It was like a miracle. Heck, it *was* a miracle. One minute he had been a drowned thing. Dead. Ended. Finished. And the next, he was alive. Grace hugged herself against the cold, offering a silent prayer of thanks to the distant stars above.

"What . . . happened . . . ?" Mr. Fox's rusty voice trailed uncertainly. He made an effort to push himself up.

Grace bent over him reassuringly. "It's all right. You're going to be fine. Just rest here. I'm going for help." She patted the long fingers that clutched weakly at her wrist.

"Wait—" Mr. Fox broke off to shiver convulsively.

Shock and the damp could undo all that she had fought for. Gently Grace freed herself, rising from her cramped position. "I'll be right back," she promised. "Just take it easy."

Picking her way blindly over the roots and grass, Grace at last found the path and started back to the inn. She walked as quickly as she dared over the uncertain terrain, back toward warmth and light and people.

But a few yards down the trail a feeling of alarm swept over Grace. It wasn't logical, it wasn't even something she could explain, but she plunged back the way she had come, feet pounding the dirt, dropping to her knees once more beside Mr. Fox.

Tentatively she touched him. He was still breathing; she wasn't sure if he was conscious or not. Grace chewed her lip, trying to decide what to do. Intently she listened. Nightfall pressed in on them from all sides.

It was too silent. There was the sound of the stream chuckling away, the sound of their own soft breathing, but nothing else. Not a cricket. Not a bird. Not a leaf stirring. To Grace's overwrought nerves it seemed like the night was listening.

It was silly. She tried to shake off her unease, but at a tiny crackling sound she felt the small hairs on the back of her neck rise. Something was out there.

Something stood in the trees beyond her range of vision, something that watched and waited.

Waited for what?

For Grace to leave.

But that was nonsense! While she sat here imagining things, Mr. Fox was probably catching pneumonia. She needed to go. Now.

Still, she waited.

So intensely did Grace listen to the sounds of the night that she nearly jumped out of her skin when Mr. Fox spoke.

"What is it?" he mumbled.

"Nothing. I . . ."

Mr. Fox's hand went to the back of his bloody head. "What happened?" he questioned again, more forcefully.

"You fell in the stream."

"Fell in the . . ." His voice dwindled away. "Like hell," he said suddenly.

In the gloom Grace could just make out his eyes blinking up at her. Irrelevantly she wondered what color they were.

Watching Mr. Fox slowly assessing the damage to himself, Grace wondered how a man who fell facedown in a stream managed to hit himself on the *back* of his head?

As this sinister discrepancy trickled through her brain Grace heard the hoot of an owl some distance away. Abruptly the night seemed alive with sound: crickets, frogs, rustlings in the undergrowth. She knew with certainty that whoever had watched and waited was now gone.

Probably a tramp, she told herself.

Mr. Fox made an effort to rise. He sank back. Grace slid a sturdy arm behind his shoulders. He leaned heavily into her and swore.

Her arms full of damp, long-limbed man, Grace experienced a confused rush of sensations. The body pressing into hers was all hard angles. He smelled of water and earth and something uniquely, cleanly male. His breath filtered through the loose cotton of her sweater, warming her skin. It was . . . sort of intimate in a weird way.

Mr. Fox reached behind, once more checking the back of his skull. He brought his hand away and stared at his blood-smeared fingers. Grace craned her neck trying to see. She knew head injuries bled a lot. The fact that he was alive and conscious had to be a plus.

"It probably looks worse than it is," she offered by way of comfort.

Mr. Fox muttered something unintelligible and likely unprintable, and peered into Grace's face, trying to focus.

"Do I know you?" Though gravelly, his voice was stronger. Grace thought that they should probably stop clinging to each other, but didn't like to withdraw support first.

"I'm staying at the Tinker's Dam, too."

"Are you?" He sounded vague, searching his memory. "The American girl with the hair?"

"Well," Grace admitted, "I'm American and I have hair."

At the moment Mr. Fox had his face pressed into her neck and the aforementioned hair. He was a heavy weight in Grace's arms and on her breasts as he continued to rest against her, apparently at ease. His complete lack of self-consciousness confirmed Grace's initial impression, which had been formed in the inn's dining room while observing the waitresses engaged in a Laurel and Hardy routine of sideswipes, narrow misses and dropped plates whilst trying to catch Mr. Fox's preoccupied gaze.

"That's an intriguing fragrance you're wearing," he mumbled after another spell.

"Eau de stream water."

Mr. Fox snorted, a sound that Grace recognized for a laugh. She felt his muscles bunch as he gathered himself to rise. Standing with him she watched suspiciously as he wavered and then steadied himself.

It seemed that he was going to walk away from what should have been his death scene. The man had incredible luck—stamina—or both.

On his feet and feeling in control of the situation once more, Mr. Fox offered Grace his hand.

"Miss—or is it Mrs.?"

Grace shook hands firmly. "Ms. Hollister. And I already know that you are Mr. Fox."

"Peter, please," Mr. Fox corrected. "I can hardly stand on ceremony with the lady who fished me out of the stream. My thanks, Miss Hollister."

Why the pointed "Miss," she wondered? What was he, some kind of throwback? And then, to Grace's amusement—and confirming her suspicions—he raised her hand and kissed it.

It was so smoothly done, so clearly practiced, that it should have been corny. Instead, the sensation of Peter's warm lips against her skin sent a frisson down Grace's spine.

She said feebly, "You're welcome, Peter."

He patted down his Levis, checking his wallet. "Nothing seems to be missing," he murmured, thumbing through the bills. "I don't suppose you saw who coshed me?"

At Grace's silence he glanced up attentively. "Did you see something?"

"N-no, not exactly." Grace was nonplussed at the way Peter instantly assumed he had been attacked. Was that the normal conclusion to draw? Apparently Peter could put two and two together faster than most.

He turned and started down the path. Grace followed. Their feet sounded dully on the hard-packed earth. After a moment Grace sucked in a deep breath and said, "There is something. Whoever hit you put your head under the water deliberately."

If she had expected protest, or even a reaction, Grace didn't get it. There was simply an unusually long pause before Mr. Fox said calmly, "Why should you say that?"

"If you had slipped—"

"I never slipped," he interrupted flatly.

That Grace could believe. Even now he moved with cat-footed confidence, although Grace suspected it took all his energy and concentration to do so.

"If you had slipped," Grace continued, "you would have put your hands out to catch yourself, but your arms were at your sides as though someone had dragged you over and left you there. Besides, if you had fallen forward you wouldn't have cut the *back* of your head."

"But why should someone want to murder me?" He sounded more interested than perturbed.

Murder. No mincing words with Mr. Fox.

"Is that question rhetorical?" Grace asked in her best professorial manner, trying to match Peter Fox's dispassionate tone.

"What's that supposed to mean?"

Grace shrugged. "You must know if you have enemies."

It seemed a strange conversation to be having, but then Grace's vacation had definitely take a strange turn from the moment she stumbled across Mr. Peter Fox bobbing for stream pebbles.

"Your Yank candor is so refreshing," Peter bit out. "Mind if we stop for a minute?" He dropped down on the grassy verge, resting his head on his folded arms. He took slow, deep breaths.

"Do you want me to run ahead and get help?" Grace hovered indecisively.

"No, I do not." The vehemence of this was lessened

by the fact that he had his head between his knees.
"Damn, damn, damn it to hell . . ."

Men, Grace thought sardonically. It didn't matter
how old they were—and she guessed Peter Fox was
somewhere in his late thirties—when it came to the
male ego they were all sensitive boys.

Patiently Grace waited while Mr. Fox continued
his deep breathing exercises. The night air tasted of
approaching autumn, wood smoke and the bite of
moldering fennel and mint. Grace kept her ears
pricked for anything out of the ordinary, but there
was nothing to hear but the chirp of crickets.

"What did you say your Christian name was?"
Peter asked, his voice muffled.

"Grace."

"Grace," he repeated. "Saving Grace in this case."
Even half fainting he had a flip way of speaking that
reminded Grace of those drawling rakes in the Regency novels to which she was secretly addicted. No
one really talked like that; probably not even Regency
rakes, but Peter was certainly lifelike in all other aspects. Grace could feel the heat of him emanating
through his wet clothing, and she could recall what
his hard male body had briefly felt like in her arms.

"My mouth tastes as though I'd been sucking the
bottom of the streambed." He wiped his hand over
his mouth and then pushed himself upright once
more with a less than fluid movement.

He walked on and Grace followed.

The narrow path gave way to a dirt road which

Peter and Grace followed across a humpback bridge, at last putting the woods safely behind them. Ahead stretched a meadow, colorless in the moonlight.

"What exactly were you doing out here by yourself?" Peter inquired, his voice sounding stronger.

"Walking. Enjoying the scenery." Through the trees Grace spied the lights of the Tinker's Dam. Laughter and voices carried across the meadow. Moonlight gleamed on the cars in the crowded car park. A weathered sign painted in fading colors portraying a skinny gray mare hitched to a gypsy caravan hung above a lighted doorway.

Peter had no comment to Grace's answer, and in silence they crossed the meadow and walked up to the inn.

"Do me a favor," Fox said, his hand on Grace's arm as she moved toward the entrance of the pub. "Have a drink with me."

"A drink?" Alcohol and concussion was a bad mix, she was thinking, but no doubt Peter Fox had been around enough to know that.

"Yes." He rubbed his solar plexus absently. "It's beginning to sink in that you . . . er . . . probably saved my life. The least I can do is stand you a drink."

"Oh well, that's not . . ." What was she saying? A goodlooking, intriguing man was asking her to have a drink. "I mean, happy to oblige, as you British say."

Peter Fox's wide mouth twitched humorously at this. He said only, "I'll run upstairs, have a wash and join you in a couple of minutes."

"Aren't you going to call the police?"

The slanted brows rose. "The police? No."

"But someone tried to kill you!"

"There's no point involving the police."

Grace realized she was gaping. She quit gaping and said, "And you Brits talk about Americans' blasé attitude toward crime!"

"My dear woman," Peter said patiently, "the police will simply think I slipped and then rolled over in a semiconscious state. Even if they believe your story, the tramp or juvenile delinquent who hit me has long since scarpered. What's the point then wasting the rest of our evening chatting with the local constabulary?"

"Aren't you at least going to have a doctor look at your head?"

Peter Fox smiled. His long, thin fingers caressed and yet seemed to warn as he pushed Grace toward the doorway.

"I'll be down in ten." As an afterthought he added, "Keep your eye on the door. I want to know who comes in after us."

Grace went inside the smoky, crowded pub. It was a comfortable room with dark wood paneling and mullion windows. There were hunting and fishing prints on the wall. The Tinker's Dam had been serving pints since before America was a colony. It was the kind of place Grace adored.

Squelching across the polished wood floor, she decided on a dash upstairs to change out of her muddy things. After all, her travels had not abounded with handsome, intriguing men inviting her for drinks; she might as well make the most of this.

It was quiet in her room; the genial hubbub of the bar was muffled beneath the thick floorboards. The old-fashioned lamp cast an amber light as Grace ran a brush through her hair and quickly dabbed her mouth with lipstick. Even as she made these cursory preparations she shook her head. She prided herself on being "serious-minded" (as Ms. Wintersmith, the principal at St. Anne's Academy for Girls, would put it). She was not a woman to get thrown into a flutter by a good-looking (and probably aware of it) man. She was not strictly on vacation, after all. Well, she was, but her vacation did have a higher purpose—and that higher purpose did not include meeting men. (Although, in her friend and traveling companion Monica's case, it had.)

Grace pulled on clean slacks and a fresh shirt. Refusing to reexamine her reflection—or her thoughts of Peter Fox—she headed downstairs to the taproom.

She ordered a lager and lime and sat down in a high-backed booth facing the door. Sipping her drink, Grace studied the room. Everyone in the pub looked as though they belonged—or at least, had been there all evening. A couple of men were playing darts by the fireplace. At an oak table a group of ruddy-faced men in tweed caps were discussing sheep. At another booth sat a younger group, hikers and rock climbers, laughing about the day's exploits.

If anyone was out of place, it was herself, the

eccentric American "professor" tracking down the haunts of long dead Romantic poets.

Peter Fox sat down on the bench across from Grace, startling her out of her speculations. He had showered and changed into a black turtleneck sweater and jeans faded almost white.

"What are you drinking?"

Now that she had a good look at him in the light, Grace was struck by the odd attractiveness of his face: elegant bones, thin yet sensual lips and heavy-lidded eyes of an arresting blue beneath the black V of his eyebrows. His hair, damp from the shower, fell across his forehead in straight golden strands. The contrast of blond hair and dark brows was unusual but not unappealing.

Realizing that Peter was waiting for her reply, Grace made a negative gesture. "I'm fine."

Peter headed for the bar with its gleaming brass fixtures and rosy-cheeked barmaid, who he immediately engaged in smiling banter.

Grace skeptically studied the neat white strip of adhesive behind his ear. Obviously the man was able to take care of himself. By rights he should be in a hospital bed, not chatting up giggling barmaids.

Peter returned to the booth with what looked like a strong one.

"Cheers." Touching his glass to Grace's, he took a long swallow, then leaned back. "So tell me all about yourself, Miss Grace Hollister from America. Where in America exactly? The West Coast?"

Grace nodded. She thought it was interesting that Peter did not ask whether anyone had entered the bar. He seemed prepared to forget all about his close call.

"There's not much to tell," she said slowly. "I'm thirty-three, single. I teach English literature at St. Anne's Academy for Girls. I'm working on my doctorate." She shrugged. "This is my first trip to Britain."

"Then this is a business trip?"

Grace grinned. "To be honest, I could do my research in the States but it wouldn't be nearly as interesting. Or as much fun."

"And what brings you to this particular neck of the woods?" Beneath hooded lids Peter's eyes were as intent as a cat scoping a mouse hole.

"The Romantics are my period. Wordsworth, Coleridge . . . so naturally I wanted to visit the Lake District." Actually it was Byron, Shelley, and Keats who fascinated Grace, but it sounded too unintellectual to confess a secret passion for the bad boys of poetry.

"Ah." Peter smiled enigmatically and quoted, "That blended holiness of earth and sky."

As Peter's rather husky voice unself-consciously quoted Wordsworth, a strange emotion fluttered through Grace. If he had quoted Shelley or Keats she probably would have fallen in love on the spot.

"That's it exactly," she said, leaning forward in her eagerness. "I've never been anywhere quite so . . . romantic. Even the names of the places are poetic: Windermere, Seathwaite, Derwent Water."

Peter smiled again and sipped his brandy. "You're traveling alone?"

"Yes. Well, not exactly. I came over with a friend of mine, Monica Gabbana. We both teach at St. Anne's. Monica was here years ago as an exchange student. Anyway, we were staying in Surrey when we ran into an old friend—actually, a college don of hers." Grace laughed and made a face. "You know what they say, two's company, three's a crowd? So I'm seeing the Lake District on my own."

"I take it the friendly old college don was male?"

"Yes. They realized they had some unfinished business."

" 'Unfinished business.' My God, what an American way of putting it."

"How would you put it?"

Peter smiled a slow, deliberate smile that was as seductive as a kiss.

Remembering the feel of his soft lips on her bare skin, Grace blinked.

"Anyway," she continued at random, dragging her eyes away from the peculiar pull of Peter's, "it's been a great trip so far. Yesterday I saw Dove Cottage, where Wordsworth lived for several years. He was so poor at the time he had to line the walls with newspaper to stay warm." She shook her head a little at the thought. "The garden is so lovely and the museum has one of the greatest collections of manuscripts, books and paintings relating to British Romanticism. But it's the cottage that I found amazing. It's just as it was in

Wordsworth's time. His spectacles are still lying there just waiting for him to walk in and slip them on."

"Yes?"

"And I saw Rydal Mount where he lived when he was poet laureate. Oh, and I saw St. Oswald's church-yard where he's buried."

"All the high spots, in fact."

No doubt it sounded pretty tame to Peter Fox. He did not look like the academic type. Who would have thought twenty-four hours ago, when Grace had finally resigned herself to spending the remainder of her vacation alone, that tonight she would be having drinks with a devastatingly attractive man who could quote the Romantic poets?

Peter drained his glass. "Ever tried something called a Gypsy Queen?" he queried.

"I don't think so."

"Let me see if they can make one up." He quirked one brow. "You look a bit like a gypsy with all that red gold hair and those sparkling earrings." He rose once more and made his way to the bar.

Grace contemplated her half-empty glass and tried to decide whether she was being seduced. Either way, things were definitely livening up. She was still smiling when Peter returned with their drinks.

"Something funny?"

"I don't know if it's particularly funny. I was just thinking what a strange evening this is turning into."

"Mmm." Peter nodded as Grace took a cautious sip. Her eyes widened. "How's the drink?" he inquired.

"Wow. What's in this thing?"

"Four parts vodka, one part Benedictine, a dash of orange bitters."

The door to the pub opened with a sudden gust of cold night air. Two men made their way through the room to a small table near the fireplace. Something told Grace they were strangers to this quiet agricultural community.

Watching Grace's face, Fox grew alert. "Who's just come in?" He continued to turn his glass in one tanned, well-shaped hand.

"Two men."

"Describe them."

Grace tried to study the pair without being obvious. "They're both . . . um . . . Caucasian. One's small, middle-aged. Kind of wizened looking. Bottlebrush mustache. The other's taller, younger. He's got a sad sort of face. Big mournful eyes."

From the way Fox's expressive brows drew together Grace gathered that none of this sounded familiar. "What are Mutt and Jeff doing?"

"Who?"

"Mutt and—" He cocked an eyebrow. "You sheltered academic types. It's an American comic strip from the 1920s."

"A little before my time, thank you very much." She peeked once more at the men across the room. "They're arguing, I think."

The smaller man spoke out of the side of his mouth in an aside to his partner who grew even more lugubrious.

Peter said with decision, "I'm going to the bar. Watch for their reaction."

Sliding out of the booth, Peter made his way yet again to the crowded bar. He was a tall man, a man with presence; people edged out of his way. Mutt and Jeff noticed him immediately.

Their reaction was instantaneous. Mutt knocked over his ashtray. His gnomish face puckered like a perturbed monkey's. He hissed a warning to his companion. Jeff, however, had already spotted Fox. He was staring, mouth ajar, eyes enormous.

Mutt muttered another something out of the corner of his mouth, tugging the bill of his tweed cap low. Jeff was already sidling out of his chair.

The door closed behind them just as Fox turned away from the bar.

"They've gone," Grace informed him as he set their drinks down on the polished tabletop.

"Yes. Cheers, Esmerelda." He touched his glass to hers.

"Queen of the Gypsies?" Grace bit back a laugh. Maybe it was the drinks but she felt as young and carefree as one of her own pupils. Adventurous. Not at all like the mature career woman she was. Suddenly she didn't care that Mr. Peter Fox was apparently trying to get her drunk. She didn't care that something fishy was going on. She didn't care that Peter Fox was not what he seemed . . . not that she had quite worked out what he seemed.

"Your hair is quite lovely," he informed her. "The

color of firelight." He seemed to be settling down to some routine flirtation. Grace was not so easily distracted.

"Do you know those men?"

"No."

"They know you."

"It does look that way."

"They were certainly surprised to see you alive and kicking."

"Were they?" The subject appeared to have lost interest for Peter.

Grace considered her companion. "So, Peter, what is it that you do?"

"That I *do?* I do a number of things." And all of them quite well, his tone implied.

"For a living." She somehow couldn't imagine him working a nine to five job; perhaps he was independently wealthy.

Peter said vaguely, "A little of this, a little of that." It wasn't so much that he seemed rude as preoccupied.

Surprising herself, Grace persisted. "You live around here?" She would have liked to ask whether he was married, but there really was no way of asking that without sounding personally interested in the response.

His restless gaze lit briefly on her own. "Yes." His eyes flickered. "No. That is, I live in South Cumbria."

"Oh, South Cumbria!" Grace was enthusiastic. "I was hoping to stop by the Abbots Reading Farm Museum, but I understand that's no longer open.

But there's still Levens Hall with its topiary garden. And Furness Abbey, of course."

"And the Laurel and Hardy museum."

She couldn't tell from his tone whether he was mocking her or not.

"And bookshops!" she exclaimed. "Lots and lots of lovely bookshops. I'm almost afraid to give in to the temptation."

He opened his mouth, seemed about to say something, then changed his mind.

"And it's not just the books and the writers," Grace went on, reaching for her glass once more. "The Lake District is famous for so many things. Um, Carr's Biscuits, Kendal Mint Cake, Grasmere gingerbread."

"Would you like me to order something to eat?" Peter offered. He glanced toward the bar.

Grace chuckled. "No, I had a wonderful dinner. People always say British food is so bland, but the beef is terrific!" She had another long draw on her Gypsy Queen. When she came up for air, Peter was eyeing her with that private amusement.

"Tasty stuff?" he suggested.

"Yes indeedy." Grace thought perhaps she had better slow down, and replaced her glass on the table.

"Besides your traveling companion, have you friends in this country?"

"No. I don't know anyone. Well, you. You and Monica."

"And you're staying how long?"

"Another . . ." Grace glanced at her watch. "Nine,

no eight days. School starts the fifth, but we, the staff, I mean, have got to be back early to prepare." This time she let herself drink from her glass.

Peter said lazily, "You know, the Chinese believe that when you save someone's life you ever after become responsible for it."

Grace choked on her drink.

2

$\mathcal{G}$race woke to the whisper of rain against windowpanes.

She spent several moments blinking up at the ceiling beams. Six hours and four Gypsy Queens later, she was lucky to be waking at all. Carefully she sat up, and was amazed to find the room stayed stationary. Her head throbbed, but moderately; nothing that a cup of tea and a bottle of aspirin couldn't fix.

A cautious turn toward her traveling alarm clock warned Grace that it was eight-thirty. She was to meet Peter for breakfast at nine. She tossed back the white comforter and climbed down from the four-poster bed, padding over to the dressing table.

"How's Esmerelda, Queen of the Gypsies, this morning?" she asked her reflection.

The reflected Esmerelda looked Grace up and down critically. Medium height, womanly contours;

Grace had the gift of so many American women: great skin and straight, white teeth. Her eyes were green and long lashed, but Grace considered her strong points to be her legs, which were long and shapely, and her hair, which was very long, auburn and naturally curly. Grace's hair was the envy of her tenth graders; her legs, the envy of her twelfth. Even old Esmerelda could not fault these.

Frowning, she tried to remember how the night before had ended. Toward the bottom of the fourth Gypsy Queen things had gone a little fuzzy. One thing stood out in her mind: Peter had not been trying to seduce her. He had been charming and attentive; he had bought her drinks and paid her compliments, but nothing in his manner had suggested he wanted to know her more intimately.

In fact, as ridiculous as it seemed in the gray light of morning, it seemed to Grace that Peter, if anything, had been trying to . . . well, pump her for information.

Good luck to him if that was the case, Grace reflected. Unless Peter was a rival scholar planning to refute her thesis, he would have found last night's conversation of little practical use. The more Grace drank, the more enthusiastically she had babbled about her dead poets, about literature and about the glories of the English countryside. Not that Peter hadn't egged her on. He had asked all the right questions and listened attentively to her answers. He had laughed in all the right places, and made Grace laugh (too much) as well. By the time they had said good night, Peter Fox knew all there was to know about Grace Hollister. Grace knew nothing about Peter Fox.

Grabbing her sponge, bath gel and towel, she stepped out into the hallway. She still found it strange sharing a bath with other guests. It brought back memories of college dorm life, though she had discovered English plumbing to be more eccentric than American.

The plumbing at the Tinker's Dam was no exception. Although the inn boasted a shower, a blast of scalding water drained away to a trickle. Muttering under her breath Grace fiddled with the knobs and was rewarded with a burst of ice-cold rain.

After the first shriek, she endured the cold wash, rinsing shampoo out of her hair as quickly as possible, teeth clenched.

A brisk towel down helped to restore circulation, and the cold water had taken care of her headache. Grace wriggled into coffee-colored jeans and an oversize cream sweater. Fastening her hair into a loose braid, she opened the door into the drafty hall.

At the far end of the hallway a room stood open. Grace could see that the bed was stripped. A maid was running a dust mop along the floorboards. The room was Peter Fox's.

Slowly, Grace walked down the corridor.

"Excuse me." And as the maid looked up inquiringly, "Has Mr. Fox checked out?"

"Yes, miss."

"But . . . when?"

The maid looked surprised. "This morning, I suppose."

"Do you know if he left any kind of message?"

"I couldn't say."

"We were supposed to have breakfast together."

The maid looked doubtful. "You could ask downstairs at the desk, miss."

But the word at the desk was no more reassuring.

"Left during the night," Mrs. Tompkins, the comfortable wife of the innkeeper, informed Grace. "Bit funny really. Just packed up and left."

"But his bill—"

"Oh, that's all right," the woman said easily. "He paid cash for the room."

"In advance?"

Mrs. Tompkins shrugged. "Some folks do."

Wild improbabilities flitted through Grace's mind: panicked flight, abduction, murder. Foul play, in short. But he paid for the room in advance, which probably meant he had planned to leave early anyway. She tried to remember whether they had made firm plans for breakfast or left it open. The shank of the evening was a little fuzzy. Still it was odd . . .

"Did Mr. Fox leave an address?"

"Oh, I don't know about that, miss."

In her best schoolmarm manner Grace said, "I *completely* understand, but Mr. Fox fell and hit his head last night. I just want to make sure that he's all right. It doesn't sound as if he is. You know, wandering off in the middle of the night. He might have a con-cussion or something."

"I'm sure it was nothing like that, miss." But Mrs. Tompkins' eyes slid uneasily toward the register book.

Grace tried to look as sincere and responsible as she knew how. The kind of woman parents entrusted with their impressionable daughters.

"We were supposed to have breakfast together," she offered.

Mrs. Tompkins wavered. "As to that, you wouldn't be the first lass stood up by a man," she pronounced. "Alls the same, I can't see what harm it would do. You two seemed cozy enough last evening." She dragged over the register book, heavy with years of guests, and ran a work-worn finger down the page.

"Here we are. Mr. P. Fox, Craddock House, Innis-dale Wood, Cumbria. Sounds familiar, that."

"Sounds like a relation of Peter Rabbit," muttered Grace, jotting down the address.

Stolidly, on cue, Mrs. Tompkins returned, "I wouldn't know about that, miss."

While Grace ate her breakfast of Irish oatmeal and boiled egg in a china cup she studied Peter Fox's ad-dress. Having got hold of this information, she asked herself, what am I going to do with it?

As Mrs. Tompkins had tactfully pointed out, it wasn't the first time in the history of man that one of them had skipped out on a date. If she could only be sure that they actually had made a plan to meet. Had the thing been left more casually than Grace remembered? There had been no need for Peter to suggest breakfast, let alone sneak off in the dead of night to avoid sharing it with Grace.

Last night had, thanks to the Gypsy Queens no doubt, a dreamlike remoteness, but Grace knew that she had not dreamed resuscitating Peter Fox. Someone—Mutt and Jeff?—had tried to kill him.

And sometime during the night Peter had disappeared.

Were the two things related?

Peter Fox might have disappeared for his own reasons. What those reasons might be, Grace couldn't imagine, but then she really knew nothing about Peter Fox. She didn't even know if he was married, although he didn't wear a ring.

She did know that he had not seemed at all worried or afraid yesterday evening. She deduced that since he had not wanted the police involved last night, he would not appreciate her going to them now with vague suspicions and rash conjecture. Grace suspected that even if Peter *had* been kidnapped he probably wouldn't want the police involved.

So that left two possibilities. Grace could either forget about Mr. P. Fox of Innisdale Wood, and continue her vacation, or she could try to reach him at home in West Cumbria.

Grace had still not made up her mind which course to follow when she checked out of the Tinker's

Dam and began driving once more. She found herself turning southwest, but she had wanted to see
this part of the Lake District in any case, although it
wasn't actually on her itinerary. Two and a half weeks
was not nearly long enough to spend, although Great
Britain had looked so small on the maps in Monica's
living room that she had truly believed they could
completely cover England and still have two days left
for Scotland.

The best-laid plans, Grace reflected as the green
fields and hedgerows of Kentmere fell behind in the
rainy mist. The hamlet nestled in a valley that had
once been under a lake. Decades earlier, the waters
had been drained away to provide valuable grazing
land. She passed herds of black-face sheep with curling horns and red markings on their shaggy coats.
She passed the inevitable cyclist, one or two hikers, a
few other cars.

The rented "mini" hugged the narrow winding
road as Grace drove, windshield wipers keeping time
to the Irish reels playing on the tape deck. Grace
concentrated on shifting gears with her left hand. It
had taken a while to get used to driving on the
"wrong" side of the road in the wrong side of the car,
but she had finally grown comfortable enough to appreciate the scenery as she steered.

Perhaps I could add an extra day or two in West
Cumbria and give up Scotland, she thought, as the
road sign advising the way to Hill Top, the farm once
belonging to children's author Beatrix Potter, flashed

by. The car seemed to be of the same thought, because they were certainly headed south, although Grace still told herself she hadn't made up her mind. Of course, were she to stick to her original plan, next on her agenda was Samuel Taylor Coleridge, but he had lived in Keswick, which lay to the north.

She comforted herself by the recollection that by the time Coleridge had moved to the Lake District, he was addicted to opium and his greatest poetical works lay behind him.

Aside from losing Monica to Love's Young Dream Revisited it had been a great holiday, and after all, she and Monica had spent the first week together visiting Kew Gardens on the outskirts of London, the Geffrye Museum, and Charles Dickens' house at 48 Doughty Street. Just as they had planned for the past fourteen months they had savored buttered crumpets and tea at the Maids of Honour, and tried out the sticky toffee pudding at Pophams. Best of all, on Saturday they had prowled the antique market at Portobello Road where Grace had picked up three etched glass apothecary bottles to keep bath salts in, and an eighteenth century tea chest made of rosewood and lined with green felt.

It was after this high point that they had hit Surrey, the literary southeast, where Monica had bumped literally into Professor Calum Bell who had once been her don at Oxford. After that Monica had not even shown interest in visiting Elizabeth Browning's childhood home in Herefordshire—shocking when one considered that the Victorians were her period.

Not only was it lonely, it was a little awkward because Monica was the one who knew her way around Britain. Grace missed not having anyone to share her adventures with, but she felt she was managing pretty well. If Monica had been with her yesterday she probably would not have taken that twilight stroll, and Peter Fox would be dead, and Grace would have missed an entertaining evening. So perhaps things were working out for the best.

After stopping for a quick lunch at Lakeside Pier on the southern end of Windermere, Grace resumed driving. Despite the leaden skies, traffic was heavy through this popular holiday resort. Visitors piled in to see the Steamboat Museum and The World of Beatrix Potter, one of the ten most popular tourist attractions in the entire country. Grace was not fond of tourist attractions. She longed to see the Lake District known only to the local residents, not the guidebook's recommendation for day-trippers and summer folk.

The silver water of England's largest natural lake was dotted by boats of all kinds, including old-fashioned steamers chugging out toward the Victorian-styled village of Bowness-on-Windermere. That famous stretch of water, coursing through densely wooded banks and secluded islands, still functioned as a public waterway, just as it had been used since the days of the Romans.

There were at least two used bookshops in Bowness that Grace would have liked to visit. There really wasn't a legitimate reason to be rushing along, ignoring breathtaking scenery and missing all these once-in-a-lifetime opportunities, and yet, Grace felt impelled to hurry.

It was nearing teatime when Grace spotted the van. Several miles back on the empty road, it gained quickly, the tires eating the miles between. As the van drew near it flashed its lights; the driver blasted his horn.

With drystone wall on one side and a steep embankment overlooking somber woods on the other, Grace had no choice but to step on the gas. Her speedometer climbed as the blue mini bounced along over the narrow, potholed road.

It had been a mistake to speed up. The van stayed right on her tail, lights flashing, horn blaring.

God help them if they met opposing traffic. The driver of the van had to be crazy, Grace thought, concentrating on keeping the mini under control. Up ahead it looked like there might be room to pull off where a dirt lane turned off into the woods.

The mini flew, rattling as it hit another missing chunk in the road. The van stuck to Grace's bumper like glue. As Grace risked a peek in her rearview she glimpsed what appeared to be an old woman crouched over the van steering wheel. The woman's long gray hair flew around wildly. Another lumpish figure sat beside her.

The van drew closer still, its black face filling the rear window of the mini. To Grace's angry amazement she felt a tremendous bang as the van rammed the bumper of the mini. It was not a hard hit but the mini swerved, its left fender screeching horrendously as it scraped along the stone wall to the accompaniment of whirling Irish fiddles.

Grace wrenched the car back on course, trying not to panic as the van loomed behind her once more. Once again the van slammed into the mini's bumper and she fought for control.

The turnoff lay just a few yards ahead.

Three yards.

Two yards.

Grace cut the wheel sharply and the mini spun out, gravel spraying beneath its tires. Very nearly turning over, the mini rocked back onto all four tires, managing to stay upright, and sat there, its engine running.

Shaking, Grace leaned over the wheel, fully expecting to see the black van go hurtling past in her side mirrors. Instead the van screeched up perpendicular to the mini, effectively blocking entrance to the road. The cab doors flew open and two men got out, striding to where Grace idled.

Shock held her speechless. For a moment she thought it might be Mutt and Jeff, but no, something about their height and builds didn't match up. One of the men was a little taller, one was a little broader. They were dressed in dark casual clothes, jeans and sweaters, and they wore wigs and Halloween masks: the taller man, a flop-eared hound dog; his stockier companion, a beaming caricature of the late Queen Mother.

The driver, the Queen Mother, reached the mini first, and yanked on the passenger door handle, which was fortunately locked. Belatedly Grace's survival instincts kicked into gear. She turned the key in the ignition, which was already running, causing an alarming grinding of the engine.

Fumbling, she found the unfamiliar shift and threw the car into reverse, dislodging the second man who was tugging on the handle of her door.

As the first man thumped hard on the windshield, Grace looked up. He was pointing an enormous black gun at her. The glass between them seemed like no barrier at all as he made a convincingly threatening gesture.

Grace didn't know what to do. In her entire life she had never faced a genuinely violent situation—barring the occasional brawl between the young ladies of St. Anne's. She had never held a real gun, let alone had one pointed at her. Staring wide-eyed, Grace tried to think with a brain that felt freeze-dried.

"Get out of the car!" The man on Grace's side pounded on her window. He wore black leather gloves, deadening the sound of blows heavy enough to break the glass.

Grace turned off the engine and the car shuddered to a stop. Numbly she felt for the seat belt release. She unlocked the door. What choice did she have? They could shoot the tires of her car and smash the window in. They could shoot her through the window for that matter. Even if she could get past the guns, she wasn't going anywhere with their van blocking the main road.

The man sporting the hound dog mask jerked open the car door and grabbed Grace's arm, dragging her out of the mini. Grace fell against the side of the car.

The other man, the one with the Queen Mother mask and the gun, came around the hood of the car. He said, his voice muffled through the mask, "Where is he?"

"Who?" Grace gasped.

"The fox."

"The w-what?"

The Queen Mother turned to the hound dog. "This is the right bird? You're sure?"

"It's her all right."

The Queen Mother slapped Grace hard, open palmed. Grace's head rocked back. She saw stars.

"Don't mess me about," he snarled.

"I'm n-not!" Tears of fright and fury sprang to Grace's eyes. Her teeth felt loose. She put her hand up to her jaw. One thing burned in her brain, she was not going to cry in front of these animals.

"Where's Fox?" the other man chimed in. "We know you're in it together."

"What are you talking about?" Grace cried. But her mind began to turn over. Not *the* fox, as in a four-footed woodland creature, but Fox, as in Peter. As in the man who didn't want police involved even after an attempt on his life. A man who disappeared in the middle of the night—apparently with good reason.

The guy in the dog mask began to rummage through Grace's purse in the front seat. The other man waved the gun before her nose. Behind the mask his pale eyes were cold and menacing.

Grace chattered out, "I don't know him. Last night was the first time I ever laid eyes on him. I don't know where he's gone. I don't know anything about him."

The man in her car turned his head, his mask askew and said, "I saw you kissing the life back into him last night."

"That was mouth-to-mouth resuscitation! I never saw him before," Grace insisted. "I'd have done the same for anyone."

"Why did you follow him out there if you didn't know him?"

"I didn't! I was out for a walk. I just found him in the stream."

The Queen Mother said slyly, "Teach you to mind your own business then, won't it?"

"She knows him all right," the dog mask interrupted triumphantly, holding aloft Grace's copy of *Walker's Britain*. "His address is scribbled here." He indicated the flyleaf where Grace had jotted down Peter Fox's address.

Both masks turned accusingly to Grace. She said helplessly, "I don't know him."

The Queen Mother uttered an ugly chuckle. "That's

your story, you stick to it. I suppose you don't know anything about gewgaws either?"

This can't be happening, Grace thought dizzily. *I'm dreaming.* The rain pattering on her face, bouncing off the cars, soaking the ground where they stood told her she wasn't.

"Nothing in here," the man in the car continued, rifling the contents of Grace's shoulder bag. He pulled out her passport. "Grace Hollister, thirty-three. She's American." He made a sound of contempt.

"Save the inventory," barked the Queen Mother. "Fox won't have left the stuff with her." He jerked his head toward the van. "Come ahead, we can't stand about all day. Someone's liable to come by." He reached out a massive, gloved fist, and Grace shrank back.

Grabbing Grace's braid, he hauled her face up to his plastic one. The Queen Mother's face smiled benignly, at odds with the threats issuing through the molded lips. "Listen up, ducks, you do what I tell you and maybe you won't get hurt."

"What do you need her for?" objected the hound dog.

Blue eyes shifted briefly from Grace's. "Use your loaf," he snarled. "We'll trade her for the gewgaws."

"Fox won't go for that."

"He'd better." The mask turned back to Grace. "For your sake."

"You're making a mistake," Grace got out desperately.

Neither man listened. The Queen Mother shoved Grace forward toward the van.

In less than a minute Grace found herself facedown on the grease-stained carpet in the back of the van. She could hear the mini's engine gunning as the van doors slammed shut. Rain rattled on the metal roof.

"Keep your head down," the Queen Mother ordered, settling in behind the steering wheel. "Try to see where we're going and I'll break your nose for you."

Grace believed him. She cradled her head on her arms as the van's engine roared into life. The van backed up sharply and she dug her fingers into the carpet, trying to keep from tumbling forward. A moment later tires skidded back onto the main road, and they hurtled down the highway.

For what felt like ages they drove, the van clattering alarmingly as they banged down on potholes. The driver did not speak, fiddling incessantly with the radio knobs, finally settling on a talk show.

As Grace's initial shock and fear wore off she was able to think rationally, and the first rational thought that occurred was that if her abductors bothered to wear masks and didn't want her to see where they were headed, then there was a good chance they did plan on letting her go.

On the other hand, if her rescue depended on Peter Fox's cooperation . . . ?

Grace could not imagine what her Good Samaritan stunt yesterday had involved her in, but apparently attempted murder was just the beginning. Pulling Peter Fox out of that stream just might have been the biggest mistake of Grace's life.

Would Peter Fox be willing to trade gewgaws for Grace? What were gewgaws exactly? Jewels? Or was it some modern slang for drugs?

Perhaps these two had attacked Peter last night, and not Mutt and Jeff. Could two separate sets of thugs be after the man? Just who was Peter Fox? What had he involved her in?

Fingers clenching the diesel-smelling carpet as the van fishtailed left and right, Grace no longer doubted the seriousness of that attack on Peter's life. *Had* he left the inn last night of his own free will? Maybe he was already dead.

Then again, maybe he was on the run. If so, how would he find out about Grace's plight? If Peter Fox did know Grace was in trouble, maybe he didn't care, especially if he were a crook, too.

The van finally left the main highway, bumping along a dirt track; Grace tried to keep straight which direction they were traveling in, but the smell of dust and exhaust fumes under the rear doors made her a little nauseous. She reminded herself that if she did survive she would need to know where to bring the police.

Grace could only rely on herself. Monica wouldn't worry if she didn't hear from her until Grace missed their flight. That was eight days—no, seven days now—away. By then Grace could be long dead.

With a suddenness that took her by surprise, the van lurched to a stop. How long had they traveled west? At least an hour. Motionless, Grace waited for the next development.

The driver turned around in his seat, commanding Grace to stay down. She obeyed, listening as he climbed out, hearing the crunching of his feet on gravel as he came around to the rear of the van.

The mini's engine whined as it parked behind the van.

The next instant the back doors of the van flew wide. Before Grace could sit up she was hauled out into the misting rain, and shoved against the bumper. All this pushing and pulling was beginning to make her mad, a healthy reaction to being victimized. She leaned against the van and glared at the two men in their silly masks.

"Look, you have got—"

"No, you look," the Queen Mum shot back. Twisting Grace's arm behind her back he swung her about so that she had a clear view of the abandoned farmhouse and outlying buildings. "Take a good look. What do you see?"

Despite the pain in her arm and shoulder, Grace looked. It was obvious the whitewashed buildings had not been inhabited for years. Weeds overgrew the vegetable garden and flowerbeds. The yew trees surrounding the house were wild and brambly. The house had a couple of broken windows and a tumbledown chimney. Slates were missing in patches from the roof.

There was not another house as far as the eye could see, nor even another road. Nothing but rainswept empty hills disappearing into gray mist.

"Nothing," she bit out.

"Too right," said the Queen Mum. "Nothing. No phone, no gas, no electric and *no body*. There isn't anyone to hear you scream, so scream your bloody head off. And there isn't anywhere to run, so don't get any bright ideas. You'll be wasting your time—and mine. And I don't like people who waste my time."

Together they trooped into the house. Uneasily Grace gazed about. Mildew stained the walls, cobwebs draped from light fixtures. The floor was beginning to rot.

Marched up a narrow flight of stairs, Grace found herself thrown into a room with multi-paned windows looking over the outlying sheds and lonely moors. In one corner of the room stood a cot; in the other, a metal bucket. That completed the furnishings.

The door locked behind Grace.

Picking herself up, Grace examined her prison more closely. In the dying light she could see faded wallpaper peeling from the walls in sheets. The wooden floor was thick with years of dust and dirt. Listening to the pinpricks of rain against the windows, Grace was nearly overcome with despair.

Angrily she pushed these feelings aside. Feeling sorry for herself would accomplish nothing. She had to start using her head. Going to the window, Grace stared out through the tangle of tree limbs. She felt round for the catch. It took her several minutes in the fading light to identify the old-fashioned latch. By the time she found it, Grace had also noticed bright shiny studs fastening the sill down.

Frustrated, she stood back and studied the window. It was made up of four panes of glass, each about two-by-two across. Voices drifted eerily up from downstairs. She traced their source back to the heating register on the floor. Kneeling down beside the fancy iron grid covering what must have once been the heating duct, she listened tensely.

"When will you be back?" It was the other man. The dog mask man. Grace's heart lifted. One less kidnapper improved her chances of escape fifty percent. And if she had to be left alone with one of them she preferred Man's Best Friend to the gun-toting Queen Mother.

The Queen Mother growled something that Grace couldn't pick up through the air shaft.

"What if he doesn't come through?"

"He will."

"Maybe she's telling the truth. Not much his usual style, is she?"

"They're all his style."

More that Grace couldn't hear. Then one of them, she thought the Queen Mother, snarled, "I'll bring something back. Don't be a bloody nit. One of us has to watch her. You might be recognized."

"Twenty years later? Not bloody likely."

Their voices faded. They must be walking out toward the cars.

Grace hopped up, swiftly crossing to the cot and grabbing the moldy mattress. She dragged it under the window. Wildly, she visualized shoving the mattress out and jumping after it, her fall cushioned by the rotting stuffing. A quick reality check stopped her. The branches against the windows were too close to throw anything down—even if she could stuff the mattress through the small frame, which was unlikely.

Wrapping the blanket in a great swath around her arm she returned to the window.

There would be noise. There was no way around that, Grace thought. Most of the glass would fall to the ground outside. But now, while they were on the other side of the house, while the rain drummed down on the roof and thundered on the gravel, now was her best opportunity. Taking a deep breath and turning her face away, Grace tapped lightly at the corner windowpane. Breaking windows did not come naturally to her. She feinted again, patting the pane with increasing force.

On the fourth blow the glass cracked across like a spider web. A few pieces fell tinkling to the mattress. Grace stopped, waiting rigidly.

She could hear nothing but the rain. Reaching with the blanket, she pulled loose the broken shards and tossed them to the ticking. When she had worked most of the glass free she wiped her thickly blanketed arm around the casement, making sure all the splinters were removed. Roughly, she dusted the sill.

Grace hastily gathered all the broken pieces of glass off the mattress and piled them in the corner behind the door. One of those shards would make a brutal weapon, though she couldn't imagine slicing at someone's face or throat, and that's what it would come down to if she tried to make a fight of it. Her only thought at the moment was escape.

She tiptoed over to the heating duct and listened. She could hear someone moving downstairs. No sound of alarm. No sound of anyone coming to check on her.

Grace went back to the window and stared out at the mist-shrouded fell. She felt rain against her face. It was oddly comforting, a taste of freedom. *Nightfall opens the door . . .* Who had written that?

It would be hours before it was actually dark, thanks to the lingering English twilight. She was afraid to chance an escape without the cover of night. But in a few hours the Queen Mother would also be back, and if she feared one of them more than the other, it was he.

Desperately Grace tried to think. Run or wait? If she blew this chance she would be unlikely to get another. Everything in her screamed to go now, but a flicker of caution—or maybe sheer fear—held her motionless.

At last, Grace lugged the mattress back to the cot.

The hours passed slowly. The room slid into complete darkness. Grace paced up and down to keep warm. It was cold, almost bitter, for summer.

She heard the stairs creak beneath heavy feet. The key in the lock had Grace's heart leaping in her mouth. There was no disguising the cold air gusting through the room from the broken window, nor the rain pooling on the floor, but in the darkness her jailer might not notice. Surely his attention would be on her.

Grace moved over to the cot, settling her back against the wall.

He stood in the doorway holding a kerosene lantern. The sight of the lugubrious dog mask in the flickering light had Grace biting her lip on a hysterical bubble of laughter. He began to back out of the room.

"I'm freezing up here," Grace chattered out between teeth clicking as much from nerves as cold. "Could I have my jacket? And a light?"

"You don't need a light. Go to sleep." He shut the door and relocked it.

Well, it had been worth a try.

A few minutes later the lock scraped, the door opened a crack, and her duffel jacket flew in like a wounded bird, landing on the floor. The man closed and relocked the door before Grace could stir.

Gratefully she shrugged on her jacket and huddled back into the blanket. She resettled on the mattress to wait.

The hours crawled by.

The rain slowed, stopped. The wind sent skeletal fingers clawing at the remaining panes of glass. The rain began again.

Grace heard the van's return across the echoing emptiness of the valley. Her heart began to slug against her ribs. Rising from the mattress she returned to her listening post by the heating duct.

Not long to wait before she could hear them moving below, their voices distorted by the sounds of rustling paper and the wind in the heating duct.

"What the hell do we do now?"

"—tomorrow—" That was the one with the gun. The Queen Mother.

The other man's voice rose nervously. "What if we can't? What if he's gone to earth? What does the man say?"

The scent of curry wafted up through the vent. Grace's stomach growled a hungry response so loudly she wondered the men downstairs didn't hear.

Her lunch at Lakeside Pier was a fond memory now. Grace fantasized about the rashers of thick bacon she had left untouched at breakfast. The voices downstairs droned on unintelligibly. Grace heard something about "Delon." Was that a person or a place? Obscenities seemed to have the best carrying power, she noted, and the two downstairs lavishly sprinkled their conversation with them.

"What do we do with the bird?"

As tensely as Grace listened she could not catch the reply to this. There was more undertone talk. The first man's voice rose and was cut off by the Queen Mum's stream of swearing.

"—ice Fox—"

Grace's blood ran cold. "Ice Fox?" She'd watched enough TV to know what that meant.

"You're off your bloody nut! I knew this would never work. If you cross him and—"

"Do you want to cross the man?"

Sharp silence followed.

The Queen Mother said scornfully, "You don't think big enough, that's your problem."

"You think we should go into business for ourselves?"

"I think—options open."

The voices faded out again.

After a while Grace gave up and returned to her nest on the mattress. An hour passed. She listened to the minutes tick by on her wristwatch as the house sank into uneasy slumber.

There had not been a sound from downstairs in ages. Nothing to indicate her captors were not sleeping. The first hours of sleep were the deepest. If she was going to make a try at escape it should be now. Now with darkness to cover her and the drumming of rain to deaden the sound.

Grace crossed to the window and stared down. It was about a twelve-foot drop. Far enough to break an ankle or leg, if not her neck.

In her navy duffel coat and jeans she made a suitably dark silhouette, but the bulky coat added too many inches to squeeze through the small window frame. Grace stripped off the coat, shoved it out into the tree branches where it dangled precariously and fell to the ground.

Agonizing seconds passed while Grace waited for signs of alarm. There was nothing. She decided to go ahead. She studied the window opening. Should she try head first or feet first?

A nosedive out the window did not appeal, but the other way she had no way of spotting a foothold. There was no sill as such on the outside of the window, and no screens.

Grace finally decided on headfirst. Squeezing her arms and shoulders out through the open window she groped for a branch strong enough to take her full weight. It was like trying to find an opening in a wall of brambles. Putting her eye out was a real possibility. Ducking her head Grace reached still farther till she found a limb that felt thicker than the others and grabbed on tight.

Now what?

Twigs poking her head, hair and shoulders already soaked, Grace pushed the rest of the way through the window. The branch she clung to dipped with her weight. Grace found herself in a vulnerable position, spread-eagled across the drop between tree and house.

Don't look down, she warned herself doggedly.

The tree limb sank and sprang back, and Grace had a vivid picture of herself bucked clear over the roof of the house. She bit her lip against a hysterical laugh, but all humor fled as the branch gave an alarming crack. Grace hoped to heaven the storm howling around the house would mask the sounds of her clumsy escape.

She pushed off from the windowsill with a silent prayer.

Clinging monkey-style, she shinnied toward the

tree trunk, shoving through the twigs catching at her hair and clothes. She balanced unsteadily on her wooden perch. Dead leaves and sticks rained to the ground.

Grace stared down. Light from the kitchen window pooled on the ground below. Stealthily she lowered herself to the next branch, twigs snarling her hair and pulling her sweater. When she was near the ground she half fell, half dropped out of the tree, landing on her haunches in the soft mud.

Grace picked herself up off her soggy behind and hustled into the duffel coat, fingers fumbling with cold and fright as she drew the hood down over her hair. She hoped with her head covered, the long line of the navy coat and her dark jeans would present only a shadow to any watcher.

Creeping to the window, Grace leaned against the stone wall, panting softly. Fear warred with the knowledge that if she could get her car keys, her chances of escape would be much better. On foot out in this wilderness what chance would she stand once her flight was discovered? She didn't even know what direction to run in.

Inch by inch Grace raised her head until she could peek over the windowsill. Her heart froze.

One of her captors sat at a table reading *The Sun*, and smoking. Facing the hall and the stairs leading to Grace's prison, his back was to the window where Grace stood, otherwise her escape would have ended then and there. He read on unperturbed.

Grace spotted a wig and rubber mask tossed carelessly amid the Indian take-out containers. She studied the square set of his shoulders. He had long dark hair in a ponytail with a thick gray streak down the back. Grace was sure she would recognize him by that distinguishing feature alone.

Her eyes darted around the room. Her suitcases were tossed carelessly in the corner. Everything had been dumped out and pawed through. She could see one of her little apothecary bottles smashed on the floor. The two Regency romances she had brought were sitting on the table next to the man's elbow. She did not see her purse or keys anywhere.

Perhaps they were still in her car? She weighed the risk of creeping round to the front of the house on the slim chance that her captors had conveniently left her keys in the ignition. What if the man in the house noticed she was gone? What if the Queen Mother returned? She could only too vividly picture herself caught in the headlights of the Queen Mother's van.

Grace turned from the window and picked her way on tiptoe through the overgrown vegetable patch. Behind a broken-down shed she located a footpath and ran, pushing through the bracken, heading for the hills.

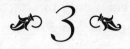

3

"*I*'m sorry, Miss Hollister, there's no answer."

"Can't you send someone out there?" Grace demanded, her fingers tightening on the mug of hot tea she held between both hands.

P.C. Kenton looked uncomfortable. "The thing of it is, miss," he began to explain, "Mr. Fox left word with the Innisdale police that he's away on business till next week. A buying trip of some sort. They've left a message on his machine. There's really no point in sending anyone over."

And you don't believe me anyway, Grace thought bitterly.

She had walked for hours in the rain last night, covering miles of lonely dirt track before a dairy truck had picked her up.

The driver clearly thought she was yet another demented Yankee tourist, and at the first village they had come to had been only too happy to hand Grace straight over to the police station.

The police, or P.C. Kenton as it turned out, had been shocked and sympathetic. He had energetically wasted several hours with Grace exploring the country's back roads (and getting lost several times) before finding the right deserted farmhouse. Grace's car had been parked out front, keys hanging in the ignition. Her packed suitcases were inside.

"My suitcases were in the house," Grace told the constable. "They put them here for some reason."

"For what reason, miss?"

Grace shook her head.

The house itself was locked. Inside there was no sign that anyone had been there except for footsteps in the layers of dust and some rice grains on the battered table in the kitchen.

"There will be glass from the broken window upstairs," Grace told the constable, reading the doubt on his face.

They trooped upstairs, and sure enough there was a small pile of glass glittering in the dust behind the bedroom door.

"There, you see!" Grace said triumphantly.

P.C. Kenton nodded. He seemed more uncomfortable than reassured.

"Shouldn't you at least take photos of the footprints?" Grace urged.

P.C. Kenton had obligingly taken photos, but it was clearly to humor Grace.

"It's not that I don't believe you, miss," P.C. Kenton added now, hastily, as though reading Grace's face. "It's plain as punch you've been through . . . well, *something*. But the thing of it is . . ."

"Yes, I know," Grace sighed. "I've got my car back and most of my belongings, and since there's no trace of anyone at the farm, and I wasn't actually harmed, why make a fuss?"

"I never said that," protested the constable. "Kidnapping's a serious offense. If this *was* a kidnapping and not a—a—?"

"A what?" inquired Grace. "A prank? They've taken my passport and my wallet. And my airline tickets." And two romance novels, but why confuse the issue?

P.C. Kenton suddenly brightened. "Perhaps they were terrorists, miss! Did they say anything to indicate they might be terrorists?"

Grace shook her head. "No. I'm sure they weren't terrorists."

"There are a lot of terrorists about these days."

"They weren't terrorists. They weren't pranksters either."

"Then you must see how it is, Miss Hollister. If they weren't amateurs and they weren't terrorists, then the lads who picked you up were pros. They didn't leave so much as a cigarette butt at that farmhouse. They'll have worn gloves, everyone does these days. You yourself said you'd only a glimpse of the back of one chap's head. I just don't see—we're not Scotland Yard, miss!"

Grace gave it up. It was no use asking a village constable to sort out attempted murder and "gew-gaws." The fact was, P.C. Kenton had his hands full with a missing cow and graffiti on a church wall. Grace thought grimly that it had never really been a plan on the part of the kidnappers to snatch her. The farmhouse room had been selected to imprison a man. A man whose wide shoulders would never squeeze though a box-sized window, and whose six-foot frame could never be supported by a half-dead tree. Perhaps, having lost Grace, her captors would return to their original plan of finding Peter Fox.

Of "icing" Peter Fox?

Grace set down the mug of tea and rose to her feet. "Thank you for all your help, P.C. Kenton," she said. "I think you're right. I think the best thing to do is put this out of my mind and get on with my vacation."

P.C. Kenton looked relieved. "That's the ticket, Miss Hollister. I'm sure those two scoundrels have re-alized their mistake. They know the police have their description. You won't be bothered again."

Right, thought Grace. The police will be looking for a giant dog and the Queen Mother. Why worry?

The message on the answering machine of Mon-ica's friend Calum informed all and sundry that the professor had gone to Scotland for the weekend.

"Monica, I could murder you myself," Grace mut-tered inside the red kiosk. She hung the phone up with a bang.

Now what? she wondered. Climbing back into the battered mini, she unfolded a road map, blearily studying it. She was not at her best and brightest this afternoon. She had blisters on her feet, scratches on her face. She looked like a bag lady. She felt like something a bag lady would turn up her nose at.

Surely her "responsibility" to Peter Fox (assuming she had any) ended once she had gone to the police? She had told P.C. Kenton everything she knew, which was not much, and P.C. Kenton informed the chief constable of the county. The matter was now in the hands of the local authorities.

P.C. Kenton believed Grace was the victim of an elaborate but random tourist mugging. He seemed sure Grace was leaping to all kinds of wild conclusions in connecting Peter Fox's accident to her own misadventure. And it did sound awfully far-fetched, Grace had to admit. She rested her forehead on the steering wheel and tried to think. She was so tired. She wanted to believe the constable. She wanted to believe it was all over. But she couldn't quite convince herself.

They had taken her passport and airline tickets. Why? So she couldn't leave the country? They had to know that she didn't have whatever it was they were looking for. Had they taken her tickets and passport for spite? Was this the reaction of the thwarted criminal mind? Grace sat up.

So now what? She couldn't get hold of Monica and she couldn't get hold of Peter Fox. The police told her she was perfectly safe, but unless she drove straight to London and grabbed the first available flight out of the country (which she could hardly do without her passport and airline tickets), Grace feared she might still be in jeopardy.

She smothered another tearing yawn that was half exhaustion, half nerves. What she wanted was a hot bath, a thick steak with all the trimmings, and twenty-four hours of undisturbed sleep.

P.C. Kenton had alternately believed Grace to be the victim of a prank—given the Guy Fawkes masks—the impulse mugging of a helpless tourist, or a terrorist attack.

"They were probably drunk, miss," he had offered by way of comfort, so maybe in the end he had believed Grace was the victim of crazed alcoholics.

But they had not been drunk and they had not mistaken Grace for anyone else. They had been dead serious, and Grace knew they were not going to give up so easily. With a sigh she put the key in the ignition and began driving once more.

It was late afternoon when Grace stopped in Innisdale, a storybook village of white cottages with slate roofs. Pots and window boxes bursting with Fall flowers decorated stoops and sills. Smoke from cozy hearths drifted into the darkling skies. Grace found the tourist information center without trouble. A two-story pink building with a giant one-armed clock facing the village square, the center shared cramped lodgings with the post office. Her inquiry brought the welcome news that her quest was nearly done. Craddock House lay less than ten miles away.

Grace got back in her car and crossed a stone bridge beneath which swans glided on peaceful water. Leaving the village behind, she drove on through a small, dark wood. Grace came upon Craddock House at the precise moment the sun drifted out from behind thunderclouds to bathe the glen in golden radiance.

For a moment Grace simply sat there blinking. It was the most beautiful house she had ever seen. From the road the ground level was half hidden behind trimmed hedges and banks of flowers, both cultivated and wild, a riot of color against the whitewashed walls and silver slate roof. Grace could count at least three chimneys and numerous diamond-paned windows. Behind the house hedges and shrubs gave way to more forest.

Grace parked well off the road under the low-hanging trees, got out of the mini and walked up the hillside path of flagstones. The afternoon smelled of wet grass and cool flowers. There was the bite of wood smoke in the air. As Grace drew near she realized the first floor of Craddock House had been given over to a shop. A long rectangular sign hung over the door. Gold script on black wood pronounced, "Rogue's Gallery." In a huge bow window pranced a full-sized merry-go-round charger, black mane flying, gilt hooves pawing.

An antique shop, Grace realized. She read the

placard in the window beneath the charger's hooves:
CLOSED.

What had she expected?

Automatically she tried the door handle. To her surprise the door swung open with a soft jingle of bells, as though it had not been latched properly.

Grace stepped inside the shop, looking about herself uneasily. She was a law-abiding woman, and breaking and entering was not part of her makeup.

The room was an antique lover's dream. A book lover's dream. Directly over the shop the entire second story was paneled in towering bookshelves, accessible only from the narrow landing. A staircase led up to the second floor; a doorway on the landing led into what must be Peter Fox's living quarters.

Grace's eye fell on a fan-shaped display of war axes and pikes hanging above the staircase. One set of hooks was conspicuously bare; a recent sale perhaps.

The room felt cold and smelt of old books. Grace absently chaffed her arms as she stared about herself. There was no sign of anyone. The room, the building, felt empty. She glanced up. A ship's figurehead hung suspended from the high vault ceiling, a full-breasted mermaid in dark wood appeared to be diving down into the room.

Grace tried to connect all this with what she knew of Peter Fox. An antique dealer? Somehow that didn't seem to fit, and yet this hodgepodge of collectibles and curiosities did.

There were Chippendale and Prince of Wales chairs,

a muffin stand supporting a large Egyptian resin cat. On the wall by the bay window were several Japanese kabuki masks. Directly across hung a very old map in muted tints, beautiful and highly inaccurate, Grace thought with a mental smile.

Her eyes fell on a squat oak dresser supporting a variety of Staffordshire pottery in blues, reds, and browns; four sixth century Grecian urns, and two grinning skulls. *Memento Mori.* Grace shivered and walked toward the counter at the back of the shop.

"Hello?" she called. "Anyone here?"

Her voice sounded loud in the vintage silence. For some reason Grace began to feel anxious. Although the shop seemed empty, there was something peculiar . . .

She turned, starting up the stairs to the doorway on the second landing. The stairs creaked and Grace glanced over her shoulder half expecting to see some shadowy figure detach itself from the corners of the showroom below.

Reaching the top landing, she tried the door. This, too, opened. The man was clearly uninterested in security, she decided.

For what felt like a long time Grace simply stood on the threshold, weighing her options. And then she walked into an airy whitewashed room with high ceilings, dark, open beams and bare wood floors. It was an elegant room but at the same time a masculine room. The furniture was comfortable and old, dark woods and red leather. With unabashed curiosity she gazed about herself. There was a glass-topped curio case serving as a coffee table. A huge moon-faced grandfather clock stood against one wall. A mounted telescope aimed out of white-framed Georgian windows at the road and wood-line beyond. Books were everywhere: on shelves, on the polished floors, on a seven-foot tall chinoiserie cabinet. A pair of Wellington boots stood beside the door.

Grace's brows rose. "Hel-low?" she called, but more softly. Although she was here on a mission, in Peter Fox's private rooms Grace was unhappily conscious of being an intruder.

She walked quickly through the rest of the flat, a couple of bedrooms, a bath, laundry room, pantry and kitchen. The kitchen, like all the rooms, was large and airy. Gleaming kettles hung from above. Scrubbed pine table and chairs were ensconced in a cozy nook overlooking the rose garden below. Oak-leaf china shone from behind glass-fronted cupboards. An answering machine sat on the counter, blinking away in the tidy quiet.

After a hesitation Grace pressed playback.

"Peter, you *naughty* man," trilled one of those imperious feminine voices. "What do you mean leaving town without a *bye*-word? You never said about the Huxleys on Wednesday, darling. Call me!"

"Peter," breathed the next voice in what Grace supposed were dulcet tones, "you *are* an angel. Thank you so much. I'll be wearing it Wednesday at the Huxleys'." This was followed by kissing sounds.

"Double booking," Grace muttered. "No wonder he thought he'd better skip town."

These calls were followed by several business calls regarding pieces other dealers thought Peter might be interested in, and buyers asking him to scout around for various things. It certainly sounded legitimate.

Next up, the first woman's voice, now petulant. "Peter, *darling*, I know you're there! The lights are on. Are you avoiding me?"

When had this been, Grace wondered? Had Peter possibly returned home and left again?

Two hang-up calls followed, then a voice Grace recognized and which sent chills down her spine. "Nobody home? Pity. I've got an item you'll be interested in, Fox. An American export. I'll be in touch."

Then, another message: "Don't mess me about, Fox. I'm not a patient man. Ask your mate Delon. The item for exchange has an expiration date."

The hair on the back of Grace's neck stood up.

There was one more hang-up call before a new voice came on, ponderous and authoritative. "Mr. Fox, this is Chief Constable Heron. We should be obliged if you would ring the station when you get in, sir. Thank you."

The machine beeped one last time signifying the end of messages. Her nerves jangling, Grace went back downstairs, closing the door to the flat behind her.

She had not been imagining things, she had not been mistaken. Her abduction was directly linked to Peter Fox. Apparently he had something the Queen

Mother and cohort wanted. Or at least they believed he had something, which was pretty much the same thing.

Where Mutt and Jeff figured in, Grace could not imagine. Frankly she didn't want to know. She was already too deeply involved. These thugs knew her name, had stolen her passport so she could not escape out of the country. They knew what flight she planned to be on. Given the time they'd had to plow through her things they might even have figured out where Monica was staying, Grace thought in alarm.

With difficulty she reined in her panic. Even if her abductors traced her to Monica, the bright spot was that Monica was undoubtedly in Scotland with Calum Bell. Monica should be safe enough for the time being.

It also meant Grace was on her own. The one person with all the answers was Peter Fox, and Peter Fox had apparently—as one of the thugs put it—gone to earth.

But sooner or later he would return home. Should she leave him some kind of warning message? Grace hesitated, trying to think. Her lack of sleep was catching up. Belatedly it occurred to her that the first place the Queen Mum would think of looking for her would be in the fox's lair. He had believed from the first that they were in it together; so to him it would make perfect sense that Grace would try to rendezvous with Peter.

She had to get out. Fast.

Grace made her way downstairs, and hurried along the aisle crowded with furniture and a bronze bust of—for a wonder—Romantic poet Lord George Gordon Noel Byron.

She couldn't explain what kept her exploring when she knew that even now her attackers might be closing in on the house. Curiosity, or perhaps some half-formed notion of leaving Peter a note caused her to slip behind the counter and follow a short hallway into what appeared to be a back office. It smelled . . . unusual. She couldn't place the odor. The deepening gloom made it necessary to turn on a light.

The office seemed to also serve as storeroom. Crates and boxes filled metal shelves. There was a suspiciously neat desk, a computer, and several broken pieces of furniture. Nearly backing into a mounted lion's head, Grace sucked in her breath sharply. Her nerves had about had it.

Grace tried to open a drawer, looking for blank paper. The drawers were locked. The desk was locked but he left his front door unlocked? Something odd about that.

An old Vuitton steamer trunk sat on the floor. Inside a nest of papers was a headless marble torso with an impossibly perfect set of breasts. A somber picture of Dutch windmills stood propped against the trunk. Beside it on the floor lay a leather-bound ledger.

Grace knelt and picked up the ledger. A bold,

elegant hand had scrawled notations a cryptologist wouldn't have been able to decipher. Grace started to tear a page out of the ledger when something caught her eye.

She stared at the wall in front of her. At first it appeared that one end of the shelves crammed with china figurines and record books stood out from the wall, but looking more closely she realized that the wall itself was crooked. There appeared to be a narrow opening between the wall and the shelf.

A secret passage?

Grace scooted over and examined the opening carefully. The shelf was bolted to the wall, the china figurines and record books glued to the shelving. Grace tugged on the shelf and a portion of the wall swung soundlessly out, revealing a doorway about four feet high.

The doorway led off into darkness.

Grace ducked under the doorway and stood, peering into the gloom. She seemed to be in a passage. Grace caught her breath in horror at what she could make out in the light from the storeroom. Now she recognized the dreadful scent stealing through the shop.

A man lay sprawled on the bare stone floor. This time it was not Peter Fox, and this time the man was definitely dead. His staring eyes testified to that.

The cause of death was unmistakable as well. Buried in his chest was one of the decorative-looking battle-axes from the stairwell display. There was blood everywhere. Blood on the stone walls, blood pooling beneath the body.

It looked as though in his dying moments the man had tried to write something on the wall in his own blood.

Ignoring the buzzing sound in her brain, Grace leaned forward to try and make out what was written. She heard a soft click as she brushed against the doorway. The significance of that sound did not register until a moment later when the door swung silently shut behind her, shutting off all light.

The last thing Grace saw before the passage plunged into blackness was the bloodstained word *Astarte*.

Grace opened her mouth to scream. Nothing came out but a whisper. She tried again. It was like in a dream when no sound would come. Her vocal chords felt paralyzed. She couldn't seem to get enough air to yell. She tried again, and again there was only a frightened choke of panicked sob.

Grace turned, falling to her knees and scrabbling at the door.

She believed it was the door; in the pitch blackness it was impossible to tell. Not a glimmer of light revealed the entrance frame. With desperate fingers Grace felt along the stone. There had to be some clue. She pried and clawed at what felt like an indentation. Nothing happened. But there had to be something, a hidden spring or button . . . *something*.

Grace forced her thoughts away from the thing

that lay in the darkness with her. Hysteria would not save her. Tearing her hands to pieces on century-old stone would not help.

Taking a deep shuddering breath, she made herself stop. She sat back on her heels and tried to think. She was in no immediate danger. Despite the rank smell, she wasn't going to suffocate. The dead man couldn't hurt her.

But what if his killer came back? He would find her trapped here . . .

Was she trapped? She tried to visualize what she had seen before the lights went out. Had she seen a staircase in the shadows beyond the corpse?

Grace scrubbed at the tears blinding her. It sank in on her that she still had her shoulder bag slung over her shoulder.

With shaking hands she opened the flap and sifted through the contents till she felt her keys. On the key ring was a tiny pocket flashlight. Grace switched it on. A beam of light about the circumference of a quarter cut the Stygian gloom.

The light had an immediate steadying effect on Grace. Yes, there did seem to be a steep flight of narrow stairs winding out of sight but it was not a proposing sight. More calmly, though her hands still shook, she tried once more to find the hidden catch.

Twenty minutes later she was still trying.

At last Grace was forced to admit that either there was no way out from this side of the secret panel, or that she had been repeating the same motions for so

long she could no longer tell what she was seeing
and feeling.

She got to her feet, leaning against the cold stone,
telling herself she could step over the thing blocking
the stairs. A stairway had to lead somewhere. She
might have more luck at the other end of the passage.

Swinging the pocket flashlight toward the stairs,
Grace's breath came out in a shuddering gulp as she
took a long look at the body. He was a small man of
about fifty. His artificially red hair was oiled flat. His
sunken dark eyes stared up in an expression of terror.

There was no telling how long he'd lain there—not
by Grace anyway, who wasn't getting any closer to
him than she had to. The blood on the wall had dried,
the blood pooled beneath had congealed. Grace stared
at the word written in blood. What could Astarte, the
Phoenician goddess of love and fertility, have to do
with any of the events of the past days?

Had Peter Fox killed this man and then fled on a supposed business trip? Or had this man been killed in mistake for Peter Fox? Grace had no idea and she didn't
care. She wanted only to escape Rogue's Gallery, get to
the nearest police station, and from there to the American Embassy and an airport.

Passionately she wished she had never met Peter
Fox. Never gone for a walk in the woods of Kentmere, never come to the Lake District—or England.
It was knowing Peter Fox that had gotten her into
this mess. Peter Fox was a dangerous man to know.

Grace directed the pinpoint of light to the stairs once more. Steeling herself, she stepped over the body, hopping a little to avoid the blood. Her feet echoed emptily on the narrow stone. The steps were deep and there was no railing. Grace kept one hand against the wall to guide herself and climbed cautiously. Her initial surge of adrenaline had faded. She felt she was moving in a haze of weariness.

Maybe I'm dreaming, she told herself. Maybe I'll soon wake up and find myself still in bed at the Tinker's Dam.

Some way up, the staircase made a sharp turn. Grace's flashlight picked out a recess like a shelf or a deep window built into the wall. She would have missed it if she hadn't been climbing so slowly. The stairs wound out of sight in the inkwell of blackness.

Grace played her flashlight over the recess before her. Was this an opening of some kind? Perhaps another door? Grace crawled on to the shelf, which was about as large as a steamer trunk, and traced the flashlight beam slowly around the corners.

Grace could detect no latch, nothing like that. But unlike the passage opening downstairs, this panel was wooden. If nothing else, she thought, she could kick it in, if necessary. As she felt around the edges Grace felt the panel move. Her heart leapt. The mechanism was so simple, so neatly constructed that she had nearly missed it.

With delicate fingertips Grace slid the panel to the side. It moved soundlessly into the wall revealing what appeared to the ray of her flashlight to be the inside of a tall narrow box. "Coffin" came to mind, and she hastily banished the image.

Grace inspected the box with her flashlight. There was a simple turn latch. Grace flipped it over and the door swung open. Meeting her astonished gaze was a stretch of crimson-and-peacock Oriental carpet. A telescope pointed out of the white Georgian windows of Peter Fox's living room.

She crawled though the case of the grandfather clock, and got to her feet. The weighted door swung shut behind her. At the soft click Grace nearly jumped out of her skin.

Dusk now shrouded the still rooms. She could hear rain brushing softly against the windows. Grace snapped off her flashlight and headed for Peter's kitchen. She was just lifting the phone receiver when she heard a door shut downstairs. The sound of whistling carried clearly through the wooden floor, floating nearer.

Grace froze. Her eyes flew around the room seeking another exit. She heard the scrape of a key in the lock. Carefully Grace replaced the phone and darted behind the kitchen door. She wasn't sure if her reaction was guilt or fear.

Through the crack she spied the living room door swinging open. A light switched on, bathing the room in homely glow.

Peter Fox was home. Grace relaxed a fraction.

He wore Levis and a brown leather flight jacket.

He carried a black Gladstone bag. He was staring down, frowning at his keys. The rain spangled his fair hair and the shoulders of his jacket. From behind the door Grace caught a hint of wet evening and clean male.

She tried to decide what to do. The body in the basement changed everything. She couldn't be sure Peter had not killed the man. Warning Peter now seemed second priority to escaping this house and getting to the police.

Fox's light, restless gaze swung around the room. *He's wondering why the door wasn't locked*, she realized, holding her breath.

But he seemed to find nothing amiss. He dropped the Gladstone, and pulled some envelopes out of his pocket, shuffling through them absently. Grace, her thoughts flying ahead in panic, concluded, *he'll come into the kitchen to check his phone messages . . .*

Her eyes raced desperately around the kitchen. There was no way out. Even if she could get to the window without being seen, she couldn't leap two stories down.

Grace's eyes zeroed back to Peter Fox. She watched him toss his mail to the glass-topped curio table. He walked out of Grace's line of vision. She waited tensely. Where was he? What was he doing? Should she make a run for it now?

Her tension spiked as he began whistling that same jaunty tune. He must be in the bedroom, she decided, gauging the sound. The whistle faded. Grace heard the muffled rush of running water, the rumble of old plumbing.

It took every ounce of courage she possessed to slide out from behind the door. She stuck her head out the kitchen doorway and peeked around.

The light in the bedroom was on. There was no sign of Peter Fox, but she could hear him walking around, opening and closing drawers.

Slipping off her shoes, Grace sprinted noiselessly to the door, every moment expecting to hear a yell behind her. Fingers unsteady, she turned the knob and eased the door open. Not daring to close it, she hurried, still on the balls of her feet, down the staircase. Her legs trembled with both fear and exhaustion.

Below her, the showroom lay in darkness, the eyes of the merry-go-round horse glinted in the light from above. Grace was just tiptoeing past the display of pikes and axes—with that conspicuous bare spot—when a voice floated down from above, "Well, well. If it isn't Miss Hollister, wandering lonely as a cloud."

With a squeal of panic, Grace bolted down the rest of the stairs toward the front door.

But she had not realized how fast and silently he moved, so silently that he seemed to barely stir the air. Grace's fingertips grazed the front door handle as his hand fell heavily on her shoulder.

She screamed and whacked at him with her shoes. Her shoes were yanked from her hands so hard she nearly fell. She tried to fight back, but was hindered by the sliding strap of her purse. It was happening so fast. Grace screamed again, and tried to swing her bag at her attacker. Everything she had ever learned about self-defense came to her in a confused rush. She kicked, trying unsuccessfully for that most vulnerable part of the male anatomy. She flailed furiously. But above all, she screamed, breathlessly, hoarsely for help.

From a distance she heard Peter Fox yelling at her to shut up—shut up or else. Somehow he held on to her, his hands punishing as Grace turned and twisted frantically, still kicking out. She was fighting for her life. Yesterday she had been unprepared for violence; today was another story.

"Damn you, stop it!" swore Peter Fox. "What the hell is the *matter* with you?" He shook Grace so hard that her head bobbled back and forth.

"Let go of me!" She clawed at his face.

He slapped her.

As a slap it was not much. The Queen Mother could have taught Peter Fox a few things about hitting women. However, it was the second time in as many days that a man had struck Grace, and instead of seeing stars, this time she saw red.

Like a professional boxer, she hauled off and swung, her fist connecting to Peter's jaw with a force she felt all down her arm.

The silence that followed was as shattering as the previous pandemonium. It didn't take Grace long to get her breath back. She was way past fear.

"Don't you ever, *ever* hit me again, you swine!"

"Why, you bloody lunatic!" Peter broke off, uncharacteristically at a loss for words.

By now it had sunk in on Grace that if Peter Fox had killed the man in his secret passage he would not have been yelling what was the matter with her. He would not have wasted a minute wrestling with Grace when he had plenty of other weapons within grasp. She was not naive enough to imagine she had actually held her own in physical combat. The fact that even now, following their impromptu brawl, he merely stood there rubbing his cheek and glaring, told Grace all she needed to know about Peter Fox and the dead man in his stockroom.

"You were hysterical," he stated.

Voice wavering, she got out, "I don't care if I'm foaming at the mouth, no one is ever laying a hand on me again!"

Peter quit rubbing his cheek and gaped indignantly. "You silly bitch, you're lucky I don't wring your neck. Who do you think you are?" He took a menacing step toward Grace. "And what the hell are you doing in my house?"

All at once Grace felt perfectly calm. Rational. She willed away the vision of how she must appear to him, Mr. Rochester's crazy wife in her livelier moments, and pronounced, "I came to warn you."

"Of *what?*" Clearly he thought the warning had to be as bad as whatever she was warning against.

"It's a long story. I think you'd better . . ." Like a figure of doom, Grace pointed toward the back office.

Peter stared, following the traverse of her finger, then glanced back at Grace. "If this is some kind of joke . . ."

Grace shook her head.

Keeping a wary eye on her, Peter started toward the back room. Grace followed. She saw him pause a fraction of a second when the smell hit him. He muttered something she didn't catch.

Flicking on the light, Peter stared around the office with narrowed eyes. Grace hung back in the doorway; he crowded the little room. She gestured toward the shelves with their faux ledgers and glued-on gimcracks.

"In there."

He looked pale. She thought, he already knows what that scent means. Tersely, he asked, "How do you know about the passageway?"

"It was open when I arrived this afternoon."

"Make yourself at home," he muttered, crouching down before the shelf. Reaching behind, he released some catch and swung the case toward himself as though he were opening a door.

The passage mouth gaped blackly before them.

"Well?"

"He's in there." She shivered, hugging herself against the memory of the thing at the foot of the stairs.

"He?"

Frowning, Peter reached in, and to Grace's chagrin, snapped on an overhead light. She could not see his face, but she saw the set of his shoulders go rigid. His whole body was perfectly still for a moment and then he moved toward the stairs and out of Grace's line of vision.

Footsteps dragging, Grace entered the stockroom and dropped down at the bare desk. She could not see what was happening in the passage, but Peter's out-loud thought reached her ears, "You greedy little sod, what have you done?"

She waited, staring unseeingly at the painting of Dutch windmills. How had she not known that unmistakable smell the first time? The pungent, metallic odor of blood and other. The less definable scent of death.

A moment later Peter ducked out of the passage. His eyes, meeting Grace's, looked electric blue in the pallor of his grim face.

"Would you mind explaining how you figure into this?"

All the lazy charm of their first encounter was gone. This, Grace thought, was the real man: tough and rather cold.

"I was hoping you could tell me. Since I pulled you out of that stream I've been run off the road, abducted by men with guns, and held prisoner in an abandoned farmhouse. Today I found a dead man in your secret passage."

Peter's eyes flickered. "What were you doing in my secret passage to begin with?"

"I told you, I came to warn you."

"Warn me of what?"

Grace spluttered, "Of—of *that!*" She waved at the passageway with its gruesome contents. "I heard them talking—"

"Heard who?"

"The Queen Mother and the other one."

"The . . . !" Peter's expression said it all.

"A man wearing a party mask," Grace corrected with asperity. "Look, I know I'm not telling this very coherently. There isn't time. One of the men who grabbed me said—well, actually I overheard him talking about 'icing Fox.' *You.*"

A strange expression crossed Peter's face.

Grace said impatiently, "I've gone through this with the police. They didn't believe me, which is why I had to come myself." She put a hand to her forehead. "What are we wasting time talking for? We've got to phone the police now!"

She reached for the phone on the desk.

Peter's hand covered hers, forcing the receiver back in its cradle.

"What are you—?" she broke off, frightened by the odd look in his eyes.

"No police," Peter said in a flat, still voice.

4

"What are you talking about?" Grace exclaimed. "We've *got* to call the police. This is murder!"

"Yes. Let me think." Peter's hand, still covering Grace's, felt warm and capable. But capable of what? Maybe Grace wasn't thinking clearly; she had gone nearly forty-eight hours without sleep, and practically that long without food. But she could not come up with any reason that an innocent person would not call the police. It was a gut reaction, not reasoned argument, that had her jerking her hand away from Peter's.

She pushed back in the chair, on her feet in one movement.

"Whoa. *Whoa!*" Peter's hands forced Grace back into her seat. "I didn't kill him, Grace."

"Then who did?"

"I don't know." His long, thin fingers absently

massaged her collarbone through the loose-knit sweater.

There was something hypnotic about that soothing touch. Grace felt as though her muscles were melting along with her resistance.

"Then what is going on?" she whispered.

"I don't know. Straight up." His eyes held hers for a moment, then he moved away, closing the passageway on the thing it held. He pushed the shelf back into place, and glanced at Grace, still motionless with indecision.

"Come on, let's go upstairs and talk this through."

"We can't just leave him there!"

"We don't want him upstairs."

The callousness of that held Grace silent. She stared into Peter's face, trying to read his expression.

"Come." Count Dracula couldn't have put it more convincingly, and his hand on the small of Grace's back seemed to leave her body no choice but to obey. She preceded him out of the office and down the narrow aisle of furniture and statuary.

In the showroom she waited while Peter moved soundlessly through the crowded darkness, relocking the front door, rearming the burglar alarm.

"So that's how you knew I was here," she commented, thinking aloud.

His voice carried to her across the aisle. "That's how I knew someone was here. I was expecting to be charged with a battle-ax though. Little did I think it was my own Miss Bluestocking from the colonies."

Being a fan of Regency novels, Grace knew that a "bluestocking" was a not particularly flattering term for a female academic. Irritation pricked her weary apathy.

"For a man expecting to be charged by an ax-wielding burglar you seemed pretty cool. You must lead an interesting life."

"It has its moments." Peter appeared beside her in that noiseless fashion that sent her nerves snapping like there was a short in her wiring. "After you," he invited.

Inside the flat, Peter waved her to one of the comfortable oversize chairs. She ignored this, trailing him into the kitchen, watching as he plugged in the electric teakettle.

"Tea?" she said disbelievingly. "We're going to have tea?"

"If you'd prefer something stronger—?"

"There is a body downstairs with an ax in its chest. Someone scrawled the word 'Astarte' in blood on the wall, and you're concerned with *beverages?*" Grace's voice shot up an octave.

Peter's brows rose with it. "Definitely something stronger for you."

He brought Grace a brandy. "Drink up, there's a good girl," he ordered. "My nerves can't take another bout of hysterics."

His nerves? The man didn't have a nerve in his body.

Grace snatched the snifter and drank the brandy in two gulps that left her gasping beneath Peter's gaze. "I'm not hysterical," she informed him. "And even if I am, I have every right to be."

"Certainly. We'll hear about that in a minute." Peter pressed replay on his answering machine. While he listened to the messages he prepared a tray for tea. Watching him Grace felt as though she had wandered through the Looking Glass. Not even the Queen Mother's snarl of a voice caused him to turn a hair as he calmly filled a bowl with lemon wedges, placing fragile porcelain cups and cake plates on a tray.

Exasperated beyond belief, Grace hobbled after him into the living room, sinking wearily into a deep, leather chair. He set the tea tray on the curio table.

"Cream and sugar?"

Maybe I *am* dreaming, she thought foggily. Perhaps it was the brandy kicking in, but she decided to go with the flow. "Please."

There was something fascinating about such a virile man performing so civilized an act as pouring tea. Grace observed his long brown hands deftly moving the delicate cups. She found herself wondering what those hands would feel like on her body. She tore her thoughts away, shocked.

Distractedly, Grace drank the tea. It was hot and strong and refreshing. She ate some chocolate hazelnut cake, and remembered that she was starving. The last real meal she'd had was now but a fond memory. She had been running on adrenaline and caffeine for the last few hours, and now she was running on empty: physically, mentally and emotionally. She had believed she was too stressed to eat. She served herself another delicious piece of cake.

Peter watched her tuck it away without comment. He served her a second cup of tea, and waited till Grace leaned back in the chair with a heartfelt sigh, before commenting, "Suppose you start at the beginning."

As coherently as possible, Grace related her adventures. After the brandy, tea and cake, she felt better. Much better. Stronger. Calmer. She did not trust Peter Fox, but oddly enough, she felt safe with him.

He heard her out from beginning to end with only a couple of questions. There is something very flattering about being given a handsome man's undivided attention. Grace experienced the same tug of attraction she had felt at the Tinker's Dam.

"*Were* we supposed to meet that next morning?" she asked as an afterthought, as she wound up her story.

Peter's lashes lowered, veiling his eyes. He said evasively, "I thought I might do well to check out a couple of things first."

So all that charm of the night before had simply been to pry information out of her. Grace recalled the feminine voices on his tape machine, the waitresses at the Tinker's Dam vying for his attention. Whatever happens, she warned herself as though advising one of her girls, you must not fall for this man.

"And what did you learn?"

Peter shrugged. He leaned back in his chair, stretching his long legs. He wore denims that hugged every move his lithe body made, and a moleskin shirt of palest baby blue, which played up the color of his eyes and the gold glints in his thick hair. He was not classically handsome, but there was definitely something about him.

Grace, on the other hand, knew she looked like she felt. She needed a shower and sleep. She was still wearing the clothes she had made her cross-country run in, and if her hair did not actually have leaves and twigs in it, her braid was as frayed and tattered as her nerves.

"Tell me this," he said offhandedly. "Did your constable happen to mention who owned that farmhouse in the middle of nowhere?"

Grace thought it over. "If he did, I don't recall it. The place had clearly been abandoned for years. But I suppose you're right. The owner might provide some kind of clue to the identity of those thugs who nabbed me."

He seemed to have no further comment.

"Wait just a minute," she responded to Peter's reticence, "it's your fault I'm involved in this. I have a right to know what's going on. If you know, you need to tell me. You owe me that much."

Peter sat forward, putting that husky, beguiling voice to good use. "I know. I do apologize. But trust me on this, Grace; the less you know, the better."

"That's ridiculous!" Grace glared at him. "The more I know, the better my chances of protecting myself. That's just common sense. Quit carrying on like someone out of . . . of Sax Rohmer, and tell me what's going on!"

Peter had drawn back warily at this unexpected attack. Now a faint smile curved his wide, rather mocking mouth. "Actually, I haven't a clue what's going on," he admitted. "Your guess is as good as mine."

"Swell."

"Don't trouble yourself. Tomorrow you'll be on a plane heading back to the States."

"I wish." She sighed, leaning back in the butter-soft leather upholstery, and added, "It's going to take the consulate a couple of days to issue me a replacement passport. I can't afford to buy new plane tickets. I don't even know if I can get my old tickets replaced." She rubbed her head as though she could stimulate her thought process. "Who was that man downstairs? Did you know him?"

After a moment, Peter said reluctantly, "His name is—was—Danny Delon. He's a petty thief. Strictly small-time."

"What nice friends you have."

"He was more of an acquaintance."

"Then what was he doing in your secret passage?"

"I've no idea."

"Do you have an idea of who killed him?"

"No."

"Or why?"

"No."

"You must have *some* idea."

Peter looked annoyed. "This interrogation technique might work wonders with the belles of St. Mary's or wherever the hell it is—"

"St. Anne's."

"—but I don't appreciate it."

"I don't appreciate being slapped or having guns pointed at me or being run off the road or kidnapped. What is it those men wanted in exchange for me?"

Peter gritted his teeth. "I do not know."

"You *must* have some idea. They said, 'ask your mate Delon.' "

"Unfortunately, he's not talking. As you may have noticed."

Years of dealing with devious adolescents had equipped Grace with a built-in lie detector. Peter Fox was good—a born liar in fact—but Grace knew what that slant of eyes to the left meant. He might not be lying, but he wasn't telling the complete truth.

She asked tartly, "And I suppose Astarte is the name of the person who killed him?"

For one fleeting second he actually seemed to consider trying it on. He replied shortly, "You know as well as I do Delon never lifted a finger after that ax was planted in his chest."

Grace swallowed a lump in her throat. "So what does *Astarte* mean? Is it a warning?"

"I suppose so. I don't know. About a week ago

Delon came to me with a story of a valuable something he'd managed to lay his hands on."

"Something stolen?"

"That would be a safe bet." Peter's left brow rose in a gesture Grace was beginning to recognize as characteristic.

"What did you do?"

"I told him I thought he was in over his head. I told him to get rid of the goods."

"And instead someone got rid of him. Who? Mutt and Jeff? The Queen Mum?"

Peter said crossly, "Would you stop calling that bloke the Queen Mum? It's distracting."

Grace was not listening, busy tabulating facts. Fact: Danny Delon, a small-time hood, brought stolen goods to Peter Fox. Fact: Peter Fox did not want to contact the police; not when someone tried to kill him, and not even when he found a corpse in his home. These facts did not add up to a very flattering portrait of Peter Fox.

"Why can't you go to the police?" she inquired.

"I prefer to handle this my own way."

"Dead bodies in the secret passage all in a day's work for you?"

The blue eyes gleamed with dislike. Grace prodded delicately, "Are you . . . er . . . ?"

"Known to the police?" Peter finished dryly. "Yes, Miss Hollister, in a manner of speaking, I am. Which is why I didn't want any part of Delon's find, intriguing though it sounded."

"You're a crook?" Grace abandoned tact.

"No, I'm not a crook!" Peter rose and then seemed to have nowhere to go. Restlessly he prowled the spacious room. No further explanation seemed forthcoming.

A crook with tender feelings? Grace prodded, "Then what?"

Peter stared out the window at the black silhouette of wood line. He said finally, "It was over five years ago, but . . ." He sighed. "Take my word, I cannot go to the police."

"Even over something like this?"

"Trust me." He said it as though he fully expected her to do so.

"What happens if the killer comes back?" Grace speculated aloud, "Now that I think about it, you have four people that I know of wanting to kill you."

"Not 'ice' as in kill," Peter clarified reluctantly. " 'Ice' as in diamonds. Ice Fox. It's an alias. A bit of youthful cheek."

Even if the Queen Mother and cohort had not planned to kill Peter, someone had. Someone had deliberately put his head underwater. Mutt and Jeff? Someone had certainly killed Danny Delon.

"What about Mr. Delon?" she pointed out. "Was he killed in mistake for you?"

"You're joking. No one could mistake Danny for me."

He had a point. It would be like mistaking one of the dwarves for Prince Charming. Even if the murderer had never seen Peter, he had to have a general idea of what he looked like. Had Danny Delon actually been the intended victim? Then why the attempt on Peter's life? Were the two things *not* connected? Given Peter's (she suspected) unsavory past, maybe people frequently tried to knock him off. It would explain his sangfroid about the incident.

Were the "gewgaws" the intriguing "stuff" Danny had got his hands on? Where did Astarte fit in? Where did Grace fit in?

"If Astarte isn't a person . . . ?"

"I don't know if Astarte is a person," Peter informed Grace. He flopped down in a chair and raked a hand through his fair hair. "I doubt it, since I've never met anyone named Astarte."

"Maybe it isn't 'Astarte'?" Grace suggested suddenly. "Maybe the murderer was interrupted before he could finish writing out the message."

Peter studied Grace as though she were from another planet. "Just out of curiosity, what message do you imagine he might have been writing? 'A-start-e . . . ?' 'E' for what? Elsewhere? As in 'A start elsewhere might be a good idea'?"

"No, but—oh, all right! It was just a thought."

Peter shook his head. "What an imagination. You're wasted teaching dead poets to hormone-riddled adolescents."

Some connection between dead poets and Astarte clicked in Grace's brain, but before she could pin it down, it was gone.

"Well, if it's not someone's name, and it isn't part

of another message, it must be whatever the murderer was after. Astarte. Maybe you have a statue of Astarte? Or maybe Delon did. Or perhaps the gewgaws, the jewels, are in a statue of Astarte?"

Peter put a hand to his head as though it hurt. "I don't have a statue of Astarte. I don't have anything connected to Astarte. I never did have the item, whatever it is. Delon did."

"But Delon came here. Maybe he brought it with him?"

"In which case whoever killed him has it now, and wrote 'Astarte' to warn us off."

That made sense. Grace liked that scenario. For one thing it meant the affair was now over—other than the minor detail of Danny Delon's dead body. She smothered a yawn triggered as much by nerves as fatigue.

Peter said abruptly, "You're dead on your feet. Why don't you have a wash and a lie down. I'll see about . . . dinner."

Grace suspected he had been about to say something quite different. She shuddered and said weakly, "I don't care about dinner. I don't think I could eat a bite."

Peter's eyes fell on what remained of the cake. He said solemnly, "Naturally. But you have to keep your strength up."

Meeting his gaze, Grace surprised herself with a laugh. Twenty-four hours ago she had believed she would never laugh again.

"You know, Mr. Fox, if you had been honest that first night you might have saved us both a lot of trouble."

"I didn't know whether you were involved the first night," Peter admitted. "I didn't know what was happening myself. I still don't."

"Well, I'm involved now."

"Not for long. Tomorrow we'll have you on your way home."

Grace doubted it, but it was reassuring to hear. With both hands she smothered another of those engulfing yawns.

"Where are your keys?" Peter rose in one of those restless movements that had her overwrought nerves twitching like jumping beans. "I'll bring up your bags. Where did you park?"

Grace told him, fishing her keys out of her purse. She tossed them to Peter who caught them one-handed.

"The bath's through there. Towels are in the cupboard," he informed her on his way out the door.

Despite the old-fashioned porcelain and brass fixtures, the bathroom was modern and utilitarian. The man believed in his creature comforts, Grace reflected. There was plenty of hot water, fluffy giant bath towels, and bars of vanilla-scented French-milled soaps.

A few gallons of hot water soaked the ache out of her tired bones and tense muscles.

Grace took her time, lathered in vanilla suds, leisurely massaging shampoo through her hair, and using a hot spring's worth of H_2O to rinse away the grime and fear of the past days.

Feeling pleasantly drained she wrapped a towel around her hair and padded into the bedroom to find her suitcases lying on Peter Fox's four-poster bed. Rosy light from a silk-shaded lamp cast mellow warmth over the masculine furnishings. The bed looked big and inviting.

Grace changed into a fleecy pair of navy sweats with St. Anne's logo, and poked her head out the bedroom door. The tea things still sat on the glass-topped curio chest. There was no sign of Peter. It didn't take much imagination to guess where he was. Dismissing her queasy stomach Grace cleared away the tea tray. The man was mad. You couldn't conceal a murder. What honest person would want to?

"Mad, bad and dangerous to know." Wasn't that what Lady Caroline Lamb had written about Lord Byron? It might as easily have been written about Peter Fox.

There was still no sign of Peter by the time Grace finished washing up the tea things. Weariness dragged at her like Jacob Marley's chains. She felt as though she were moving in a fog. No wonder she couldn't think straight.

Checking the front door to be sure it was locked, Grace wandered into Peter's bedroom with its oyster watered-silk wallpaper and dark, heavy furniture.

She shoved her suitcases off the bed, crawled on the too-firm mattress and snuggled into the eiderdown. In seconds she was fast asleep.

Grace came slowly back to consciousness.

It took her a few moments to think where she was. Her eyes traveled around a softly lit room. A wood-block print of a mill hung over a tall bureau. A man's plaid bathrobe hung on the back of the half-closed door.

From the rooms beyond came mouth-watering aromas and the muted beat of rock music. Grace sat up in bed. She caught a glimpse of herself in the oval dressing mirror. Her cheeks were flushed with sleep, her long hair tousled. She looked more like one of St. Anne's students than a staid instructor.

Wandering into the kitchen she found Peter cooking at the old-fashioned gas range. "There you are," he greeted Grace. "I was just about to call you. How are you feeling?"

Grace pulled out a chair, sitting down, folding her arms as she studied Peter. "Much better. That smells great. What is it?"

"Grilled veal chops. Leek and brie soup."

"You cook, too?" She had to admit she was impressed. Chaz, her sometime escort's idea of cooking was reheating take-out. Surely a man who could cook like this and quote Romantic poets couldn't be all bad?

"I find cooking relaxing. I do my best thinking when I'm cooking."

"What a coincidence. I do my best thinking when I'm eating." Absently she took note of the oak-leaf china, gleaming flatware and crisp linens on the table set for two. Everything in Peter's flat, and even the shop below, was so perfect it was like a stage set. Peter had created an atmosphere so civilized it was unreal. Even murder couldn't touch it.

Only the music seemed out of character. It should have been something classical, something refined and passionless. Instead it was a raw, primitive sound with a beat that had Grace's foot unconsciously keeping time on the floor. She recognized the Irish group Waterboys' version of "We Will Not Be Lovers." Chaz was fond of Irish music. She tried to recall the lyrics. Something about words being weapons and lies being a defense.

Before she had time to explore this thought, Peter was serving dinner.

First came the soup made from new potatoes, leeks, spinach, brie and vermouth. Grace licked the tip of her spoon and sent her compliments to the chef. Next up: grilled chops and a salad of chilled artichokes, asparagus, and green beans in a ginger and carrot vinaigrette. The food tasted as perfect as it looked. As perfect as the setting looked. As perfect as the man looked.

"What did you do with the body?" Grace questioned.

Peter didn't even glance up. "Let's wait till we've eaten to discuss it."

Probably a reasonable request, yet it struck Grace

as bizarre under the circumstances. She finished her vegetables and remarked, "You do appreciate the finer things, don't you?"

He read the underlying criticism of that correctly, and after a pause, replied, "I once spent fourteen months in a Turkish prison. I suppose you could say I've learned to value life's little civilities."

Grace, feeling that a piece of artichoke had lodged in her throat, swallowed hard, and got out, "I didn't mean that as a—a—reflection—"

Peter's smile was odd, his eyes the color one of Grace's dead poets had once described as "the witchery of soft, blue sky."

"No?"

"No. Of course not. Why shouldn't you enjoy beautiful things?" She wondered what he'd done to get himself thrown into a Turkish prison. Smuggling drugs? That was the usual reason, wasn't it?

Her discomfiture seemed to amuse him. "It's quite all right. I'm not sensitive." He refilled her wineglass. "Tomorrow, first thing, we're putting you on a plane for home."

"You keep saying that. It must be wishful thinking. What about my passport?"

"I can get you a replacement. I called a mate of mine while you were dead to the world."

"You mean a *forgery?*" Grace gawked at Peter who stared back unmoved. "No. *No.* I can't do something like that! Something illegal. What if I was caught? I'd go to jail. I'd lose my job." Grace realized this probably did not impress a man who'd spent time in a Turkish prison.

"You won't be caught."

"Yes, I will. I could never pull off something like that. One look at my face, and they would instantly know something was up. I have that kind of a face."

"Criminal?"

"Yes. I mean, no! You know what I mean. Besides, my getting caught isn't the only consideration. I don't *want* to do something illegal. I'm—I'm a law-abiding person. I've never even had a parking ticket. I turn my library books in on time."

Peter's mouth twitched with some private amusement. No doubt he was the kind of person who found ethics impractical and morality comical.

"Besides," she finished quietly, "I'm not a total coward, you know. I don't want to give in to intimidation or—well, terrorism. I don't want to flee the country because of a case of mistaken identification or something. You said yourself, it's probably over; that they probably have whatever they were looking for."

"I never said that."

Hadn't he? She thought he sort of had, but maybe she had been hearing what she wanted to hear. "You said whoever killed Delon probably has whatever they were looking for."

"I was speculating."

"It makes sense."

"Then why kidnap you?"

"Who's to say it was the same person? The Queen

Mother . . ." Grace broke off at Peter's expression. "The men who grabbed me aren't necessarily the men who killed Delon."

" 'Ask your mate Delon?' " quoted Peter. "I think they were watching me, which is how they hit on the notion of using you as bait when they let me slip."

"But if they were watching you, who tried to kill you? Mutt and Jeff?"

Peter shrugged.

"Who are all these people? You said Delon was a small-time thief. What could a small-time thief have that would interest so many other crooks? What could be worth *murdering* him over?"

"You'd be surprised," Peter said cryptically. "Look, that's what I intend to find out, and—I can't put this more tactfully—your presence restricts my options."

"If we went to the police—"

"No police. How many times must I say it?"

"Then what *are* you going to do?"

"That needn't concern you." He spoke with cool confidence. "Believe me, I'll handle it."

She was silent. "I could help you," she said at last.

The winged brows rose.

"Seriously," Grace said. "I could help. I've seen these men, you haven't. I got a better look at Mutt and Jeff, too." At his expression, she said defensively, "One thing is definite: I am not trying to board any plane with a forged passport, so either let me help, or send me on my merry way." Into his formidable silence she added, "Frankly, I think once I'm away from the Lake District I won't have any more problems."

"You really don't get it, do you?" he commented. "Listen, my dear, I owe you for saving my neck. Allow me to repay that debt by getting you back home in one piece."

Irked, Grace replied, "Believe me, my dear, it was *nothing*. And I don't need you to break more laws in order to shove me on a plane like I'm some half-wit who can't take care of herself, merely because you don't wish to feel guilty if I get hit by a bus or something."

She stopped for breath, but before he could respond, she was off again, "And furthermore, I take full responsibility for my actions and my safety. I don't need you limiting your 'options' on my behalf. I came to warn you, not ask for your help."

"Am I arguing?"

"You're too busy trying to think of something to convince me. Or scare me."

Peter laughed. "Why, Esmerelda!"

"Oh save it!" Grace shook her head. "I'm really not as naive as you seem to think. I prefer honesty to that facile charm you dish out with the Gypsy Queens."

For a split second he looked taken aback. Then he said simply, "We're both in trouble here, Grace. Believe it or not, I am doing my best to get you out of it."

The sincere way his eyes held hers, the huskiness in his voice, had an undermining effect on her that was very aggravating. Grace said gruffly, "Well, we're going to have to think of another way. My friend Monica is over here. I can't just abandon her. What if these thugs go after her?"

Peter said wearily, "One problem at a time."

It was at this point that the burglar alarm went off downstairs.

5

*I*n Grace's opinion a normal person would have jumped to his feet or made some exclamation or done *something* as alarm bells clamored through the house. Peter did not move a muscle. In fact, he went very still, his lean face taking on a peculiar listening intentness.

The next instant he was out of his chair and easing open the door of the flat. "Stay here," he ordered Grace in afterthought, and with that, was gone.

Not so long ago Grace would have obeyed. But as Peter slipped silently out of his quarters she left the table and followed him onto the landing. It took her eyes a moment to adjust to the gloom. Peter was already on the ground floor, a shadow gliding through the other shadows. Grace crept down the staircase on stockinged feet.

A scream, high-pitched and terrified, came from outside, only to be choked off.

"Peter!" gasped Grace.

She spotted him racing toward the front door. The door opened onto an Arthur Rackham nightscape: gnarled black apple trees stood silhouetted against a golden lantern moon. Shape-shifting clouds drifted across the sky. Grace abandoned stealth and thudded down the stairs. She paused before the display of weapons, her hand hovering as she realized that the missing ax had been replaced. Polished steel gleamed in the light from the landing.

Commotion at the shop entrance startled her. Peter reappeared, supporting a moaning woman. The woman clutched her dark head with one hand and Peter with the other.

"He hit me," she mumbled.

Peter helped the woman to the nearest Chippendale chair. "Run get some ice," he told Grace.

Grace ran. When she returned with ice wrapped in a towel the other woman seemed to have recovered slightly although she was still clinging to Peter's shirtfront, and making tiresome noises into his chest.

She was a "handsome" woman of about forty-five, Grace estimated, handing over the ice pack. She had dark, shoulder-length hair, and a tall, model-thin body. Opening hazel eyes, the woman squinted painfully at Grace.

"Who is *that?*" She struggled to sit up.

"Take it easy, Al," Peter said, solicitously applying the ice to what, Grace had to admit, was a goose egg-sized bump.

"But who is she?"

"This is Miss Grace Hollister from America." Peter's eyes met Grace's briefly. "Grace, this is the Honorable Allegra Clairmont-Brougham."

"But who *is* she?" pressed Al plaintively. "Why is she here?"

Grace thought she recognized Al's too-too-refined accent from Peter's answering machine. Al was the gal who thought "naughty man" Peter was avoiding her phone calls. The Hon. Al's dark clothing and the hour of the night she'd chosen to come calling indicated romantic reconnaissance. Grace felt sorry for the woman.

She felt even sorrier for her when Peter said brusquely, "She's staying with me, Al."

"She's . . ." Allegra sat up, holding fast to the ice pack. "But I thought you and Mimi—that is—" She turned her disbelieving gaze to Grace. "But Peter, you never have anyone *stay*," she protested.

"Grace is different." Peter ignored the daggers of Grace's stare.

Al dropped back against his broad chest with a pained sound. Grace scowled at Peter over Al's bowed head. *Cad,* she mouthed. He looked blank. She was tempted to snatch one of the skulls off the nearby dresser and crown him. *Memento Amoure* in this particular case.

Ignoring Grace's ire, Peter was querying, briskly but not un-sympathetically, "What happened, Al? Did you see who coshed you?"

"Not clearly. I came round the back—I thought I heard something—and I saw a man with a crowbar at the window. Then the alarm went off. After that it's all a blur." Falteringly she put a hand to her head.

Grace was relieved that Peter had enough tact not to question the obvious. Perhaps he was used to suspicious lovers skulking outside his windows.

"You didn't recognize the man? What did he look like?"

"A shadowy figure, that's all. Tall. Very tall." She seemed to hesitate. "His face was all blacked."

"What else?"

"Nothing really. Just the way the light fell."

"Spit it out, Al. What did you see?"

Al said uncomfortably, "I rather got the impression . . . you'll think me mad, but I . . . I thought he was wearing a turban."

Peter's eyebrows shot up, mirroring Grace's own expression.

Allegra opened her eyes wide and murmured, "Oh, Peter, *why* didn't you ring?"

"I wasn't home."

"But I saw your lights on."

"When?" Peter and Grace asked in unison. They briefly exchanged looks.

"Yesterday evening. Thursday." She focused on Grace and said pettishly, "I suppose that was you?"

Grace's reply was forestalled by Peter's warning glance.

Al said, "I've been staying with Auntie Venetia

while the chimneys at the Carriage House are being cleaned. But the place is like a tomb. *Too* dreary." Her fingers crept up to play with Peter's collar. "Do you suppose . . . Peter, if it's not too terribly much trouble *could* you run me home? I don't feel quite up to driving." She fluttered her eyelashes.

Grace decided it would be ridiculous to be annoyed by the Hon. Al's ploys; despite Peter's deliberate attempt to make it look otherwise, Grace was not involved with him and had no intention of becoming involved with him. What sane woman would want to be involved with a man who clearly couldn't commit to anything but a life of crime?

"You should have your head examined," she heard herself say. Both Al and Peter looked her way. "First," Grace amended hastily. "You should *first* have someone examine your . . . um . . . head."

Al peered at her through pain-narrowed eyes, and then said to Peter, "Peter, how can you be giving Mimi Kenton-Kydd antique pendants one minute, and living with American girls the next?"

"Yes, I'm curious, too," Grace remarked.

The look he shot her promised retaliation. To Al, Peter said, ruefully, "I'm rather afraid it's going to be less of the former and more of the latter now that Grace is here to keep me in line."

Al was still trying to do the math as Peter helped her to her feet once more.

"Are you sure it's safe?" Grace asked under her voice, holding the door for them.

Peter's nod was curt. "Keep the doors locked. Don't open for anyone but me."

"I was thinking of *you*. Could he still be out there?"

She was rewarded by an unexpectedly engaging grin. "And I was beginning to think you didn't care."

Al stopped clinging long enough to scowl at Grace.

"I'll wait up, shall I?" Grace added for Al's benefit. She was instantly ashamed.

"Do." To her openmouthed surprise, Peter kissed her.

The next moment he had vanished into the night with the Hon. Allegra Clairmont-Brougham in tow.

As a kiss it was too brief to analyze, but as Grace went slowly up the stairs to Peter's flat, she had the funniest impression her lips were tingling.

Inside Peter's quarters, Grace switched on the electric teakettle and cleared away the dinner dishes, putting the leftover food away. Finishing, she went into the living room and sat down to wait. Her eyes roved the room and settled on the curio table before her. She wondered if the items collected under glass were a clue to Peter Fox's character. Among the odds and ends gathered were a child's spyglass; a browned traveler's diary with faded writing; another book, this one gilt-stamped and calf-bound; a silver compass; assorted shells and stones and antique coins; and a jade-handled knife. So much *stuff*.

She glanced across at the moon-faced grandfather clock and saw that it was nearly midnight. Grace decided that with a computer at her fingertips she could log in a little research time. Mr. Fox, Do You Yahoo? He *had* to have Internet access.

It was nearly dawn when Peter unlocked the door to his flat. He was vaguely surprised to find the lights still on. It had taken two hours and twenty minutes to smooth Al's feathers. That was two hours longer than he wanted to spend. The peace talks had been followed by the even more disagreeable task of shifting the mortal remains of Danny Delon.

For a moment there in the passage the old panic had swept over him, the sensation of walls closing in, of suffocation, of being buried alive. The cold, crisp night air had helped to clear his head.

Surprise stopped him midway through a jaw-breaking yawn as Peter took in the clutter of tea tray with its empty cake plate and teacup on the table. Stacks of books towered like Grecian ruins, and Esmerelda lay draped over the couch like somebody's virgin sacrifice. Peter's thin mouth quirked as he studied the sleeping *Ms.* Hollister. Chestnut hair framed her flushed face in a silky cloud. She was wearing a pair of round spectacles and some kind of white, ruffly night thing. She clutched a gold-tooled volume to her breast.

She looked rather like a scholarly angel—except that Mary Shelley's *Frankenstein* was not suitably cherubic reading. Not that there was anything particularly ethereal about the long, slender leg resting outside the tangle of afghan and nightshirt she had cocooned herself in. Nor in the swell of breasts gently rising and falling. Earthly delights these.

Peter had an uncomfortably vivid memory of resting his face against those firm breasts. He recalled the warm scent of her skin and the silken feel of her hair against his lips.

Her gentle limbs she did undress and lie down in her loveliness.

He approached the couch, all his defenses intact. Grace never stirred. Peter studied her without expression. Then he dropped down on his haunches and with light fingers removed her spectacles, laying them aside on the table. Her skin was soft to his fingertips. Baby skin. She didn't really look old enough to teach teenage girls anything, although he had to admit she did possess an unexpectedly sharp mind. And tongue to match.

Peter continued to study Grace, feeling the light warmth of her breath on his face. Her mouth was pink and moist, slightly parted.

This was a complication he did not need. Peter rose and walked into the bedroom, shutting the door gently behind him.

"Fertility clinics," Grace informed Peter at breakfast the next morning. "Fertility clinics and designer plus-sizes. That's all I could find last night on the Internet."

"Huh?" Peter asked intelligently, his mouth full of Canadian bacon.

He was wearing a dark plaid robe over what

appeared to be yellow pajamas. Grace refused to think about the fact that she was having breakfast with a pajama-clad man she barely knew. There was gold bristle on his jaw and his hair was ruffled. It was so . . . personal.

She pulled her own plaid robe—a different tartan, mind—closer.

"Relating to Astarte," she clarified. "There's an on-line magazine for something called the Goddess Woman. And there's a place in San Francisco called the Astarte Fertility Center which provides an integrated online list of egg donors and invitro fertilization and long-distance treatment plans."

Peter chewed, swallowed, and said, "I don't have a clue what you're talking about."

"I thought maybe I could help by researching the Astarte connection. I used your computer last night; I hope you don't mind. The thing is—" She leaned forward on the table. "There *is* something called the Astarte Lodge in Berlin. Their site says they celebrate the Gnostic Mass and offer classes to initiates on the Qabalah, ritual techniques, yoga—it's a bit New Agey, but there could be a connection."

Peter studied her thoughtfully. "Are you like this every morning?"

Grace sat back in her chair. "Like what? Awake? Most people are, who don't come waltzing in at four o'clock in the morning."

"Three-thirty. And I was not waltzing. If you were in a noticing mood, you'd have seen my feet dragging."

"No doubt you were exhausted." Grace bit into a muffin, all her white teeth showing.

Peter chuckled and refilled her teacup. "What are you insinuating? Believe me, you couldn't be further from the mark. The woman is a nuisance."

"You're all heart." Grace downed the last bit of muffin. It took her a moment or two to clear her air passage enough to speak. "Anyway, I couldn't care less about your love life. I just want to solve this thing and save my skin. Not to mention, my vacation."

"I think the vacation is a scrub," Peter informed her. "But I'll see what I can do about your skin. It's a rather nice hide, I admit." He winked at her across the breakfast dishes.

Not used to being flirted with over eggs and bacon, Grace momentarily lost her train of thought.

Peter finished his coffee, put the cup down and said curiously, "Were you really thinking you could find the reason for your being kidnapped on the Internet?"

"It's quite amazing the things you can find on the Internet," Grace defended. "I found some pictures of statues believed to represent Astarte; they looked a bit like little chicken-headed figures wearing dunce caps. They're incredibly valuable though. And I found directions on how to perform the Rite of Astarte. You need seven green candles, dried red rose petals and fruit juice, preferably apple."

"Sounds most uplifting. I don't believe we are under attack by renegade Gnostics however."

The phone rang and Peter rose to answer it.

Grace watched his face turn into a mask of elegant bones and hollows. After a moment he replied expressionlessly, "I appreciate your concern, Chief Constable."

Silence.

Peter's gaze shifted to Grace. "The young lady is with me now."

A longer silence.

Peter's jaw clenched but his voice was smooth and civil as he cut in, "Let me save you the trip, Chief Constable. I planned to drive into—" A pause. "I look forward to it."

Peter slammed down the receiver. *"Bloody hell!"*

"What is it?"

"Why the hell did you have to go to the police?"

The unfairness of this attack had Grace spluttering, "What was I supposed to do? I was kidnapped; of course I went to the police. How could I know you have a—a rap sheet!"

"A what?"

"A police record."

Peter pinched his bottom lip, scowling. Meeting Grace's concerned gaze he said, "Suit up, Esmerelda. The cops are coming."

Grace was coiling her hair in a French chignon when Peter tapped on her door.

"Let me do the talking, right?"

"What do I do if the constable asks me a direct question? Pretend to be mute?"

"There's a thought." He studied Grace critically, from the pristine white linen blouse to the Laura Ashley print skirt. It was the kind of ensemble Grace typically chose for parent-teacher conferences. She knew she looked feminine and sensible. The kind of woman who did not get involved in police investigations. Frankly, she thought Peter could do better than jeans and a lapis lazuli-colored shirt. Chaz would never wear such a shirt, she reflected. It almost looked like *silk*.

Peter had punctuated her dressing by calling bits of information to her: Chief Constable Heron had received a call from P.C. Kenton relating Grace's misadventures and her concern for Peter's safety. When Grace Hollister had promptly disappeared, the forces of law and order were perturbed in their phlegmatic British way.

"We simply need to let them see that you're all right and everything's under control." It was the third time Peter had said this and Grace wondered whom he was trying to convince?

"Everything is *not* under control," Grace had to point out.

Peter stalked away from her bedroom door.

Though everything was not under control, against her better judgment Grace was going along with Peter. She knew what she would say to one of her girls running around with a strange man (strange in more ways than one) conspiring to deceive the police force of a foreign country. No one who knew her would believe she was agreeing to this insanity voluntarily: not her family, not her colleagues, not Ms. Wintersmith, headmistress at St. Anne's, who was grooming Grace to replace her in some far distant future—and certainly not Chaz, who on more than one occasion had praised her "dependability." Grace found it hard to believe herself.

Of course it hadn't helped that her morning phone call to the American Embassy had ended in the news that it would take several days to issue Grace a replacement passport—and this was assuming there were no "glitches." How could there *not* be glitches in a situation like this one? Glitches were a guarantee. Grace could flee Innisdale, but for the time being she was stuck on this blessed plot, this earth, this realm, this England . . .

And to top it all off, it wasn't like Peter Fox *wanted* her. The fact that he needed her help even to this extent clearly pained him.

From the landing she watched him admit the police. A rosy-cheeked constable started up the long staircase, followed by an older man who looked like he had escaped out of an Agatha Christie novel (right down to the wax on his handlebar mustache). This had to be the chief constable.

"Well, Miss Hollister, it's a relief to find you in good health."

Grace shook hands. "Sorry for the mix-up. I didn't realize anyone was expecting me to turn up at a certain time or place."

The chief constable shook hands with Peter. "Mr. Fox." His tone was decidedly cooler.

They settled in Peter's comfortable living room and the two policemen looked about themselves. The chief constable said, "You won't mind showing me some ID, Miss Hollister?"

"That's just it," Grace said, "The men who grabbed me stole my ID. My passport, my money, everything."

"Of course. I'd forgotten." Heron twisted the ends of his mustache and Grace realized he hadn't forgotten at all. Was it some kind of test?

Peter said lazily, "Perhaps you'd like Grace to recap her . . . adventures?" He apparently couldn't help that tone of voice, but Grace noted it didn't go over well with the officers of the law.

Heron's black-cherry eyes rested on Peter's face. "Hmm. We've got it on record. Miss Hollister, you've known Mr. Fox how long?"

"About three days."

"What has that to do with anything?" Peter inquired.

"Just wondering why, after all she'd been through, Miss Hollister would come to you rather than ourselves."

"I believed Peter's life was in danger."

At last Heron looked her way. "Why?" he asked bluntly.

Grace chose her words carefully. "They—well, someone had tried to kill him once. I gathered the only reason they were bothering me was they believed I was involved with Peter." She began to see the danger in this line of questioning. "They seemed like dangerous men," she said at last. The young constable smiled at her sympathetically.

"You didn't trust the police to warn Mr. Fox?"

"I—yes, but I wasn't sure you would be in time."

Peter reached across and squeezed Grace's hand. "I'd told Grace the night before she had a standing invitation." The sheen of violet silk made his eyes shine like amethysts. "I was delighted she took me up on it."

Grace smiled feebly. "Yep," she said.

Heron cleared his throat. "I see." He glanced at the constable who handed him a sheet of paper. "And what may I ask is this item you were supposed to exchange for Miss Hollister?"

Peter's thin strong fingers tightened unconsciously on Grace's. "There was no item."

"Come, come, Mr. Fox. It's right here in Miss Hollister's account of her abduction." He ran a thick finger along the typewritten sentence.

Grace interjected, "I . . . might have misunderstood on that point."

"Why should you say so, miss?"

"Because she was rattled," Peter said. "These yobbos abducted her, terrorized her—are her listening skills really the issue?"

Peter's sarcasm had little effect on the stalwart minions of the law.

"No, Mr. Fox." Heron returned equably. "No, I believe the young lady reported exactly what she heard, and I believe she heard the truth. You have something these miscreants want."

Miscreants? Grace felt her confidence in local law enforcement waning. These gentlemen were so different from the trim, efficient LAPD back home. Plus they seemed convinced that Peter was the biggest threat to her safety.

"I have a question for you," Peter said. "Did you happen to discover the identity of the owner of the farmhouse where Grace was held?"

Heron took this one in stride. "Indeed we have. The house was formerly owned by a Miss Barbara Hopkins. Miss Hopkins was an elderly spinster lady, and when she passed on, she had no relations to bequeath the property to. There was a housekeeper who apparently lived on there for some time, but she's also long since deceased."

"What was the housekeeper's name?"

"Why?" Heron asked bluntly.

"Mild curiosity. These chaps seemed to know me. I wondered if I might recognize a name that could help the police in their investigations."

The last bit was mockingly said, but instead of being offended Heron said quite cordially, "The housekeeper went by the name of Ames. Ring any bells?"

"No."

"Quite certain of that, Mr. Fox?"

"Granted, life is full of uncertainties, Chief Constable, but I'm fairly certain the name Ames carries no special significance for me."

Peter rose. "If that's all, Grace and I have some business to attend to."

"Actually, Mr. Fox, there is one thing more."

Grace, who had started to rise, sat back down as though the strength had melted from her legs. She looked at Peter. Peter was watching Heron with narrowed eyes.

"And that is?"

"Do you know a Mr. Danny Delon, sir?"

After a moment, Peter said, "He's a former business acquaintance."

"When was the last time you saw Mr. Delon?"

Peter flicked an imaginary speck of lint from his sleeve. "Why?"

"Answer the question, Mr. Fox."

Grace's heart began to pound so hard she could hardly hear Peter's indifferent, "About a week ago."

"That was the last time you saw Delon? You haven't seen him since your trip?"

"No."

Grace inwardly cringed at this lie. Something in Heron's tone warned that this was not a casual question. That it was, in fact, a trap.

"Are you going to tell me what this is about?"

Peter sounded just right, a little bored, a little impatient. He seemed unconscious of the three pairs of eyes pinned on him.

Heron also rose, saying bluntly, "We received an anonymous tip, sir. The caller said that if we searched this house we would find Mr. Delon's body."

6

Grace could not help the squeak of alarm that escaped her. All three gentlemen turned her way and waited politely. When she did not continue, there was a sort of pause.

"Be my guest," Peter drawled with a languid wave of his hand. One of Georgette Heyer's Regency bucks couldn't have done it better.

Heron glanced at his trusty constable. "We have your permission to search the premises?"

"If it will amuse you."

"Amuse us? No, sir. We're simply doing our duty."

Peter's expression grew mocking, and Heron reddened.

"I'll just finish packing," Grace suggested, edging off toward the guest room.

"Packing, miss?"

"Miss Hollister hopes to meet up with friends in Scotland."

"I see."

"Is there a problem?" Grace asked nervously.

"I'm not sure, Miss Hollister." Heron turned to Peter. "Will you accompany us downstairs, Mr. Fox?"

"Certainly." Peter headed for the door, impatience vibrating in his step.

Grace watched them out of the room. The official march of feet on the stairs sounded ominous.

They did not expect to find anything, Peter thought, and that was all that saved him.

They did not like anonymous phone calls, but they were conscientious and thorough. He watched them opening cupboard doors and checking in cabinets, even looking down the neck of a man-sized Satsuma vase. When the constable lifted the lid of a fan-shaped Yixing teapot, Peter could not restrain himself.

"Are you searching for bodies or bargains? Because I've a business to run here, and it seems only fair to let the other shoppers in."

The youthful constable blushed.

"What's in this room, Mr. Fox?" asked Chief Constable Heron.

"It's the stockroom. I store all my murder victims there."

"There's no need to be sarcastic, sir."

Peter followed them into the stockroom, watching them poke around. His nerves tightened as the constable glanced over the shelf in front of the passage-way, nearly knocking over an art deco figurine. Peter had learned the hard way how to conceal his feel-ings. He swallowed over the rock in his throat and remarked, "You break it, you buy it."

The constable and his chief exchanged looks, hav-ing seen some of the price tags in Rogue's Gallery.

Some more poking and prying, and then at last Chief Constable Heron said, "Thank you for your cooperation, Mr. Fox."

"Satisfied?"

The older man eyed him levelly. "No sir. That I am not. Not by a long shot."

Peter closed the door on them and leaned against it, eyes closed, breathing hard and fast, and very qui-etly, as though he'd run a mile and was still being pursued.

When he'd had a minute to gather himself he went upstairs. Grace was in the guest room. For a moment he observed her. She was painstakingly packing everything in little uptight bundles that couldn't breathe. Wedging them in together . . .

With an effort he controlled himself again.

Grace was staring at him. "What is it? Did they find something?"

"No, of course not. There's nothing to find."

"You look . . ."

He probably looked like he felt: ill. Just the thought of it, the thought of being locked up, confined, closed into a small space. Sweat popped out on his forehead in memory.

"Everything's fine."

She did not look reassured, and he did not blame her.

"You moved the body?"

"Last night."

She pressed her hands to her eyes for a moment. "This is bad: not telling the police, disturbing evidence. We could go to jail for that alone."

"I know."

She closed the neatly packed suitcase. Locked it. "I think I should try to locate Monica as soon as possible, and then go to the embassy. They must be able to fix me up with some kind of temporary passport." She lugged the bag toward Peter, who took it from her.

More curious than anything else, he queried, "What happened to not running away?"

"That was before I was facing jail time." She tried to imagine Ms. Wintersmith receiving a phone call that Grace had been arrested. The picture this conjured caused her to blurt out, "Given the circumstances, I don't think I have any choice."

"I'm not so sure."

He had to be the most contradictory creature on the planet. One minute he couldn't wait to get rid of her, the next . . . A little exasperatedly, Grace questioned, "What aren't you sure about?"

"Let's think about this for a moment. Someone

kills Delon and leaves him in my home. First, why do they kill him?"

"To get the . . . the gewgaws."

"Maybe. Then someone tips the police off that the body is here. Why?"

"To frame you."

"Yes, but why?"

"To keep you out of the action?"

"I think so, but again, why?"

Grace studied him gravely. "Because he—she—they—think you could be a problem. *Or* because they didn't get the gewgaws when they murdered Delon, and they think you have them—it—the object in question. And they want time to find it."

"Which means someone thinks it's still here."

He watched the way her eyes widened; she was a rather pretty girl, although maybe it was an odd time to notice. A bit Victorian-looking with her Dresden doll face, rosebud mouth, wide eyes, and that veil of sorrel hair now done up in a sophisticated roll that made her look older and more conservative.

"In the shop?"

"Maybe. I suppose it's possible." He scrutinized her from beneath his lashes. "You see what I'm saying though? All this would indicate that they are watching me and this house."

"And me." Grace worked it out. "You think they'll try for me again, when I leave here?"

"I don't know. It's possible. My inclination is to let them have what they want."

"Me?"

His lips twitched. "No. Access to the house. The shop. If Delon hid something here, let them find it. Let them take it. Let them keep right on 'round the bend."

This seemed to breach some suburban ethic. "But you can't! It's—it's—Not only that, suppose they wreck the place during their search?"

"My guess is that they'll try to be subtle about it. They won't want us to know that they know that we've still got the goods. But if worse comes to worse—" He lifted his shoulders. "It's insured."

Grace was staring at him as though he hailed from another planet.

"Besides, Delon couldn't have had much time to stash the goods. It won't take them long to find what they're after." He loved this house, loved the beautiful, old things he had filled it with, but he had learned the hard way that these things were not important. Life and limb; this was what counted. And in the final instance: life.

Grace was still viewing him with consternation. "But you can't just let these felons take what they want. You can't give in to them."

"I admire your spirit." Actually he seemed amused by it. It seemed odd to her that someone who so obviously valued material things should dismiss the idea of fighting to protect them.

Grace opened her mouth, but he brushed her objection aside. "We'll discuss it later." He checked his watch. "It's time to open the shop."

"You're working?"

"They don't actually pay me to get knocked over the head and thrown in streams."

"But what am I supposed to do?"

"Do you know anything about antiques?"

"Well, no."

"It's your neck. If it were mine . . ." With a meaningful look he set Grace's suitcase back inside the guest room.

"But what will the police think? I can't just—" She was talking to his back.

It seemed to be business as usual at Rogue's Gallery. Tourists came, they saw, and were conquered. Peter was an effective salesman. He flirted lazily with the women and rattled off appreciating values to doubtful husbands.

Late morning, a van rolled up filled with old furniture, the result of Peter's recent buying trip. So at least he had not lied about that. Grace watched him unpack assorted pieces of china and pottery, a stack of fashion magazines from the 1920s, and various tables and chairs in all sizes and styles. Much of the antique business seemed to consist of tables and chairs.

Grace couldn't understand him. She felt they should be searching the premises for the item Danny Delon had died for. Especially since Peter had indicated he didn't plan on mounting any great resistance. How long could it take to find the item with both of them hunting? Granted, it was awkward not knowing what they were hunting for. And there were so many places to hide in Craddock House and Rogue's Gallery. Then again, maybe Peter was right. If they *were* being watched, then perhaps there was some sense in pretending to carry on as though everything were normal. She just didn't know. She tried to think how she would advise one of her girls, but frankly she hoped none of her girls was ever dumb enough to get into a situation like this.

Since Peter didn't require her help downstairs, she returned upstairs to his living quarters, changed out of her skirt and blouse and into jeans and a T-shirt. She unpacked her suitcase and put her things away in the cherry-wood armoire in the guest room.

She wasn't sure at which exact point during her conversation with Peter she had made her mind up to stay. Or, more exactly, to postpone leaving. She was certainly afraid of the police and of getting involved in any kind of scandal, but she was even more afraid of bumping into the Queen Mother and his partner. (Or even Mutt and Jeff.) And it was difficult to get real protection from the police without revealing the extent of Peter's involvement—which she didn't want to do. It was pretty clear to Grace that Peter was not popular with the local fuzz.

So she told herself, as she emptied her suitcase, that her decision was of a purely practical nature. Grace prided herself on being practical. She dismissed the idea that perhaps there was some little tiny part of her that was sort of enjoying having an adventure.

Her bags unpacked, Grace decided to occupy herself by searching the Internet once more. Peter could
scoff all he liked, but men in turbans indicated cults
to her. This time she concentrated on the religious
aspects of Astarte.

Astarte, aka Astoreth, Ishtar and Ugarit was a Phoenician fertility goddess worshipped around 1500 B.C.

Considering how often her name showed up in
connection with occult-related sites, Grace wondered
if her hunch about cults wasn't correct.

Astarte was the goddess of the Evening Star, of
love and of war. And she was one of the earliest aspects of the Great Mother.

"What else is there?" Grace wondered aloud,
clicking on a link.

The link opened on the image of a naked woman
riding a horse. She wore a horned crown and bran-
dished barbaric weapons.

"Hello, Muddah," murmured Grace, and jotted
down notes on a legal pad.

The sun made a brief appearance in the early afternoon, traveling slowly across the floorboards. The
shadow of the wisteria outside the windows dappled
the white walls. It was so peaceful that it was hard to
believe only two days earlier she had been held prisoner in a dirty, drafty abandoned farmhouse.

She was leaving another message on Calum Bell's
answering machine when Peter carried in her lunch
tray. Shepherd's pie made with chicken and vegetables, and a cold lager.

"I suppose you don't have any diet cola?" Grace inquired, eyeing the lager with misgivings.

"You suppose correctly." He glanced at the computer. "Having fun?"

"On a scale of one to ten—ten being kidnapped— I'm having the time of my life." Grace pushed her specs up on her forehead. "How's business?"

He shrugged. "It's a living."

"A very nice one by all appearances." She sampled a forkful of mashed potato topping. She recognized hints of Parmesan and buttermilk. If only this man would use his talents for good instead of evil.

His grin was wicked. "Do I detect a note of disapproval? Do you suspect I'm living off my ill-gotten gains? I assure you, I'm strictly legit these days." He glanced at the phone receiver. "Who were you calling?"

Did he not trust her?

Grace explained once again about Monica running off to Scotland. "I don't think they could track her, but I'm not sure. Maybe Calum's neighbors know where he's staying. Or maybe they'll break into Calum's flat and find some clue to tell them where they've gone."

"Ease up," Peter advised. "You're flooding the engine." He considered her troubled features. "I thought all you Yanks carried cell phones."

A mouthful of potato made it hard to articulate. Grace swallowed and got out, "That's just an ugly urban legend." She ignored the memory of the cell phones that both she and Monica did carry when on home soil.

He shrugged and said, apparently untroubled by the thought of other people in danger, "You've done what you could. When they get back she'll know where to find you."

Peter only stayed to chat another moment or two. Grace could see that he didn't expect her to find anything, but was relieved to have her out of his hair. Spurred on by the desire to prove him wrong, she kept on at the computer until it was getting dark.

Dusk was falling when she finally heard the last car drive away in the Cumbrian evening. This was followed by Peter's quick light tread on the stairs. The living room lights came on and with them the stereo and the restless beat of The Waterboys once more. It was strange hearing music that she knew from another time in her life. She recognized the song: "Be My Enemy," and the remembered lyrics brought a reluctant grin. Something about finding goons on one's landing and thieves on one's trail and nazis on the phone—at least they didn't have to worry about nazis dialing in. Something to be grateful for!

You be my enemy and I'll be yours.

Love in the twenty-first century, Grace thought. She tried to imagine Keats or Shelley or Byron penning rock lyrics. After all, they had sort of been the equivalent of rock stars in their own era.

She logged off the computer, pulled off her glasses and joined Peter in the kitchen where he was having a beer and staring out the window at the indigo tarn and the dark woods beyond.

"Buy you a drink?" he offered, holding up the bottle.

"Er—no thanks." She was conscious that tonight she would sleep under this man's roof again. It would be easier if she wasn't so maddeningly *aware* of him. "Do you want to know what I found?"

"Sure. But later. Let's eat out tonight."

"Is that wise?"

Peter drained the last of his beer and said, "The important thing is to keep up a normal front. We don't want anyone watching us—cops or crooks—to see anything out of the ordinary."

"That in itself is suspicious with what's been going on here," Grace pointed out.

As though she hadn't spoken, Peter said, "What are you in the mood for? There's a marvelous little Indian place down the road."

"You *hope* they'll break in!" Grace accused.

He studied her quizzically.

"And don't give me that look!"

Peter felt his jaw as though checking his "look." "Let's examine this from a practical standpoint," he said. "Our friends are convinced that whatever they're after is here. Myself, I think Danny probably was smart enough not to walk around carrying the item on his person, but these chaps aren't going to give up on the idea till they've had a chance to check for themselves. Since they won't take no for an answer, and since someone—one of us, I fear—might get injured trying to prevent their search, I say we give them enough time and plenty of space to make sure for themselves."

"That is the craziest plan I've ever heard!" Grace exclaimed.

"You need to get out more," Peter replied quite seriously.

The lowering sky was fading from pewter to lavender as they drove across the little stone bridge into the village of Innisdale. Lights glowed with friendly warmth in windows, the slate roofs glistened black from the recent rain.

"What happy fortune were it here to live," Grace quoted Wordsworth softly as Peter parked his Land Rover beneath the trees on the street in front of the Hungry Tiger restaurant.

Peter chuckled. He had an attractive laugh. "You wouldn't last six months, Esmerelda. Off season, the pace here is slow and steady. Very few fax machines and even fewer cell phones."

"There are worse things."

"True."

He came round, opening her car door. No wonder he was so popular with the local ladies, she thought. Those old-world gestures did weird things to a woman's defenses. It was hard not to respond. Why, at the mere mention of dining out, Grace had jumped back into her floral print skirt and Aran-knit sweater. She had to remind herself that this was not a date.

They went inside the restaurant. It was unexpectedly crowded, and smelled of curry and incense. Sitar music played discreetly in the background.

"Welcome, Peter my friend!" a Liverpudlian accent greeted them. Grace turned around, and there was a bearded man in a coral-pink turban beaming at them. She had to stop herself from exclaiming aloud.

Peter made the introductions, apparently blind to the sinister implications of Ahmed's headgear.

Ahmed winked at Grace. Perhaps he thought she was scoping him out.

"How do you do?" she mumbled, trying not to stare at the pink turban.

"This one is different, eh, Peter?" Ahmed said.

"A proper little limb."

Proper little limb? Like he'd strolled out of the pages of Charles Dickens. Was the man being droll or was he really some kind of anachronism?

They were led through sparkling bead curtains to a dark room where wall murals of tigers and palm trees were just visible in the flickering candlelight.

"Do you think that's him?" she hissed after they were seated.

"Him who?"

"The man in the turban."

Peter laughed. "You're joking. Ahmed?"

"Well, how many people in this village wear turbans?"

Peter opened his menu. "Ahmed doesn't need to turn to crime; he's making a killing right here in the restaurant."

Glancing over the menu prices, Grace had to agree.

Ahmed materialized with two bottles of Cobra beer and some kind of fried potato appetizers. He poured the beer into glasses with a flourish. Grace sipped hers cautiously. It wasn't bad, though all these foreign beers had the same skunky taste to her.

"What do you recommend?" she asked Ahmed, once again keeping her gaze focused on his face.

"Chicken Malabar!" Ahmed pronounced sunnily. "Is not to be missed. Just like you get at the famous Malabar Junction restaurant in London."

How far a jump was it from stealing recipes to murder, Grace speculated.

They ordered, Grace going for the Chicken Malabar and Peter settling on Prawn Malai Curry. Peter requested another Cobra and Grace decided to keep him company.

She began to cheer up. After all, she was having dinner with a good-looking man who was neither married nor gay. Granted, he was a thief and a liar, but he looked wonderful across the table from her. He wore a soft white shirt beneath a navy and white Kasuri vest, which he had explained, was made from an antique kimono. The dark blue made his hair gleam like old gold and brought out mysterious depths in his eyes. She was not falling for him. She admired him like she would any work of art.

Taking another swig of warm beer, Grace began earnestly, "Hebrew scholars speculate that the Astoreth of the Bible is a compilation of the Greek name Astarte and the Hebrew word *'boshet'* which means 'shame.' That would be in keeping with Hebrew contempt for the goddess cult."

Peter said, "Yes, I've seen her image on ancient seals and tomb reliefs. Sacred lotus in one hand and entwined serpents in the other."

"Her name comes up a lot in witchcraft rituals."

"Cor! The Wicked Witch of the West is after us?"

"You weren't laughing last night."

"I'm not laughing now. I simply don't follow a connection between some dusty goddess and Danny Delon getting forty whacks with an ax in my stock-room."

"You have quite a turn of phrase," Grace said. That quelling tone worked with the young ladies of St. Anne's, but seemed to have no effect on Peter. "The only clue we have is the word Astarte."

"I think there are one or two other indicators that what we're looking for has cash value on the material plane." His long lashes threw shadows over his cheekbones.

"What about the man in the turban?" Grace's eyes strayed to Ahmed speaking cheerfully with two other dinner guests.

"Men in turbans have been known to value cash."

"You're an antique dealer; so it seems reasonable to assume that whatever this item is it's something you could fence." Briefly she considered the idea that Peter had received property stolen from an ancient tomb and now the priests of that tomb were trying to retrieve their property. Too much Wilkie Collins, she decided, reaching for the potato balls.

The conversation drifted to other things until Ahmed brought their dinners. Then Peter returned to their earlier discussion as though he had been turning Grace's suggestion over in his mind.

"There's certainly a lucrative market for stolen antiquities," Peter agreed. "But I'm not a fence."

"And there are all kinds of sculptures, plaques, glyphs and votive stelae of Astarte. Some of it dates back to the second millennium," Grace put in eagerly.

"Your reasoning makes sense as far as it goes," Peter said. "The part I'm having trouble with is your favorite 'clue.' That's an artistic touch that doesn't fit."

"Why not?"

"Because most crooks don't have much sense of humor, let alone a sense of whimsy. Did Mutt and Jeff strike you as the kind of blokes to scrawl messages in blood?"

"No," Grace admitted.

"What about the other two? The two who grabbed you. They seem like the type to leave cryptic clues?"

She shook her head. "It was meant to frighten you," she observed.

"It succeeded." He didn't look too frightened though, shoveling in prawns and green chilis with a healthy appetite.

They finished their meal and Ahmed brought Kesar Pistar Kulfi, frozen cones filled with a creamy green substance that tasted like nothing Grace recognized. Peter paid the bill and Grace said, "I'm awfully sorry about this. As soon as I can replace my traveler's checks—"

He said gravely (though his eyes seemed to be laughing at her): "It's my pleasure. After all, you wouldn't be in this predicament if not for me."

"You've got that right!" But she couldn't help smiling.

"It smells like rain," Peter remarked as they walked out into the damp night. Trees lining the road rustled in the night breeze. Stars glittered above the rooftops and the smell of wood smoke lingered in the air.

Across the street, Grace could see the library. A giant motorcycle was parked at the curb, polished chrome gleaming in the lamplight. A solitary lamp burned inside the library. Did the librarian drive a hog, Grace wondered vaguely.

Peter moved past Grace to get the door of the Land Rover, which was parked a few feet away on the cobbled street. There was a crunch of footsteps on loose leaves, and someone grabbed Grace from behind. A brutal hand clamped across her mouth stifling her scream. She sensed, rather than saw Peter turning back to her.

But Grace had had days to reenact her abduction, to consider all the things she should have done to save herself, and being more than a little tightly strung—and with the benefit of two Cobras coursing through her system—this time she reacted. She jammed her elbow back with all her might into the gut of her attacker. His breath came out in a hot, "Ooouff!" At the same time she clamped her teeth into the palm over her mouth.

"You bitch!" howled her attacker.

But Grace was free. Sprinting a couple of yards down the street, she put a car at the curb between herself and her assailant.

From where she stood she could see Peter still on the near side of the Land Rover. He stood motionless, not reacting to her plight. An instant later she understood why. A man stood in the shadow of the tree. Light from the windows of the Hungry Tiger gleamed off the barrel of the gun he held aimed at Peter.

"Hold it!" he snarled in a voice she remembered only too well. "Take another step and I blast him. And then you."

"Do I know you?" Peter inquired.

The man laughed. If you could call it a laugh. "Do you?"

"It's the Queen Mother," Grace said. Even she had to admit it sounded insane.

"We want the goods Delon left with you."

"I don't have 'the goods.' I don't know what 'the goods' are." Even now, Peter couldn't help sounding a little sarcastic. Grace really wished he wouldn't.

"A likely story." QM gestured to his partner who was walking up and down the length of the parked car as though trying to decide from which direction to rush Grace. "Grab her, you git!"

The man started for the hood of the car and Grace darted around to the trunk. The man turned back to his co-thug and shrugged helplessly.

"Listen, mate," Peter said, "You should have waited to chop Delon. He never had time to tell me what he was peddling."

"That's your hard luck. If you want to keep breathing, you'll find it. Fast. And for insurance, we'll hang on to your girlfriend here."

"Yeah, right," said Peter. "Get under the car!"

For a minute Grace failed to understand he was talking to her. She saw his leg come up like a mule's kick and the gun went flying out of the thug's hand and skittering across the pavement.

Absorbing at last what was happening—although she didn't see the point of crawling under the car— Grace hit the pavement, scuttling under the chassis as the other man lunged for her again.

Instantly she saw her advantage. Her attacker had to lie down to grab her and she could scoot around— painfully but efficiently enough—to kick at his head and arms. And kick, she did.

And scream she did.

"Help!" she screamed. "Fire! Help!"

It seemed hours but it could have only been moments before the door to the Hungry Tiger flew open. Ahmed stood framed in the doorway, surrounded by some of the Hungry Tiger patrons.

"Hey, man!" Ahmed yelled.

Footsteps echoed down the street and were joined by Grace's attacker who jumped up and ran as well. Rolling over with some difficulty, she saw two dark-clad figures cross the road climb into a black van parked down the street. The van roared into life, pulled a U-turn, and peeled away in the opposite direction without turning on its lights.

A moment later Peter crouched down beside the car. "All right?"

"Yes." She took the hand he offered and crawled cautiously out. He helped her to her feet. Grace found that she was shaking so hard she needed his support to stand.

"What happened? What was that about?" Ahmed demanded, joining them.

"They tried to nick her purse," Peter said. His arm around Grace felt as solid as though encased in shining armor. She understood why the Honorable Allegra Clairmont-Brougham had clung to him with such tenacity.

"Hey, Gracie, you okay?"

She assured Ahmed and the rest of the crowd that she was fine. Peter assured them that she was fine— and at last they climbed into the Land Rover and started back to Rogue's Gallery.

Grace's teeth were chattering. That made her mad and the anger steadied her. "So much for that plan!" she said tartly. "I guess they don't feel like hunting for the stuff themselves."

"I guess not."

He had little else to say until they reached the gallery. Then bidding Grace wait for him, he went inside alone.

Tensely, Grace watched the lights go on in the lower level. The moon drifted in and out of the clouds, casting deep shadows over the sleeping banks of flowers and glistening grass.

Peter was back in a few minutes.

"A-OK. No one's been inside."

Grace got out and, limping a little, accompanied him into the building. Upstairs he took her coat.

"My skirt's ruined," she said, gazing down at the oil marks on the print. Her cream-colored sweater hadn't fared much better. Peter stared at her but she could tell he wasn't seeing her.

He said grimly, "We've got to head this off now."

"What does that mean?"

"If the cops come back here with any kind of serious equipment, they'll find traces of . . ." He caught sight of her face. "These days, with the equipment they've got: DNA fingerprinting, UV, infrared—it's impossible to cover up every sign of . . . violence."

"What are you saying?" She was afraid she knew.

"I'm saying that I must go back down to the police station and file a report. It will look suspicious if we don't. We mustn't give them an excuse for coming back here. I'll say they tried to snatch your bag—that you didn't recognize them. Understand?"

"But why would the police come here?"

"They'll come. Trust me."

His features were sharp and so pale they might have been carved scrimshaw. Why, she wondered? What was he so afraid of? Grace reached for her coat. "Then I'll go with you."

"No. I'll tell them you're a bit shocky, that you'll come in tomorrow."

"I'm not staying here by myself!"

"Steady on. You said yourself you're no use at lying."

"I'm not staying here alone!"

"They're not going to try again."

"Says *who?* Is it written in the Official Criminal Bylaws?"

"Don't be daft." He added, "Wait till the reaction hits. You'll be only too glad to curl up in bed."

He had a point. Her muscles were in knots, and her body felt like a mass of bruises and scrapes.

He walked toward the door. "I'll only be gone an hour or so. You're quite safe here. The place is like a fortress."

"Tell it to Danny Delon!"

She could see he didn't like that, but all he said was, "Chin up, Esmerelda. I'll be back before you know I'm gone."

She was pointing out the obvious illogic of that statement as he closed the door.

Off he drove into the night with Grace watching from the upper story until the embers of Peter's tail-lights had vanished into the night. *The wandering outlaw of his own dark mind . . .* Grace let the drapes fall.

In the kitchen she put the electric kettle on. As it boiled, she stared at the answering machine, its red light blinking like a warning signal. She thought about the first day she had arrived and the messages on Peter's machine. That funny little good-for-nothing Mimi was still leaving him daily phone messages.

She thought about Allegra snooping around in the dark of night. How dreadful to be reduced to such behavior. Grace tried to think whether she had ever cared enough for any man to contemplate such undignified and irrational behavior. Nope. Not even as a giddy teenager. Not that Grace had been a giddy teenager. Perhaps she had read a few too many romance novels, but that was normal.

Through the years she had had one or two undemanding relationships. Like her relationship with Chaz. Theirs was exactly the kind of sensible friendship based on mutual interests and respect that Grace needed. Chaz was good company and they shared many of the same values and goals, but Chaz was not a man to inspire reckless acts or dangerous passion. Nor Grace the woman to perform them.

Which was all to the good.

But the name "Allegra" sparked a train of thought. It was not a common name, although it was very pretty. Musical, she reflected vaguely. Grace knew of one historical Allegra, and that was the illegitimate daughter of George Gordon Noel Byron, one of her very favorite bad boy Romantic poets.

Allegra had been the result of a brief union

between Lord Byron and Claire Clairmont, another writer (though not a very good one) who also happened to be Shelley's sister-in-law. Percy Bysshe Shelley was another of Grace's favorite bad boy poets. Shelley and Byron had been great pals back in the nineteenth century. In fact, their whole literary circle had been almost incestuously intertwined, with everyone seeming to be related by blood or sex. Sort of like that Kevin Bacon game that the girls of St. Anne's were always referring to.

Yes, it was all coming to Grace now: a textbook recounting of a centuries-old scandal. Lord Byron had sent the luckless child, Allegra, to an Italian convent where she died of typhoid in 1822.

A little light went on in her brain. Astarte. Surely there was something about Byron and Astarte?

Methodically, Grace began to work down the bookshelves in Peter's rooms. The man appeared to have a love of literature to rival her own. Or were these valuable first editions just more stage dressing?

There were innumerable volumes on art and antiques. There were philosophy books and history books. There was nothing fiction—and nothing contemporary in nonfiction. *I met a traveler from an antique land*, mused Grace. Despite his clothes and speech and obvious ease with the world around him, something about Peter Fox was not quite of this day and age.

At last Grace found poetry: Wordsworth and Coleridge, who had inspired her sojourn to the Lake

District. Staunch Sir Walter Scott. There was also a first edition of Rupert Brooks she would have killed for. There were silk-bound covers of Keats and Shelley, and finally, Byron. Grace sat down Indian-fashion on the floor, skimming through the slender volume, for once resisting the magic spell of the words.

This was all the obvious stuff: "When We Two Parted," "So We'll Go No More A-Roving," "She Walks in Beauty." For a moment Grace's eyes lingered on those lovely lines, recalling that for Byron this had been a fairly routine compliment. Resolutely she pushed on. There was no mention of Astarte in any of these. Not even in the footnotes.

Perhaps it had not been Byron? Methodically she scanned the index of the other Romantic poets. Keats was a good bet with his love of things classical. But there was no reference to Astarte in Keats. No reference in any of the other Romantics.

Grace decided her first theory had been right: Byron. Maybe it was one of the longer works. Definitely not "Childe Harold." Perhaps "Don Juan?" Or "Manfred?" There was an entire landing lined with books right outside the flat door. In one of those leather-bound volumes might lie the answer she needed.

She sipped her tea and ruminated. Would Peter consider her efforts prying? Did the normal rules of etiquette hold with a man who had been responsible for getting you abducted? Miss Manners not being available for comment, Grace knew she would have to go with common sense. Except that common sense reminded her that she didn't know where Peter had concealed the body of Danny Delon. He certainly seemed panicked at the idea of another police search. Perhaps Mr. Delon had not left the building? *There* was a happy thought.

On the other hand, Grace couldn't sit up all night biting her fingernails and waiting for Peter to come home—if he came home. Take action, she always advised her girls. Sitting here in the dead of night she was liable to start imagining shadowy figures lurking behind hedges, villains in turbans watching her window light from below. She was liable to start believing every branch brushing against the glass panes was someone prying open a window. (Come to think of it, what was the UK equivalent of 911?) She was liable to start thinking every creak of this old house was someone sneaking up the stairs to get her. . . .

Impatient with herself, Grace unlocked the flat door, and poked her head out. The darkness pressed in on all sides. She felt along the wall until she found a light switch. Light blazed down on the landing and stairs.

Not a mouse stirred. Yet she had the eerie sensation of being watched.

Suspended from the vault ceiling, the mahogany ship's figurehead hung just out of reach of the balcony. The wooden eyes met hers without emotion. But then, here was a maiden who had swum with sharks.

Grace walked the length of the landing, staring up

at the walls of leather-bound volumes. Hundreds of books. Thousands in fact. It could take days to search through all this.

She decided to start with something easy. The stack behind the railing. Squatting, she scanned the titles; there seemed to be no rhyme or reason to their order. A tome on 1950s manners, several novels, a Bible, a history of the Greeks.

Overbalancing, Grace's hand brushed against the stack. The top book slid off and fell open. Curiously, she picked it up.

It was hollow. A hiding-place book.

She set the book aside and picked up the next one. *A History of Flagellation Among Different Nations.* "Yikes," murmured Grace. But this, too, was a fake. Beautifully done, but a fake.

Quickly Grace shuffled through the stack. All the books, despite size, width, age, and title were hollowed out.

Grace stared up at the shelves towering above her, and wondered if her research might not take so long after all.

7

"*A*starte," Grace informed Peter at breakfast the next morning, "refers to Lord Byron's half-sister Augusta Leigh. References to Astarte in Byron's epic poem "Manfred" are regarded by many scholars as Byron's veiled confession of their incestuous relationship."

Peter frowned as though she had begun speaking in tongues.

"George Gordon, Lord Byron, 1788-1824," Grace prompted. "*Byron.* One of the greatest of the Romantic poets and arguably the most famous, if only for his wild love affairs and passionate ideal—"

"I know who Lord Byron was. And nobody, by the way, ever called him George."

Grace allowed herself an academic smirk. "Augusta called him 'baby.' Byron called her 'goose.' "

"Here we go," muttered Peter, pouring himself another cup.

"Think about it," Grace said eagerly, leaning forward. "In 1905 Byron's grandson Lord Lovelace published the *Astarte Papers* as his grandmother's vindication for having left Byron. This is all documented fact, by the way."

Peter nodded without enthusiasm. He looked tired this morning. The tiny lines around his eyes were more pronounced. His hair, damp from the shower, fell carelessly over his forehead.

"Now, it seems obvious to me that Lord Byron and Asta—"

"It seems obvious to me," he interrupted rudely, "that you've got Lord Byron on the brain. Frankly, you seem obsessed with dead guys. It's not healthy in a woman your age."

"At what age would an obsession with dead guys be healthy?" Grace inquired, momentarily distracted. "Just for the record."

"For the record," Peter said, ignoring this, "there is absolutely no reason to suppose we are looking for a manuscript. I know that's where this is heading. I know you would love to believe we're after some priceless, long-lost masterpiece, but your mates in the van mentioned gewgaws not papers."

"But . . ."

Peter shook his head. "Jewels. For one thing, it has to be something Delon would recognize as valuable. He wouldn't have recognized a literary treasure if it had hit him between the eyes. It also has to be something Delon could easily conceal on his person."

"Why assume that? Anyway, a manuscript could be rolled up in a cylinder and carried under a jacket. And someone else could have pointed out the value of it to Delon."

"Gewgaws," said Peter.

"What *are* gewgaws?"

"Supposedly the word comes from the Middle English *giuegoue*. Meaning a showy trifle, a useless ornament, or a toy. Not, by any stretch, a manuscript."

"You're assuming the thugs who grabbed me use their nouns properly."

"I'm assuming whoever hired them can tell the difference between a book and a jewel."

Grace found Peter's reasoning oddly irritating. She wasn't used to being outargued, especially by a man.

"Fine, it's not a manuscript. So what is it? The Jewels of Astarte? There's no such thing."

Peter seemed to find something funny; what, she had no idea. He questioned gravely, "Are you sure about that?"

"Yes, I'm sure. I spent most of last night scaling your bookshelves. I've researched every major site of Astarte worship and there are no particularly valuable artifacts associated with her."

Peter washed down the last of his sausage and eggs with another cup of tea. They were enjoying a traditional English breakfast right down to the fried mushrooms and tomato. Grace was not sure about tomato at breakfast, but she was trying to be a good sport.

Tilting his chair back at a gravity-defying angle, he speculated, "Astarte or Astoreth was regarded by the Greeks and Romans as the Evening Star, and partially identified with Aphrodite. Ishtar to the Assyrians, in fact, she's the all round great female principle."

"If you already knew all this, why didn't you say so last night?"

He shrugged. "I don't know, you're rather cute when you're on the boil. In any case, literature is your field, history is mine." He drummed his fingers on the table. "I'm guessing an artifact. Probably a jewel, though I can't imagine how Delon would have access—"

"Wrong!" Grace said. "Wrong, wrong, wrong. You're taking the reference to Astarte too literally. It isn't a representation of Astarte we're after. Astarte is a symbol."

"What makes you think so?"

"Everything points to it."

"What everything?"

Grace gestured vaguely. "Your girlfriend's name, for one thing."

Peter's black brows rose in an expression of superiority. "Are we talking proof or mystical signs from on high?"

"Allegra."

"Pardon?"

"Byron had an illegitimate daughter by a woman named Claire Clairmont. That's what she called herself anyway. Actually her name was Jane, and she was Mary Godwin's stepsister. Mary Godwin was the author of *Frankenstein,* and coincidentally, Shelley's wife."

"I know who Mary Godwin was."

"She—Claire, that is—practically forced herself upon Byron who was still technically married to Annabella Milbanke—"

Catching Peter's eye, Grace returned hastily to the point. "*Allegra Clairmont*-Brougham? That's quite a coincidence. Wait, there's more!"

Grace jumped up from the table to return a moment later with a stack of weighty tomes. These she dropped on the table, rattling the creamer and sugar bowl.

Aloud she read, "*The Wicked Lord Byron. Lyrical Lords of the Romantic Age.* And here's my favorite: *He Walked In Beauty.*"

"Please, I just ate," complained Peter.

"All by your neighbor, noted Byronic scholar V. M. Brougham."

Peter sighed. "V. M. Brougham is Al's Aunt Venetia. I fail to see where this is leading."

"V. M. Brougham is a nut," Grace told him succinctly. "You think *I* have an obsession with dead guys? This woman has made them her life's work. You should read what passes for scholarship in these things. It's embarrassing."

Peter idly rubbed the side of his nose with his index finger. "That doesn't prove anything."

"There's more. In the bio notes of *He Walks,* it says V. M. Brougham is working on the definitive account of Byron's relationship with his half-sister Augusta Leigh, entitled *That Hour Foretold*. That was twenty years ago."

Peter said nothing.

"You have a Byronic scholar living on the other side of your woods—"

"It's the Lake District, Grace. It's not just the tourists who appreciate the literary history here. We've got a cottage industry based on the Romantic poets alone."

Grace stuck to her guns. "*And* there's the clue of 'Astarte' scrawled in blood. There's *got* to be a connection. At the very least, V. M. Brougham might be able to shed some light on what we're looking for. Maybe it's a letter from Byron to Augusta Leigh."

Grace's eyes blazed with a fanatical light that Peter viewed with misgiving.

"What happened to the cult angle?"

Grace shrugged.

He lowered his chair on all four legs. "Now listen," he said firmly, "I appreciate your desire to help. I value your input, but don't you think that the smartest move on your part would be to go home?"

"Certainly not! This is my field of expertise." This was the kind of thing she lived and breathed for. With the possibility of finding a literary treasure, any desire Grace had had to flee Britain for home and safety vanished. This was every scholar's dream. What were a few thugs with guns in the face of academic fame and glory? "Besides, you're the one who said they might try to snatch me if I tried to leave the country."

"I know, but I've been thinking up ways around that. I just might have a plan."

"You just *might* have a plan? That's reassuring!"

"Grace . . ."

"Peter!"

Unexpectedly he deferred to her. Grace took a deep breath. "What's the point of arguing? It's going to take at least a couple of days before I can get a new passport. In the meantime, let me help."

Still he said nothing. Was she winning him over to her point of view?

"At least grant that there is probably a connection between Byron and this murder."

He shook his head. "There's nothing to indicate a lost manuscript."

"Okay, but it is the most logical conclusion."

"It's not logical when the man specifically mentioned jewels."

Grace agilely jumped track. "As you said, literature is my field. The Romantics are my period. I can be of use to you. You're working blind."

"Don't you have family? People who are going to worry about you when you don't turn up?"

"Naturally I have a family. I have a lover." Now why had she thrown that in, for it was surely an exaggeration of her understanding with Chaz. Was this her insurance policy against her attraction to Peter Fox? "But I'm on vacation. No one's expecting to hear from me till the new term starts in . . ." She looked up at the kitchen clock and swallowed hard. "Seven days."

Seven days till the term started? Could her vacation truly have dwindled down to six days? Had she lost a day somewhere?

"Just my luck." Peter eyed her dourly.

Thinking that perhaps he was softening, Grace said persuasively, "We have nothing to lose by talking to this V. M. Brougham, surely? We could just sort of sound her out."

After a long moment Peter nodded. "Why not? Provided you agree to go home, once you see that these things are merely coincidence."

"Sure," Grace said blithely, crossing her fingers in her lap.

"Petah, dahling!" exclaimed Lady Venetia, beckoning them forward with a long, ivory cigarette holder.

"Lady Vee," returned Peter, moving forward to kiss the proffered wrinkled cheek.

Wow, thought Grace, gazing about herself in fascination. They could have stepped through a time portal into a Regency drawing room. The striped satin wallpaper, green brocade settee, black lacquer spinet: the room was perfect in every detail. Two decrepit Irish wolfhounds lay in front of the marble fireplace over which hung a huge oil painting of Lord Byron looking down his long, perfect nose at them.

In fact, the room's only anachronism was Lady Venetia herself. She was about eighty years old, tiny and birdlike. Her hair was jet black, and had been bobbed in the style of the roaring twenties. Her lips were ruby red. She wore a black beaded dress although it was just after noontime, and her red-taloned hands were encrusted with jeweled rings.

"And this must be . . . ?" Lady Vee gestured vaguely with the cigarette-holder wand. "I'm sorry dear, I didn't catch your name."

"This is Grace Hollister," Peter introduced.

Grace was offered a doll-sized hand in the royal manner. She wasn't sure if she was supposed to kiss the paw or curtsy. She settled for a firm handshake. Lady Vee winced imperceptibly.

"My *deah*, we've heard so *little* about you," she murmured. She looked Grace up and down, from the sage canvas pants to the white oversize knit shirt, and having summed her up, arched her penciled brows in disbelief.

Here we go, thought Grace. God help the woman Peter actually got involved with. She directed a dark look his way.

"You've had some little bother with the police, I believe? Nothing serious, I hope?"

Peter returned languidly, "The usual. Every time a bicycle goes missing they come to me." He shrugged as though it were no great concern.

"A bicycle?" Lady Venetia seemed to think this over. "Dear, dear. I suppose it's your wicked past catching up with you."

He had turned the full battery of his smile on Lady Vee and the old crone simpered like a girl. "I *do* hope you've brought word of that mummy case you promised me."

"Unfortunately, no."

Lady Vee pouted. When she had been sweet sixteen that sort of thing had probably been very effective. Nowadays it was scary.

"Actually," said Peter, folding his long length onto the forest-green brocade sofa, "we've come to draw upon your scholarly expertise."

"Have you? How flattering." Lady Venetia's birdlike gaze darted to Grace and then away again. "You will stay to lunch, won't you?"

"I'm afraid we've made plans," Peter regretted.

"Allegra will be *so* disappointed."

The verbal Ping-Pong continued back and forth. One of the wolfhounds groaned and rolled onto its side. Or perhaps keeled over dead. Whichever, Grace empathized. She tried to contain her impatience, studying the room they sat in. Lady Venetia's entire body of work stood behind glass-fronted doors. The Barbara Cartland of the pseudointelligentsia?

Every conceivable book on Byron weighted Lady Vee's shelves. A bronze bust of the Wicked Lord stood on a pedestal by the window. Grace was convinced that they had come to the right place.

"*Such* a pity you missed the Huxleys'," Lady Vee was saying, slanting Grace a certain look. "Mimi Kenton-Kydd was simply ravishing."

"So I've heard," Peter replied.

Grace yawned.

On it went. Lady Venetia flirted outrageously, Peter fenced. Lady Venetia rang a bell and sherry was served. Grace decided Peter had the patience of a saint—or a Machiavelli.

"Now you must tell me what little thing I can do to help you, Peter, my dear," Lady Vee said at last. "Are you thinking of writing a book perhaps?"

"Actually we were curious about one of your books," Peter said. *"That Hour Foretold."*

Lady Venetia continued to smile, but Grace caught the flicker of her beady eyes.

"My masterpiece," she murmured.

"In the course of your research did you happen across any reference to—"

"To . . . ?" Lady Vee cut in quite sharply.

"To some item of value associated with Augusta Leigh? Perhaps a gift from Byron?"

"What kind of gift?"

"Jewels?"

"Jewels?" Was it Grace's imagination or was there a hint of relief in Lady Venetia's expression. "Not that I recall. Of course B. was a generous man."

"No family jewels?"

"I'm sure you don't mean that the way it sounds." Lady Vee smiled coyly.

Even Peter looked slightly uncomfortable.

Lady Venetia refilled her sherry glass and mused aloud, "I suppose there were the Wentworth jewels, but they would have been the typical heirlooms of a noble house. You would be more a judge of that kind of thing than I." She gave Peter a sly smile. "I can't remember any particular reference to Byron's mother's jewels, nor the Milbanke woman's. No, Peter, my *deah,* I really can't think of any jewels associated with Byron. Why?"

"What about a missing manuscript?" put in Grace, disregarding Peter's look of displeasure.

Lady Vee nearly choked on her sherry. "Manuscript? What manuscript?"

"We were hoping—"

"No manuscript," Peter cut in. The look he shot Grace reminded her of the look she used with great effect on her unruly tenth graders.

"But Miss Hollister has said—"

"Miss Hollister has old manuscripts on the brain," Peter said with less than his usual charm. "They are her forte, you see. She's a highly respected professor of Romantic literature."

This exaggeration had an instant effect on Lady Vee, who froze, the thimbleful of sherry an inch from her lips. "Indeed?" she managed.

"Yes," said Peter. "Her help has been invaluable."

"Inval . . . ?" Lady Venetia blinked. "You mean in regard to these . . . these jewels?"

"Now that would be telling," Peter returned with a coyness to match Lady Vee's. He set his sherry glass aside and rose in a fluid movement. Grace had to admire both his poise and his sense of timing; the old woman was practically goggling her dismay. "A friend of mine believes such an item may soon come on the market."

"If such an item exists, and were to come on the market, I would be very much interested," Lady Venetia said. "I would hope our many years of friendship would entitle me to the right of first refusal?"

Peter, already strolling toward the doorway, tossed back casually, "You will certainly be one of the first to hear from me."

They were halfway down the grand marble staircase before Grace got out, "There! You see, I *knew*—"

"This isn't proof."

"You know darn well—if you don't believe she's involved, why did you set yourself up?"

"I didn't. I was already set up. Delon was murdered in my house, remember?"

Grace found it difficult to argue, trotting to keep up with Peter's long strides.

They went out through a brick courtyard. A section of the original stables had been converted to a garage. A silver Rolls Royce was parked in the drive. The chauffeur knelt beside it, polishing the sparkling chrome work.

Grace barely spared the man a glance, then did a double take and stopped in her tracks.

Peter's viselike grip started her moving again.

"Did you see—" She tried to look back over her shoulder.

"Later."

A wall of hedges shut the courtyard from sight. They climbed into Peter's Land Rover. Peter started the engine.

"Didn't you see who that was?" Grace demanded, turning to stare at him.

"I saw." Peter reversed smoothly in a wide arc, one arm across the back of the seat.

Grace was gazing in the rearview disbelievingly. "But Peter, it's Mutt!"

The police were dragging the tarn behind Craddock House when Peter and Grace returned, following their visit to Lady Vee's.

"What are they looking for?" Grace asked Peter's stern profile.

"What do you think they're looking for?"

She had almost forgotten about the poor little murdered man in the secret passage, preoccupied as she was by the promise of a long-lost work by Byron.

Her eyes met his. "Will they find . . . it?"

Peter turned away from the window. "If they look hard enough."

After this he opened the shop and conducted business as though nothing more were on his mind than matching the right customer to the right antiquity.

Grace amused herself thumbing through some old copies of *Punch* and reading up on the life and times of Lord Byron.

The afternoon passed without event, but toward teatime the searchers signaled a find. Glued to the window, Grace watched the commotion by the water's edge as the minions of the law bustled around the thing they had recovered from the cold deep water.

At last the body of Danny Delon was loaded into an ambulance and carted off into the dusk.

The official cars departed. The tarn was once again still as black glass, reflecting the sinking sun and crooked shadow of trees.

The guttural roar of a Harley split the silence. As Grace watched, a lone black figure on a giant chrome bike pulled out of the woods and disappeared down the highway.

"They found him," Grace informed Peter when he came upstairs for dinner a couple of hours later.

"Did they?" He seemed unmoved. "Then I suppose we can expect another visit from the local constabulary."

He went in to wash, the subject apparently closed.

"Well, Miss Hollister, what an impression of our country you must have!" Chief Constable Heron said, ushering Grace into his inner office and closing the door on Peter, who had already had his turn at being questioned. "Have a seat, young lady."

It was some time since anyone had referred to Grace as a "young lady." She decided it was sort of sweet. She had a seat and a cup of tea and tried not to let her wariness show. Heron was practically rubbing his hands in satisfaction at having separated her from Peter.

She suspected that leaving Peter to cool his heels while she was interviewed was a deliberate ploy, designed to make him fear what she might be blabbing.

She knew it was vital that she did not reveal anything about Lady Vee's connection to the lost manuscript, but she had seen enough episodes of *Columbo* to know how tricky the police could be in their interrogations. Of course she was not being interrogated, she was filing a report. Still, she felt as though she was going to be interrogated despite the tea and sympathy.

The chief constable smiled at her with fatherly reassurance, though his currant-colored eyes stayed sharp and shrewd on her face.

"Now tell me about the evening before last, Miss Hollister."

Grace related the version of events she and Peter had agreed upon.

The chief constable jotted down some notes and said, "So this man demanded your handbag, and you declined to give it to him?"

Keep it simple, stupid, Grace warned herself.

"It all happened so fast," she excused.

"Of course, of course. Most upsetting. But you did run a short way down the street? With your handbag?"

"I guess so. I don't remember that part really."

"And during this, the other man held a gun on Mr. Fox?"

"Right."

"And did you have the impression that these gentlemen knew each other?"

"The muggers?"

The chief constable frowned. "Mr. Fox and the man with the gun, Miss Hollister."

"Uh . . . well, no." She added hastily, "I couldn't hear what they said, of course."

"Of course." Heron stroked his mustache like the villain in a nineteenth century melodrama. Except Heron was the good guy and Grace was keeping company with thieves. "I imagine we'll lift a print or two off his revolver."

"Oh. Yes." Grace drank more tea.

Outside Heron's window the sun was shining and bees were humming. It was a lulling sound, but Grace knew she could not afford to be lulled. She had to stay "frosty," as her students would say.

"How well do you know Peter Fox, Miss Hollister?"

Cautiously, Grace answered, "As I told you, we only met the other night."

"The night you pulled him out of the stream at Kentmere?"

Grace nodded.

"But you are staying with him now? I thought you were going to meet friends in Scotland?"

Grace smiled and shrugged. "It's a woman's prerogative to change her mind, Chief Constable." Good God, she sounded like someone out of a book! The kind of book she discouraged girls from reading.

"Would you by any chance have an idea as to the identity of an unidentified man we found in the lake behind Craddock House?"

"Me? No. I saw you searching for him yesterday. Did someone report him missing?"

The chief constable said patiently, "If that were the case he would not be unidentified, Miss Hollister."

"Of course. I was thinking perhaps one of the village inns . . ."

"You think he might have been vacationing locally?"

"I have no idea. It seems logical, don't you think?"

"No, I don't. I believe the man was a criminal."

"Well, I guess criminals take vacations like everyone else."

Heron eyed her for a long moment, then cleared his throat. "You seem like a nice girl, Miss Hollister. Will you take a word of advice?"

"I don't know. I'll listen to it."

"Shake loose Peter Fox. He's a 'wrong 'un.' Oh, I know he seems an affable chap, but he's been involved in some most unsavory dealings."

She had been determined not to discuss Peter, but she heard herself saying, "But he's legitimate now surely?"

Heron shook his head. "Once a thief, always a thief. He's been in trouble, one way or another, since he was a boy. And now . . . well, matters may be more serious."

She knew she must not address the implication of murder. She tried to express natural curiosity. "Oh. Then he's lived here all his life?"

"Er. No. Fox is a stranger to these parts. Only lived here four or five years. But we got the complete dossier on him when he settled here." He shook his head. "Some people find that kind of thing romantic. Stealing jewels. But all it comes down to is taking what isn't yours because you don't want to do a decent day's work."

"I don't approve of stealing, naturally," Grace said. "But I do believe people can change—if they want to."

Heron said heavily, "But that's the catch, miss. How many crooks really want to?"

Peter was not in the waiting room when Grace left Heron's office. The constable looked up out of his paper and shrugged when she asked where he had disappeared.

Thanking him, Grace stepped outside the police station. Tourists strolled along the shady street carrying shopping bags and cameras. The architecture in this part of Innisdale was a little more modern, mostly Edwardian period. On the far side of the promenade was a park, and through blossoming trees, she could see a small black wrought-iron bandstand. She almost expected to hear Sergeant Pepper's Lonely Hearts Club Band tuning up.

There were a number of inviting shops housed in the Edwardian buildings: bakeries, jewelers, a confectioner, another antique store, even a fortune-teller's. There was also a Barclay's Bank, which reminded Grace that she had yet to replace her traveler's checks, although she had faithfully canceled all her credit cards after the theft.

She considered walking up the street to the library, but she had no idea how long she would have to wait for Peter. Instead, she walked toward the car park. Grace spotted the Land Rover but no Peter. She reached the vehicle and checked the doors, but the Rover was still locked. Odd.

It seemed safe enough in the broad daylight. She crossed the street and paused in front of a shop window offering hats: wonderful hats. Dream hats. The kind of hats the late Princess Diana had made fashionable once more. Hats with feathers or wisps of veil or fabulous bows. Grace gazed longingly through the glass. Inches from her nose perched a black felt wide-brimmed hat trimmed with violets and white cabbage roses and green velvet leaves. The perfect hat to go with her black dress coat at home. The hat she had been looking for all her adult life.

For a few moments Grace stared in the window reflecting that she had no money, no charge cards— nothing with which to purchase the perfect hat.

Appropriately enough, a shadow blotted out the sun. Grace realized that someone loomed up behind her. She could see his reflection in the glass. A tall, tall figure in a white suit and . . . a turban.

Grace gasped and whirled around.

The man behind her was enormous, tall and broad as a genie poured fresh from the bottle. He was Indian, perhaps that was what triggered such outlandish analogy. He was an outlandish-looking man.

His cheeks were tattooed and he wore gold earrings. He stared down at Grace, who stared up at him.

He opened his mouth. His teeth were very white. He seemed to be baring them at her.

"C-can I help you?" she got out. She spoke loudly to attract the attention of others on the street. Not that anyone seemed to be paying much attention.

The man handed her a card.

After a hesitation, Grace took it and read it: Aeneas Sweet.

She turned the card over. Written in fussy script were the words, "Come and see me. Ae."

Grace looked up to find the man in the turban threading through the crowd, escaping . . .

"Wait!" she cried.

He didn't pause, didn't seem to hear.

Grace started after him, then stopped and rethought.

Someone touched her arm and she jumped.

"What are you doing?" Peter asked. He carried two sacks of groceries. She could see a long loaf of French bread sticking out of one sack. He had gone *shopping?* It seemed so . . . mundane.

"Someone approached me," Grace informed him.

"Approached you?"

She showed him the card and watched Peter's winged brows raise.

"Well, well."

"Well, well *what?* Do you know this Sweet?"

"I know of him."

Peter nodded toward the Land Rover and they

headed across the street. He looked preoccupied.

She was getting to know his expressions. "What are you thinking?"

"It's just possible you may be on to something. I've heard Lady Vee mention Sweet. I think he's another Byronic scholar."

"Of course!" Grace said. "I thought the name sounded familiar. Sweet is the author of *The Last Corsair* and *Poet's Pilgrimage*. And he's also a neighbor?" She glanced up as a bottle-green Bentley sedately pulled past. "That's him!"

"Sweet?"

"No, the Indian!"

Peter's gaze followed the car.

"Maybe we should follow him."

"We have his business card," Peter pointed out.

Grace considered this. It seemed sort of anti-climactic.

"Well, anyway, we already have our proof. The fact that Mutt works for Lady Vee—"

"It's certainly proof that he works for Lady Vee. Other than that—"

"What are you talking about? We saw him in a pub in Kentmere the night someone tried to kill you."

"Exactly. We did not see him try to kill me."

"Oh come on! You're suggesting it was a coincidence?"

"I'm saying it's circumstantial. We need proof, Grace. We need something tantamount to a signed confession."

"Of what?"

"Of Danny Delon's murder."

Grace was silent.

Then she said, "They think you did it. The police, I mean."

"That was inevitable."

"What are you going to do?"

"I'm working on it."

"If Mutt wasn't trying to kill you, what was he doing in Kentmere?" she asked finally.

"People do occasionally go to Kentmere for other reasons."

Grace's thoughts skipped along another path. "Peter, that man must be the man in the turban who conked your pal Allegra!"

"Let's not leap to conclusions."

"Well, but seriously, how many men in turbans could be wandering around the Lake District?"

"Britain has a sizable Bengali and Indian population."

"Oh . . . get real!" Grace exclaimed, borrowing one of her students' expressions.

Reaching the Land Rover, Peter stowed the groceries in the back. Kneeling on the front seat, Grace poked through the contents of the brown bags. "Mmm. Smoked oysters, marinated artichokes, grapes. You do eat well."

"I've got a growing Girl Detective to feed."

"And I will be growing, if this keeps up."

He cast an experienced eye over her elevated derriere. "Not to worry."

Grace sat hurriedly back in her seat.

Putting the Rover in gear, Peter headed for Rogue's Gallery. Briefly Grace considered what it would be like if they were just going home to cook lunch like an ordinary couple. The idea was unexpectedly alluring.

"We could always try doing some research at the library." Being an academic, Grace just couldn't help feeling that the best place to begin any investigation was the library. "Well then, what *are* we going to do?" she queried, in answer to his look.

"Have lunch. Plan our campaign. What did the police have to say for themselves?"

"Oh. That."

Peter's blue eyes were quizzical. "Yes? I expect Heron had a fatherly word with you about me?"

"Sort of."

Peter laughed. "Anyway, he's right. The smartest thing you could do would be to grab a plane home. My offer still stands."

"Thanks, but no thanks. I'm not entering into a life of crime."

"Suit yourself. I expect your embassy could sort matters out if they had to. Why not put the pressure on them?"

"Why are you suddenly trying to get rid of me?"

Peter murmured, "My dear girl, I've been trying to get rid of you since the moment you arrived."

"Yes, but now that things are getting interesting, I resent it more."

She loved it when she made him laugh—although it was more of a snort than a laugh. "You're actually willing to risk your safety on the promise of some long-lost . . . manuscript?"

There he had said it! Instead of feeling triumphant Grace felt as though he might jinx it. She said quickly, "Of course, it might not be a manuscript. Another 'Manfred' or 'Don Juan' would be too much to hope for. It might just be . . . a letter. A poem. Heck, his grocery list would be worth a . . . a black eye."

She earned another laugh for that one.

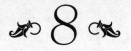

8

"*B*yron's only legitimate child was Augusta Ada Byron King or Lady Lovelace. Do you know who that is?"

"Will you be bitterly disappointed if I confess I don't?" Briefly, Peter inspected two browning steak and mushroom pies, and then closed the oven door.

"No, it's just a point of interest. Ada is best known for being the world's first computer programmer. She was a brilliant mathematician. In fact, the computer programming language ADA is named for her. Her mother, Anne Isabella Milbanke, was also a mathematician. When you think about it, that marriage was doomed from the start. A mathematician and a poet."

"How cynical. Did you want wine with lunch?"

"It'll put me to sleep." Grace finished setting the table. "Furthermore, Ada had to pawn the family jewels in order to cover the gambling debts that arose out of her experiments testing mathematical theories of probability in horse racing."

"A little knowledge is a dangerous thing." The thin mouth curved in ironic humor.

"She died of cancer when she was only thirty-six."

He made no comment to this, busy uncorking the wine.

"Byron, of course, was also only thirty-six when he died."

"I don't believe in family curses, if that's where this is leading."

"No, of course not. Ada never knew her father, although at her request she was buried next to him in St. Mary Magdalen's church in Nottinghamshire." She was thinking how odd it was that though she never noticed men's clothing, she seemed to notice everything Peter wore. Today it was jeans and a cashmere sweater. Yesterday it had been triple-pleat soft slate trousers and a white bonded collar shirt. He had dressed up for Lady Vee. She found that mildly shocking. He deliberately used his . . . sex appeal.

"Touching as hell," he said now, setting a glass of wine before Grace.

"I said I didn't want wine."

"Grace, relax for five minutes and have a glass of wine."

"I'm perfectly relaxed." But to humor him she sipped the wine. "Mm. That's pretty good. Wine and red meat for lunch. It's going to take me six months to recover from this vacation." She added wryly, "Assuming I survive it."

"You only live once."

Grace raised her eyebrows. It was the sort of thing many people said—Chaz often said it—but Peter said it with unshakable authority. She indulged in another sip. It really was a very good wine.

"Ada's mother, Annabella Milbanke—"

"A minute ago you said her name was Anne Isabella."

"It was. But she's mostly referred to as 'Annabella' in the reference texts. Maybe it was a pet name. Anyway, Byron's wife is the source for most of the information on his incestuous love affair with his half-sister, Augusta Leigh. Talk about having an ax to grind. She spent forty years writing and rewriting her account of their year-long marriage."

"Augusta Leigh being the prime candidate for Astarte?"

"Right. At least that was the family's view. I mean, needless to say, Annabella is something of a prejudiced witness. There's no proof that Byron had an affair with Augusta. They neither of them ever came out and admitted it."

There was a brief delay while Peter removed the pies and set them on oak-leaf plates. When the food was served and he was seated across from Grace he commented, "I can tell by the swamp-gas glow in your eye that you're hoping we're after some kind of written proof of this affair?"

Grace poked the golden, flaky piecrust with her fork. "Wouldn't that be incredible? To solve one of the great literary mysteries of all time?" A sudden memory occurred to her. "Oh, by the way, can we stop by a bank? In all the excitement, I forgot to replace my traveler's checks. And my credit cards are no good since I reported them stolen. I need to buy a hat."

"This sounds urgent. Getting ready for the funeral?"

"And I want to—very funny. And I want to buy a copy of *Glenarvon,* which you happen to have—dating from 1906. I've always wanted to read it."

Peter's lean cheek creased but he said only, "Have it your way, Esmerelda. Perhaps we can find a bank to rob on the way. That'll gratify Chief Constable Heron."

"The way where?"

"I was certain you were about to suggest we pay Aeneas Sweet a visit."

They drove toward the storm clouds in the west. The road was a lonely one, unraveling lazily, endlessly through fallow fields and woods turning autumn gold. The summer was over, Grace reflected as they tooled past a lone biker. In only a couple of days she would be back in the classroom and all this would be a memory. A lovely memory of lazy country lanes and ivy-covered inns, shining lakes and towering crags. Lakeland, Mountain and Fell: the guidebook had not begun to do Cumbria justice. Even Wordsworth's poetry had painted a pale portrait of this magnificent landscape.

"It rains a lot here," she commented, her eye on the pale flicker of lightning in the somber clouds ahead. The sky appeared to have an electrical short.

"You *are* a detective," Peter mocked. "It's the wettest corner of England."

He seemed in a peculiarly good mood, whistling a jaunty air as they headed for the coast.

"I like the rain," Grace said contentedly. She settled against the headrest, listening to another snatch of whistling. She remembered that tune from the night she had arrived. Right after her *Mistress of Mellyn* routine, Peter had walked in whistling that same melody. "What's that tune?"

He thought it over. "The Little Gypsy Girl."

She bit back a smile. "It sounds familiar."

"I think it's an old folksong." He quoted,

> "My father's king of the gypsies, 'tis true
> My mother, she learned me camping for
>   to do
> With my pack on my back all my friends
>   wished me well
> And I went up to London town some
>   fortunes for to tell."

Grace caught his eye and he winked. She glanced in the rearview; her smile faded. "I think we're being followed."

"The Rolls?"

"You noticed?"

"It's hard to miss. And preferable to the cops."

She hadn't even considered that the police might tail them. She wished she could be as blasé as Peter about it.

"What do we do?"

"There's no secret about where we're going. Let them follow."

"Suppose they try something?"

"They're welcome to try."

He had a point. They could probably outwalk the antique Rolls pursuing them. And would they know if the police were following?

"Can I ask you something?" she began diffidently.

"I was a poor friendless boy," he said promptly.

"Seriously. Why did you . . . ?"

"Turn to a life of crime?"

"Yes."

"Weak character."

She eyed him steadily until he shrugged. "Unfortunately it . . . appealed to me. To my adolescent love of adventure and even, I suppose, romance. And as I knew all the wrong people, it was quite easy to find steady work."

"You stole jewelry?"

"Jewels. Diamonds mostly. My least favorite stone actually."

"And you . . . kept the money?"

He smiled sympathetically. "I'm afraid so. It was my job, you see."

"Why did you quit?"

She didn't think he was going to answer, but he

said, "Things got a bit hot for me in England. I decided to travel. And while I was making the Grand Tour I realized there was a lot to be said for a quiet life. It gets old, having to look over your shoulder constantly."

Grace thought this over. She supposed there was something to be said for the fact that he didn't sugarcoat it. She glanced at his profile: Peter was whistling cheerfully once more. She could tell she was not going to get much more out of him. She was surprised he had shared this much.

Grace reached into her bag and pulled out *Glenarvon* by Lady Caroline Lamb, which she had been longing to examine all morning.

Lamb was yet another of Lord Byron's famed light o' loves (as the Regency novels delicately put it). In the early nineteenth century she had been as famous for her gothic novels as she was for her notorious liaison with the "mad, bad and dangerous to know" poet. *Glenarvon* was the fictionalized and highly overwrought tale of the love triangle between Byron, Lady Caroline Lamb, and her husband, the future Lord Melbourne. Lord Melbourne had Grace's sympathy.

Between convoluted fiction and sensational fact, it was hard to keep straight the details of Byron's life, Grace thought, turning a browned page. Byron had packed a heck of a lot of living into his brief span, and that wasn't even including his single catastrophic marriage and string of lovers.

She turned another page. Grace told herself she was looking for clues, but the truth was, she had always been curious about this scandalous novel. She offered to read aloud to Peter. He declined.

On they drove.

They arrived at Penwith Hall as the sun was setting. Grace proposed calling first, which Peter seemed to find funny. Perhaps he was counting on the element of surprise. Or perhaps he just had the worst manners in the world. Either one would not have surprised Grace.

In the uncertain light the house looked like something out of a gothic novel. *Nightmare Abbey* perhaps. Ivy entwined the shattered turrets and cracked casements. Gargoyles hunched on the rooftops. There were hundreds of windows, many of stained glass, several broken. Mist swirled in serpentine coils.

"This is cozy," Grace remarked.

"Isn't it just." Peter parked in the weed-choked courtyard and they got out beside a moss-covered fountain whispering its dying words.

The Rolls following them slid slowly past the iron gates down the end of the long drive and vanished into the gloaming.

Traversing the uneven flagstones of the court, they knocked hard on a formidable door. "Try the bell," Grace said.

"What *would* I do without you," Peter murmured, trying the bell.

A young man wearing a yellow bow tie opened the door. His expression, already displeased, grew even grimmer.

"Yes?"

"Aeneas Sweet?"

"Certainly not!"

Grace offered the card. The young man took it frowningly. He had thinning hair, a pencil-like mustache and round dark eyes. He reminded Grace of a youthful version of the Monopoly man.

"We'd like to see Mr. Sweet if it's possible," she said.

"What's the old villain up to now?" The young man eyed them suspiciously.

Peter said, "Look, mate, tell him Grace Hollister and Peter Fox have arrived."

The young man uttered a sound of exasperation and threw open the door with a ghastly screech of hinges.

"I suppose you'd better come in."

"After you," murmured Peter in Grace's ear as she hesitated.

Grace expected to be escorted in grand old tradition to a side room, there to await the master of the house's pleasure, but apparently they were to meet up on safari.

They followed their escort through an entrance hall the size of one of those playing fields of Eton—only minus the fresh air and sunshine. There were several suits of battered armor, a moth-eaten tapestry depicting a boar hunt that did not seem to be going well for any of the participants, and a gruesome assortment of gilt-framed ancestors who looked as happy to see them as the young man. The young man hurried up the monumental staircase—perhaps he was trying to lose them, thought Grace, speeding to keep up.

Down damp and dusty halls they trekked. Peter lingered now and then to examine a painting or vase.

At last they were shown into a chamber filled with antique furniture. A fire burned but it was unable to dispel the clammy chill. A tall display cabinet crowded with miniatures stood in one corner. A copy of the famous portrait of Byron in Turkish headdress hung on one wall. At least, Grace supposed it was a copy.

"You've got guests, Uncle," announced the irritable young man.

A ruined giant of a man in a paisley dressing gown rose to greet them.

"At last you've arrived!"

Aeneas Sweet had a wild mane of snowy white hair, a hawkish nose and fierce eyes. He limped toward them, his shadow looming across the wall. As he reached them he bellowed suddenly, "Ram Singh! Tea!"

Grace inadvertently stepped back on Peter's foot. He bore it stoically.

At Sweet's invitation they found seats close to the fire. The fireplace was one of those enormous constructions that reduced people to the size of andirons. As for andirons, two little gargoyles squatted in the fire leering up at Grace. A macabre touch, she thought.

The old man flung himself back on the red mohair sofa. "I expected you hours ago!"

"We only got your—um—message this afternoon," Grace excused.

Peter drawled, "So good of you to invite us."

A man wheeled in an antique tea cart. Grace recognized the Indian who had delivered Sweet's card. In this mausoleum he looked perfectly at home.

"There you are, Singh. What the devil took so long?"

The Indian said nothing. The gold earrings swung against his tattooed cheekbones as he lowered a colossal silver tray to a low table.

"Mute," Sweet informed them. "All servants should be mute. Wouldn't hurt in one's family either."

Grace glanced inadvertently around, but the young man in the bow tie had vanished. She smiled politely at the servant who gazed stonily back. The last time she had seen eyes that black and emotionless they had belonged to a figurehead in Peter's shop.

"You'll pour, dear lady," instructed Sweet. "I take sugar, lemon and cream."

It nearly took two hands to lift the enormous silver teapot. Grace poured tea into fragile little cups and handed them round.

"Have some of these savories. Singh! You've forgotten the cakes, damn your eyes!"

Grace selected one of the little fried triangles. She bit into mozzarella, peppers, black olive paste and a cup of salt. It was all she could do not to spit it back out. Peter, she noticed, had stuck to plain tea. That strong survival instinct at work.

Singh departed and the old man hissed at Peter, "Shut the damned door!"

Peter shut the door.

When he had reseated himself at the fire, Sweet demanded, "Now, have you got it with you?"

"Have we got what?"

"Don't be coy! Whatever she's offered you, I'll top it!"

"You'll top a hundred thousand pounds?" Peter inquired.

Grace held her breath.

The old man never blinked. "Opening bid at a hundred thousand, eh?" Grace had the distinct impression that he was pleased. Pleased because . . . the opening bid was *so low?* It was all she could do not to look at Peter. She was afraid her face would give her away.

"Well, well," Sweet was saying, and he could not keep the satisfaction out of his voice. "It's a great deal of money, of course. I'm not a rich man. Why, the manner in which my own kith and kin have preyed on my resources . . ." He fell silent. Studying them under white brows he said, "But you did bring it with you?"

"No," Peter said. "We wouldn't take that kind of risk."

"But you've taken a risk coming here, haven't you?" Sweet's fierce eyes bored into them.

"No."

"Heh? No?"

In the staring contest Sweet blinked first. Almost pleadingly he said, "You wouldn't sell it to her, surely? Not that . . . that . . . woman." He leaned forward and tapped Grace on the knee. "Dear lady, you've read her work?"

"I'm somewhat familiar with it."

"Ha! Familiarity breeds contempt." He drained his cup and passed it over for a refill. "Appalling lack of scholarship." He slid a couple of biscuit-shaped savories onto his plate, wiped his fingers on his robe and said, "I'm an old man. I need my rest. I sleep badly these days. You will stay for dinner, of course?"

"Of course," said Peter.

The old man waved them off wearily. "Dinner's at eight. I can't abide lateness. Singh will show you to a room where you can freshen up. And tell him to bring those cakes. The cream-filled ones."

Sure enough, Singh waited in the drafty hallway to escort them to a still damper part of the house. There, in a room with all the comfy ambience of a crypt, burned a dispirited fire in another oversize hearth.

They had a brief wait while their suitcases were brought up so that they might dress for dinner. The wind lamented down the chimney and the ivy scratched at the windows. A full-size bear rug, complete with snarling head, lay before the fireplace.

"He'd have snapped it up at a hundred thousand pounds," Grace whispered excitedly. "Did you catch that? Whatever it is, it's worth a fortune."

"To him, at any rate."

"Good point. I don't think Mr. Sweet is completely sane. What do you think?"

Peter's thin lips twisted. "I think we're going to have a hell of a time getting any more information without revealing how little we know."

"I think you're right. We could just fess up."

"We could, but he likely won't believe us. I wouldn't. And if he does believe us we'll probably not get another word out of him." He circled the enormous chamber as though taking inventory. Perhaps he was. Perhaps she should frisk him before they left this house.

"Do you think he killed Delon?"

"I don't think he's seen the light of day for the past twenty years."

"He reminds me of Miss Havisham."

Peter's mobile mouth twitched.

"You don't think he plans on our staying the night, do you?" She had been counting on spending the night at one of those cozy little inns they had passed on the long drive. Grace studied the boat-sized bed—complete with dusty canopy and faded gold hangings—skeptically. A gigantic harp crowding a window alcove had caught Peter's attention.

Quitting his examination of the harp, he ran a light hand across the old strings. Even that random chord sounded ancient. "That's worth a pretty penny."

"I think the dust here is older than anything in my apartment," Grace admitted.

Peter zipped open his shaving kit.

"Do you think he had Delon killed? That Singh looks like someone who would know how to wield an ax."

"Maybe." He headed for a side room that turned out to be a bathroom complete with a fireplace and picture window looking over the coastline. Grace followed, watching as he mixed up shaving lather in a silver cup. Over his shoulder, she could see her reflection in the mirror.

"The thing is," she said slowly, "there's still the question of the secret passage."

Peter gazed at her alertly, smoothing a dollop of white cream over his already smooth-seeming jaw.

"What I mean is, how did Danny Delon wind up dead in your secret passage?"

"I wondered when you'd consider that." He tilted his head back. The long line of his throat was exposed as he scraped the razor through the shaving lather. She thought there was something intimate about watching a man shave. "Is this one of those shadow-of-a-doubt moments?"

Grace could see herself considering this in the mirror. Peter watched her reflection, too. There was certainly plenty to doubt, but the more time she spent with Peter the more confident she felt that he could be trusted in all the essential ways.

"No, I'm just wondering how many people know about that passageway? Did Delon know?"

"I certainly didn't tell him. He could have stumbled upon it, I suppose. It's the easiest to find."

That gave her a moment's pause. Craddock House had other hidden passages?

"Could his murderer have known about it?"

"It's not impossible."

"What does that mean exactly?"

Peter shrugged. "The house is centuries old. When I purchased it the estate agent showed me that particular passage, a hidden staircase and a priest's hole. The house had other secrets I discovered for myself. And I've added a few touches of my own through the years. Anyway, it's more than possible some of my neighbors are familiar with that particular hiding place."

"Did you leave the door to your flat unlocked?"

"Of course not."

"It was unlocked when I arrived."

He thought this over. "You think Delon found his way upstairs by the secret stairway?"

"Yes. That means he could have hidden the item upstairs in your quarters."

"I suppose so. But that means Delon's killer must have had time to retrieve the item as well."

"Not necessarily. Not if he—or she—was in a hurry, and I think committing murder would tend to make you hurry. It's not that easy to find the entrance to your quarters from the passage. I found it by accident." Grace considered this. "Does anyone have a key to your shop?"

"No."

"No one?"

"No one."

That pleased her for some inexplicable reason. "So Danny must have picked the lock?"

"Picked the lock and bypassed the alarm system. It

wouldn't be hard. It's an old system. More for show than anything."

"That seems awfully trusting."

"I'm a trusting sort of fellow. Besides, we've a low crime rate in Innisdale. That's why I moved there."

"So Danny must have been wandering around when the murderer arrived. He tried to hide in the passage, but either his killer knew about it or he didn't get the door closed in time."

"Using the battleax seems to indicate a certain spontaneity," Peter agreed. "Perhaps Danny surprised this second chap."

"Perhaps. Perhaps they had arranged to meet while you were away."

Grace left him to his ablutions and opened her suitcase, shaking out the little black dress she had brought to England in hope that she might have dinner one night with a handsome and mysterious stranger. Not that she had really expected that to happen. Certainly not to this extent.

Made entirely of stretch lace, the décolleté dress had sheer lace sleeves and a body-fitted shape. She had never dared wear it before. Just owning it had seemed daring enough. Until tonight.

Peter strolled out of the bath and did a double take. "Why shucks, ma'am. Need help with any zippers or buttons, I hope?"

"Everything's under control," Grace said breathlessly. The dress was a little more body-fitted than before, thanks to her recent diet.

He quirked an eyebrow.

"What?"

He shook his head. "If we'd had teachers like you when I was a lad, I might have stayed in school."

They started downstairs, tracking—according to Peter—the savory crumbs he had thoughtfully sprinkled on their journey up. The lighting from the old wall sconces flickered spookily over the empty halls. This part of the house was nearly stripped bare; it had an abandoned air.

They passed a sizable leak in the roof. Rain trickled down in a steady stream.

Peter quoted solemnly, "Tell me how many beads there are in a silver chain . . ." He paused for dramatic effect. "Of evening rain." And Grace giggled. The sound startled her. It was such an undignified noise. She realized she was having fun. More fun than she could remember. She was having an adventure. The first in her life. And so far she was surviving it.

At long last they found the drawing room. Sweet and his nephew were already taking advantage of the cocktail hour.

The room was furnished with extraordinarily ugly Victorian furniture. Sweet, garbed in outdated evening dress, sat in a giant clawfoot chair, his feet propped on a matching footstool. His nephew, still in bow tie and sweater vest, stood staring out the window.

Outside, the rain sparkled like silver glitter.

"Good, you're wearing a frock," Sweet greeted

them. "I cannot abide women in trousers. Women in trousers are an abomination."

"I agree," said Peter.

"What do you mean, you agree?" Grace demanded.

Sweet interrupted, "You've met my nephew, Ferdinand?"

"Philip," corrected the young man turning from the window. "Delighted to meet you." Looking anything but delighted, he handed around a tray with cocktail glasses.

"Ferdy!" jeered Sweet under his breath. His gaze found Grace's. He rolled his eyes significantly. For a moment Grace thought he was having a fit. It dawned on her that Sweet was cautioning her. That he must mean he did not want them discussing the manuscript in front of Ferdinand or Philip or whatever his name was.

She glanced at Peter who dropped his eyelid in a slow deliberate wink. She sipped her drink. It seemed to consist of alcohol and ice.

"I say, are you by any chance the Peter Fox of Rogue's Gallery?" Ferdy (now Grace was thinking of him as Ferdy—he just seemed like a "Ferdy") asked.

"Guilty."

"I believe I've been to your shop. Do you ever come across oyster plates?"

"Occasionally."

"Bah!" Sweet exclaimed.

"Oyster plates?" Grace inquired.

A trace of animation entered Ferdy's manner.

"Oyster plates, yes! Decorative plates dating from 1860 to 1910 mostly. The good old days when a meal had several courses and every course had its own utensils and dishes."

"I resent that! We always have several courses," Sweet bridled. "What are you implying? You're not wasting away!"

While Ferdy defended himself, Peter explained to Grace, "Oyster plates have depressions in the shape of shells to hold the oysters and their broth. They're generally made out of porcelain, glass, pottery. I've even seen them in silver."

Ferdy's cheeks grew pink with excitement. "I recently purchased two nine-inch Haviland floral-decorated plates with two mussel wells. I should be delighted to show them to you. I've over three hundred plates in my collection, you know."

"My stars," murmured Grace. She felt as though she'd wandered into a Woody Allen movie. Even Peter seemed happy to discuss oyster plates all evening.

"You say oysters and I say bugger off!" the old man growled. "I need another drink."

Ferdinand fetched another round of cocktails. Grace, already feeling the effects of her first drink, declined.

"Very wise," Sweet said, coming up for air. "Nothing is more revolting than a woman who can't hold her liquor."

After another round of drinks and more utterly pointless small talk, they proceeded to the dining hall, which would have comfortably seated Robin Hood's entire merry band. Sweet sat at one end of the long table and Ferdy at the other. Peter and Grace were positioned midway down the table across from each other. A monstrous centerpiece made it difficult to see more than each other's eyes.

An elderly servant moved slowly from place setting to place setting. As soon as the soup was served Grace understood why getting sauced was a prerequisite for dining at Penwith Hall. The soup was a watery yellow. It tasted as it looked.

Ferdinand called to Grace, "Then you're not a dealer as well, Miss . . . Holiday was it?"

"Hollister," Grace corrected. "I'm working on my dissertation. Poets of the Romantic period."

This did not strike the noticeable dread into hearts that she had hoped.

"And have you read *my* work, Miss Hollister?" Sweet inquired hopefully, spoon poised before his lips.

From down the table Ferdy made a pained sound.

"I know that you're the author of *The Last Corsair*," Grace said diplomatically.

"Ah yes, my account of Byron's adventures in the East." Sweet smiled devilishly. "The chapter on Byron's love affair with Ali Pasha and his son Veli Pasha is a masterpiece!"

"Then you believe Byron was bisexual?"

"Of course! Byron was the supreme sensualist. He wished to experience every nuance of life, to wring from life's loins every drop of—"

Grace put her spoon down and stared at the tiny silver berries in the centerpiece, tuning out.

"The proof is conclusive," Sweet finished. "Veli Pasha honored Byron with the gift of a magnificent white horse."

"Elementary, my dear Watson," Peter's voice commented from behind the centerpiece. "You know what they say about big white horses."

The next course consisted of a slab of half-cooked meat flavored with cranberry-ginger chutney. There was a quantity of soggy vegetables, and someone had done something cruel to potatoes.

Sweet kept up his monologue, yet still managed to consume vast quantities of the dreadful food. "I suppose you have been reading that woman! She and her sisterhood want to sanitize Byron, castrate him, wrap him up in turtledoves and sticky sentiment."

"That's got to hurt," Peter put in. Through the silver shrubbery she caught a glimpse of his raised glass. Grace hoped he was not getting drunk. Not that she could blame him.

Following three kinds of moldy cheese, dessert was served: lemon tarts with poached pears—ingeniously made without any kind of sugar or sweetener at all.

Grace considered tipping her dessert plate into the centerpiece but restrained herself.

"Well, you must excuse me," Ferdy said, rising from the table.

"Yes of course, dear boy," Sweet replied with patent relief.

When the carved door closed behind the other man, Sweet knocked over his water glass, waving his hand excitedly. "Thank heavens he's gone! Now let's stop haggling. How much for it? And I warn you, I won't be swindled."

Peter said, "May I ask when Delon contacted you?"

"About a week ago, I suppose. Why?" Sweet said suspiciously, "When did he contact that woman?"

"Around the same time," Peter said as though he knew it for a fact.

"But surely it's a matter of—of—"

"Naturally," Peter said. "Out of curiosity, why did you have him killed?"

The old man's jaw dropped. "I. Beg. Your. Pardon?"

"It's one less split," Peter said. "I'm not objecting. Just curious."

"But I had no idea! None. Why should anyone kill him? You were the one handling the item." Sweet turned to Grace. She made a commiserating face.

Peter said cheerfully, "There you're wrong, I'm afraid. You see, Delon was killed before he could hand off the item."

Sweet combed his white mane out of his face as though he couldn't hear through it. "What? What are you saying?"

"We don't have it," Grace interjected. She wanted there to be no doubt. Sweet appeared exactly like the kind of wacko who would devise an abduction.

"But that's . . . that's nonsensical! What are you trying to pull?"

"It's the truth, I'm afraid," Peter said. "We're not even sure what the item is."

The old man stared at them. Then he burst out laughing. "Oh Lord, you had me for a moment!"

As though magnetized, Peter and Grace's glances locked.

The old man laughed more heartily still. "Name your price! Within reason, of course!"

"That's very tempting," Peter remarked.

"And alarming," Grace put in, thinking aloud.

"It doesn't alter the fact that we don't have . . . It."

"Bah!" The old man rose, catching the linen table-cloth and nearly dragging the place setting from the table. "Bah!"

"Nevertheless," Peter responded. His slim fingers played with the sterling napkin ring.

The old man took a turn around the room. Outside the window the night flashed white and then black. The rumble of thunder followed.

"Bah!" Sweet exclaimed again.

"Humbug," said Peter. He rolled the ring across the table to Grace. She caught it and absently tried it on for size.

"I can't think," complained Sweet. "You're up to something, I suppose. Everyone's always up to something. That damned Ram Singh has let me get drunk again. He must be up to something. We'll talk tomorrow."

"Oh! Well, actually . . ." Grace started in.

Peter shot her a warning look.

She shook her head stubbornly.

Peter nodded.

Grace shook her head more forcefully.

"What the hell are you two doing?" Sweet roared. "Save that sort of thing for the privacy of your own home." With that he banged out of the room.

"What *are* you doing?" Grace demanded. "We can't stay here!"

"We can't leave now."

"Yes we can. We get in the car and start the engine. Hey, presto!"

"My dear girl—"

"Don't 'dear girl' me. I'm a woman, not a girl. A woman who does not plan on spending the night in this house of horrors."

"Grace, we can't go haring off without the information we came here for."

"Yes we can. We can come back in the morning."

He was staring intently past her head. His nostrils flared almost imperceptibly.

"What is it?" she breathed, instinctively glancing over her shoulder.

His lips barely formed the words, "The eyes in that portrait moved."

Grace froze. *"What?* Are you trying to scare me?"

In a normal voice, he said, "Let's go upstairs."

Grace pushed back from the table. She couldn't help an uneasy look at the sallow-faced Cavalier hanging behind her chair. He bore a strong resemblance to Ferdy. Perhaps it was the eyes. Perhaps not.

"Could you tell who it was?" she asked softly as they mounted the grand staircase.

"From the eyeballs?"

"I'll bet it was that Ram Singh."

Peter didn't answer. Perhaps he was saving his breath for the climb back. It wasn't a bad idea.

When they finally staggered into their room Grace announced, "I knew it! They've searched through our luggage."

"What makes you think so?"

"My suitcase was on the left and yours was on the right. Now mine is on the right and yours is on the left."

"Maybe the maid moved them."

"What maid?"

"True." He considered and then dismissed this. "Well, if they searched our gear, it's natural enough."

"We have different ideas about what is natural when staying in other people's homes." She picked her suitcase up. "What do we do now?"

"Get some sleep." He was going through his suitcase.

"Sleep?"

"Unless you have another idea?" He winked at her in that maddening way. How he could flirt under these circumstances—but apparently it came as naturally to him as breathing.

"Uh, no. No." She studied the antique bed. "It probably has spiders."

"Very probably." He glanced at her critically. "I'd get comfortable if I were you."

"Comfortable?"

"Warm." He was pulling a black sweater over his shirt. No yellow silk jammies tonight.

"Oh." Grace grabbed her jeans and sweater and headed for the industrial-sized bath.

When she came out again Peter had turned the lights down. He was lying on the bed. She could see the outline of his body in the fireplace glow. She hesitated in the doorway.

"Come ahead. I won't bite." His voice sounded lazy and amused.

With great self-consciousness she crossed the wide expanse of cold floor and gingerly climbed into the galleon-sized bed. The mattress was feather and seemed to melt away under Grace's hands and knees. The velvet coverlet smelled dusty.

Her hand planted into something soft. She withdrew it hastily.

"Sorry." She slipped under the covers beside him. She could just make out his features in the flickering light.

Peter's mouth twitched. "You seem a little tense. Is it the spiders or me?"

Grace laughed uncertainly. "Do you suppose it's haunted?"

"The bed?"

"The Hall."

"Come here, Esmerelda." He stretched out his arm.

Grace scooted over and gingerly laid her head on his shoulder. He smelled pleasantly masculine, of soap and lambs' wool and a light spicy aftershave. She could feel him smiling. She could feel the lean strength of his body cushioning her.

Oddly enough the fact that they both wore jeans and sweaters seemed more erotic, not less. The thought of warm bodies, smooth bare skin, nakedness beneath the clothing . . .

"Better?"

She nodded.

For long moments they lay listening to the occasional pop of the fireplace, the rain against the windows.

Her stomach gurgled. "I'm starving."

"We could raid the kitchen."

"I'm afraid to find out what goes on back there."

"Good point."

Silence.

Grace's brain seemed to be in overdrive. "Did you know that due to a genetic tendency toward obesity, Byron had to diet? He periodically starved himself with soda water, biscuits and cathartics."

She felt his silent laugh.

The wind moaned drearily down the chimney.

"So you never married?" Grace asked.

The silence held a surprised quality, or maybe it was just that Grace was amazed at herself. Her uncharacteristic nosiness had to be due to finding herself sharing this man's bed, even in this weird circumstance.

"No."

"You don't seem much like the marrying type."

"Is there a type?" He sounded dry.

"I just meant that you have so many lady friends."

He seemed to be reflecting aloud. "There was a girl once. A woman, rather. We probably would have killed each other eventually."

"Oh?"

She felt rather than saw his smile. "She had red hair and the temper to match. Lovely red hair, like a fox's."

Grace discovered she had no desire to hear anything more about the woman with fox-colored hair. She was just making conversation, in any case, and wasn't really interested in picturing the woman who might one day snare Peter Fox. She deliberately summoned up the memory of Chaz and their model relationship, which was based on mutual interests and respect and friendship.

It was annoying that Chaz's face, in memory, seemed the tiniest bit fuzzy.

As though reading her thoughts, Peter said suddenly, "Tell me about the boyfriend. Chip, is it?"

"Chaz?"

"Ah. Chaz."

"It's short for Charles."

"Yes? And what does Chaz do?"

"He's a professor of mathematics at St. Anne's. St. Anne's is where I teach."

"Right." He yawned, turning his head away. "What's he like?"

"He's . . . nice. Reliable. He's an excellent teacher." Grace tried to remember. All at once Chaz seemed like someone that she had known a long time ago in another life. "We share the same interests."

After a pause, "And those interests are?" Peter sounded drowsy, like someone who was only half-remembering his cues.

"We like . . . Masterpiece Theatre and Irish music. We saw the Chieftains in concert the last time they were in Los Angeles. We like Sunday morning brunch at the Odyssey."

It suddenly seemed important to remember all the things she and Chaz shared. Peter was silent.

"In the summer we always get season tickets to the Hollywood Bowl. Usually we go with Tom and Monica. Monica is the friend I came over with. Tom is her boyfriend. He teaches P.E. at St. Anne's. And in the winter the four of us play bridge every Tue—"

She was interrupted by a gentle snore.

When she woke up all hell was breaking loose.

The room was in complete darkness. Glass was breaking, furniture smashing. For a moment Grace thought it was an earthquake. She sat bolt upright. She realized she was in a strange room.

Then she picked out the human sounds from the rest of the racket: grunting, hard breathing, the frightening sounds of fists on flesh. About the same instant she remembered where she was, she realized Peter was no longer in the bed.

Grace reached for the lamp, but the unfamiliar draperies and bedclothes got in the way.

Shadows moved past the window: two men struggling.

Grace pawed her way through the bed hangings and found the lamp as another huge crash came from across the room. The harp struck a discordant note.

Peter swore.

At last Grace found the lamp switch.

Gloomy light illuminated the long room. Peter was picking himself up out of a pile of broken Hepplewhite. An arras swung gently against the wall.

Otherwise the room was quite empty.

9

"Sleep well?"

Ferdy was having a solitary breakfast in the dining hall when Grace and Peter made their appearance. This morning's bow tie was kelly green, thus far the only bright spot in the gray day.

"Like a top." Peter helped himself to kippers. Grace's stomach growled hungrily. She couldn't support the idea of fish for breakfast—nor could she understand the point of putting toast on racks to deliberately make it cold.

"Truly?" Ferdy looked from Peter's black eye, turning an impressive purple-blue in the dawn's early light, to Grace. Respect shone in his black button eyes. "I say," he murmured.

"Do you live here year round?" Grace inquired. "It seems awfully isolated."

"I live in London." Ferdy said it as though he were

reassuring himself. "I come down to check on the old man now and again. He's the last of my family, you see, and he's getting on." He added gloomily, "Not that he wasn't always peculiar."

Grace abandoned hope of finding anything edible on the sideboard. "I guess I'll just have tea," she sighed.

"Slimming?" Peter inquired. "Perhaps they can hunt up some biscuits and soda water."

She gave him a level look. In black jeans and black lambs' wool pullover, he looked like a cat burglar after a rough night.

"The food's ghastly," Ferdy admitted, "but there's plenty of it."

As Grace sipped her tea—wondering *how* anyone could possibly spoil tea—Ferdy spoke again.

"Here, let me ask you something. Confidentially, just between us, what's he up to?"

Peter's fork paused before his mouth. "You'd have to ask him."

Ferdy colored angrily. "I like that! You see, I do have a vested interest. It's entailed. The estate, that is. This house, this land; this will all come to me one day. What's left of it. He's in debt, you know. To the hilt. So if he's off on another of these buying sprees . . ."

"Is he good for a hundred thousand pounds?" Peter asked bluntly. The crudeness of this took Grace aback.

"Is he—?" Ferdy's laughter was shrill. "He is not. He's broke, whether he realizes it or not. What is it this time? Miniatures? Is that it? Or more books? More of these damned first editions?" He turned to Grace. "Tell me this, what's your involvement?"

"Who, me?" Grace was never brilliant before her morning coffee.

"She's just a friend," Peter said.

Ferdy glared at them both for a long moment. "Right." He checked his watch. "Well, I'll leave you and your friend to it."

The dining hall was very empty after he left. Peter finished his kippers and Grace drank more tea.

She was thinking about Peter's odd behavior the night before. They had discovered a door behind the arras in their bedroom. To Grace's surprise, Peter had declined to follow their intruders through the dark passage revealed there. This perfectly rational behavior seemed out of character for Peter. If she didn't know better she'd have suspected Peter was . . . well, afraid. He had blocked the door with the harp and gone back to bed. But then, since he promptly fell asleep, he couldn't have been too afraid.

"He could be in on it," she suggested at last.

Peter shook his head. "The old man doesn't trust him."

"That could be an act."

"That's quite an act."

"They do seem to loathe each other," she admitted. "You know, what doesn't make sense to me is that they would try to search our luggage after they had already searched while we were at dinner."

Peter considered this. "What are you thinking? Two searchers?"

"Maybe the second searcher was Ferdy. He's suspicious of his uncle. Maybe he was trying to find out why we're here?"

"The bloke I tackled was no amateur," Peter said.

"Ram Singh then?" Grace asked hopefully.

"Not nearly big enough."

"Well, who then? Whoever was following us in the Rolls?"

"Maybe. But you do realize that whoever attacked us last night is familiar with this house?"

"With its secret passages, right? Does every house in England have a secret passage?"

"Only the best houses."

Grace's brow wrinkled in thought. "Maybe the men in the Rolls are working for Sweet?"

"Possibly, but in that case, why follow us? Besides, didn't you recognize that Rolls?"

"Well . . . no."

Peter's blue eyes widened. "It's a fairly unusual vehicle."

"I don't notice cars."

"Think back to the last time you saw a big silver automobile."

Grace thought back. "Lady Vee's!"

"Bingo."

"Mutt and Jeff were following us in the Rolls?"

"Not necessarily. Maybe it was Lady Vee."

An unexpected laugh gurgled up. She seemed to be doing a lot of that lately: laughing.

Peter's eyes lit with amusement; however, he said gravely, "If I had to take a guess I'd say it was our pal with the gun."

"The Que—the muggers!"

"Mm. Something else. I think I know that little runt."

"From prison?"

Peter choked on his tea.

Grace said doubtfully, "I just thought that per-haps—you had a record."

"Not in this country!"

"How should I know? The police certainly seem to know you."

"Nothing was ever proven. In this country."

"That seems like a—a fine distinction."

"It's a crucial distinction."

"Okay. No need to be so touchy. Where do you think you know him from?"

"That I don't know."

"Can't you ask around? Check with your for-mer . . . associates?"

At his expression, she said, "Look, I don't know how this stuff works!"

Sweet had still not made an appearance by the time breakfast was over and an aged pair of servants began clearing away the dishes.

"Probably sleeping it off," Peter commented.

For lack of anything more productive to do, he and Grace strolled around the grounds. Dank vapor rose from the sea they could hear but not see beyond the red cliffs. Mist cloaked the wilderness that had once been flowerbeds and lawn.

"It must have been impressive in its heyday," Grace said, staring back at the blind windows of the house. "I can see why Ferdy—I mean, Philip—resents his inheritance being squandered on an obsession."

"I don't know," said Peter. "If it were going to oyster plates . . ."

Through the sycamore trees they spied a white building looking uncannily like a miniature Greek temple.

"What's that?" Grace asked.

"The family crypt, I imagine."

She stopped in her tracks, staring at it uneasily. "Should we—?"

"No." He sounded so crisp she stared his way. His expression was odd. Possibly those kippers he'd had for breakfast hadn't agreed with him, she thought.

They trudged on, walking down some stairs into what appeared to be a sunken garden now overgrown with reeds and vines. In the center was a rectangular pool surrounded by battered and broken statuary. The half-shattered head of a helmeted statue lay beside the brackish water.

Peter quoted, "In mossy skulls that nest and lie, ever singing, 'Die, oh! Die.' "

Grace shivered. "It is eerie."

Leaving the garden, they walked a few yards into the woods, feet crunching the fallen leaves. A squat silver solid form slowly materialized. A riderless Harley motorcycle sat parked in the trees.

Grace caught Peter's arm. "Look!"

"Shhh. I see." He freed himself. "Go back to the house."

"Not without you!"

"I'm coming. I'll be right behind you." Hands on her shoulders, he turned her toward the house.

Grace took a couple of steps, then turned.

"But—"

"Go!" He had plastered himself to the nearest tree trunk. From his hiding place he scowled at Grace.

Each footstep sounded as loud as a rifle crack. A few more steps and she glanced around. Peter was gone. Grace stopped. Her eyes scanned the clearing.

"Peter," she called softly.

There was no reply; the branches swayed where he had stood a moment before.

From the other side of the clearing, a twig snapped.

Grace's nerve snapped with it.

She bolted, running for the house, feet pounding the uneven ground, heart pumping, arms close to her sides like she was trying out for St. Anne's track team. The wet grass soaked her suede flats.

The adrenaline surging through her veins sent her leaping over a fallen log like a deer. She hit the ground running, raced up the last leg of the path and reached the back terrace, breathless and spent.

Shaking, clutching the stitch in her side, Grace's eyes raked the wood line. The silence held an eldritch quality. White billowed throughout the abandoned garden, curling around the moss-stained statues. Far away she could hear the rumble of the sea.

But this is crazy, she thought. I ran from a motorcycle. It could belong to anyone. To a tourist, to a Sunday motorist. True, it didn't look like the kind of bike tourists would ride. All that bristling, bright metal had a warlike effect, and the sheer size of the thing: like a small silver buffalo . . .

But still, to run from it?

Why would anyone leave his bike there? The practical side of Grace responded, perhaps he was relieving himself or stretching his legs? But Peter had reacted to the bike, too, she reminded herself. And where was Peter?

"Peter?" she yelled, when she had enough breath to speak.

Nothing.

She opened her mouth to yell again. A window banged open above her head.

"What the devil's going on down there?" Aeneas Sweet leaned precariously out the window. "Oh, it's you! Stop that infernal noise!"

"Something's happened! I need to talk to you!" Grace called up.

"Then come up and talk to me!"

The window slammed shut.

"I have not loved the world, nor the world me," quoted Sweet. "Do you know the quotation?"

"Isn't it from 'Childe Harold's Pilgrimage'?" Grace questioned. She stayed at the window, peering out. The woods stood still and silent.

"Hey? Hmm." Sweet glowered. "You're too young to know how true those words are. Truer words were never written." He seemed to be feeling sorry for himself, for he added, "You see before you a philosopher, an idealist, a man of letters. A man who wished only to devote himself to the pursuit of intellectual studies. But fate was otherwise inclined. I had to bow to duty, to the needs of my family. And what thanks have I received?"

She wondered if Ferdy had tackled him about spending a hundred thousand pounds on first editions.

He sat before his bedroom fire in a sumptuous claret brocade dressing gown. He was drinking something out of a pewter mug. Grace was fairly sure it was not tea. "Sit down, sit down!" he commanded.

She sat down and tried to compose herself.

"Now," Aeneas Sweet said, "Seeing that this partner of yours is out of the way, suppose you and I try to come to an agreement?"

Her voice shot up despite her effort to stay calm, cool and collected as the commercials advised.

"He's not out of the way. He'll be right back! And

we told you last night we don't have it! We don't even know what it is!"

Sweet said coldly, "Lower your voice. Do you suppose I want that imbecile to know what we're discussing?"

"That imbecile is the least of your worries. There's a sinister motorcycle parked in your woods. Not to mention that Mutt and Jeff followed us down here. They're probably the ones who attacked us last night—unless that was you again. And they may have Peter."

"Mutt and Jeff?" The old man gaped at her. "Are you mad?"

"I think I'm the only one of all of you who isn't." Even if she was flinging terms like "sinister motorcycle" around. Nervously, she rose again and returned to her vantage point at the window. "I don't know why I'm wasting time. I should have followed my instinct in the very beginning. I should have gone to the police. Now they have Peter."

"The police?" gasped Sweet. "The police have Peter Fox?"

"Mutt and Jeff." Impatiently she clarified, "We call them Mutt and Jeff. We don't know their real names. Anyway, we've wasted enough time sitting around *talking!*" She remembered that in books and movies threatening the police usually ended in the threatener getting knocked off. She sealed her lips on the rest of what she had been about to say.

"Silence! I will not be subjected to the viraginous

tantrums of a woman!" Sweet blustered, "Young people have no gratitude. I invite you to my home, share my hospitality with you and that scoundrel, and this is the thanks I get? Fairy tales? Cartoon characters? Well, young woman, I daresay you see now what comes of playing one side against the other. I suggest you reconsider your position before it's too late."

He began bellowing for Ram Singh.

Grace left him to it, racing upstairs and then lugging her bags and Peter's back down to the Land Rover. She knew she should stop and reconnoiter, but she was afraid to spare the time. Every moment might mean life or death to Peter.

But when she reached the courtyard, it occurred to her that Peter had the keys. Standing there sweating in the chill morning air she tried to think what to do next.

Peter probably knew how to hot-wire a car. He knew so many useful things. The young ladies of St. Anne's also probably knew how to hot-wire a car, but what was the point of hot-wiring a car you couldn't get into?

Grace had not realized how much she had come to depend on Peter until now. She was a little aggravated at how lost—how bereft she felt without him.

She needed a plan. At the very least, she needed to take a couple of deep breaths. Then again, her course was clear. She must go to the police. If Mutt and Jeff had nabbed Peter, the rules of the game were irrevocably changed. This was not something she could manage on her own. So her plan was to go to the police.

But without keys she couldn't drive to the police.

And it didn't seem prudent to call from the Hall. Assuming they had a phone. She hadn't seen one during their stay. Perhaps Sweet kept it under lock and key lest his nephew run up long-distance bills.

She didn't have a cell phone.

That left walking.

Grace scanned the silent woods, the blood-red leaves were startling against the fog.

In the distance she heard the bad-tempered snarl of a bike engine. But that could be any bike. It didn't mean . . .

She had the most ridiculous and unproductive desire to burst into tears. That would really be the last straw.

Then, as though in a dream, Peter walked out of the woods.

Grace ran to meet him. A few feet away she stopped, aware she had been about to throw herself into his arms—and that his arms were not anticipating her arrival.

"Where have you *been?*"

Despite the black eye and supercilious expression, no one had ever looked more beautiful to her.

"I told you I was going after him."

"No, you didn't! You said you'd be right behind me!"

"And I am." He eyed their luggage. "Are we going somewhere?"

"I was going to the police."

"The police?" Peter was aghast. "Why on earth?"

"I thought you'd been—I thought something happened to you. What *did* happen to you?"

"Nothing happened. I circled round to try and ambush them but they scarpered." He unlocked the Land Rover. "Probably has nothing to do with us. Just another trespasser."

"There was a bike in the woods the day the police found Danny Delon in the tarn. I think he was watching them."

"The same bike?"

"Uh, how would I know that?"

Peter lifted a dismissing shoulder.

"Now what?" Grace inquired, hovering at his shoulder. She was afraid to let him out of her sight. Her partner in crime.

"Now," Peter said with quiet satisfaction, "we lay a little trap."

"A trap? What kind of trap?"

"Ideally, one that works."

She was so happy to have him back she didn't even object, getting into the car and sinking into contemplation.

They drove through several miles of lonely cows in lonely pastures before Peter inquired, "What's up thou still unravished bride of quietness?"

"Hmm?" she hedged. "I'm hungry."

"Get away. What else?"

Grace raked a hand through her hair. "Have you

noticed that no one has actually said the word 'man-uscript'?"

"So?"

"Everyone keeps referring to it as 'it.' Or 'the item.' Like it's an inanimate object."

"A manuscript would be an inanimate object."

"But they're not! Not in the same way." Eagerly, Grace turned to face him. "It's hard to explain, but if we were hunting for a manuscript, or even a letter, I don't think any of these people could help discussing it. Discussing the *implications* of it."

"Possibly." He shifted gears and they sped around a slow-moving lorry.

"For example, if it were a letter proving that Byron and Augusta Leigh were actually lovers, I think—scholars being what they are—"

"They would have to talk about it," Peter concluded thoughtfully. "That's rather shrewd reasoning, Professor."

"It doesn't make sense," Grace said. "These are wealthy people. Lady Venetia is anyway. I can't imagine jewels being of such interest to her that she'd be willing to risk her professional reputation—such as it is—let alone break the law."

Peter's eyes briefly left the road. "You don't under-stand the mania of the fanatic collector. These people will pay anything—and I do mean anything—for the object of their desire."

"But that's just it!" Grace exclaimed. "These peo-ple are mad about Byron, not jewels per se. I could see them doing anything to get hold of an original manuscript or something personal to Byron, but jewels? Byron was a man. What kind of jewels would he have? A signet ring? A pocket watch?"

"Are you serious?"

"Yes! What previously unknown jewels would he have possessed that would be of interest to a collector?"

"The fact remains," Peter reminded her, "that we are looking for something relating to Byron, something someone is willing to kill for. Gewgaws."

"Something probably worth more than a hundred thousand pounds," Grace agreed. She looked more closely at the rearview mirror.

"Peter . . ."

"I see them."

Like a persistent cloud on the horizon, the silver Rolls drifted behind them at a discreet distance as they tooled along.

They stopped for an early lunch at a pub, Peter parking a little out of the way in a field beside the road.

"Wouldn't it be wiser to park behind the building?" Grace suggested tactfully.

"They might miss us."

They walked across the little pasture and into the whitewashed stone building. The pub seemed to be crowded with fishermen. It was nice to see that these jewel-like lakes and streams were not going to waste, although the guidebook had noted—curiously—that the water here was so pure that apparently only fish from the ice age survived in those cold depths.

They sat down in a high-backed booth with a tartan tablecloth. Peter brought them each a pint from the taproom.

"I'd kill for a chef salad," Grace muttered. "I don't know if my cholesterol level will ever be the same."

"What was it like before?"

"I don't know. I'm betting lower though."

Chef salad was not on the menu, and Grace had to be satisfied with lamb chops, just-picked potatoes and asparagus. Wonderful food, food from a different time, a different state of mind. And to think that back home people always referred to British cuisine as blah.

When their food was set before them, Peter said, "Enjoy your lunch. I'll be back in a bit."

Grace put her fork down. "Wait a minute! Now what? Where are you going?"

"So many questions, so little time."

She stared up at him. The black slash of eyebrows and the wide ironic mouth made his face a caricature. It was not really a face to inspire trust, and yet she did trust him.

"I'm the bait?"

"More of a distraction."

"Okay, I can do that. I can distract."

"You can indeed. Wait five minutes after they come inside, then go out through the back."

"The back? What if there isn't a back?"

He gave her a chiding look.

"Why do I feel like I wandered into an episode of *La Femme Nikita?*"

He ignored this. He didn't own a TV so perhaps he didn't understand her. "Five from when they sit down."

And then he was gone. After an emotion-fraught second or two, Grace pulled out her copy of *Glenarvon*. Determinedly she affixed her eyes to the page. The book was dry but lunch was delicious.

Grace savored her lamb chops glazed in rosemary and quince. Her eyes on *Glenarvon*, she read,

> Oh I am changed, she continually thought; I have
> repressed and conquered every warm and eager
> feeling; I love and admire nothing; yet am I not
> heartless and cold enough for the world in which
> I live. What is it that makes me miserable? There
> is a fire burns within my soul . . .

The cruel antihero of the tale was naturally based upon Byron, who had quickly tired of the author and her obvious attempts to snare him. Supposedly Byron had found the novel amusing, writing that the character of Glenarvon was a "poor likeness" since he had not sat still long enough for Lamb to draw a real portrait of him. Though the affair had lasted a scant four months, Lady Caro had spent the next four years chasing Byron.

Perhaps if Byron had found the right woman,

Grace thought. Quality not quantity. Of course a happily married family man Byron would have spoiled the mystique.

Caught up in her thoughts, Grace only then noticed that Mutt and Jeff had entered the pub and were conspicuously trying to look nonconspicuous in a booth facing her.

Grace looked down into the book once more. She was afraid her expression was giving her away. She felt nakedly self-conscious.

She sipped her pint. It was impossible to concentrate. She had forgotten to look at her watch and she was afraid to look now. Of course she could count slowly to sixty about five times. She worried about it for a few minutes—hopefully five—then reluctantly taking a final bite of her broiled chop, Grace slipped her purse strap over her shoulder and slid out of the booth.

Mutt and Jeff began to whisper.

She could feel eyes boring into her back as she walked slowly to the ladies' room. She tried to look like a woman who had nothing more important on her mind than powdering her nose.

Inside she was relieved to find that there really was a window and that—as in so many British establishments—there was no screen on the window. She inched it open, dropped her purse out and climbed through. She jumped down to the ground.

Tiptoeing to the end of the building, she peeked around the corner.

The Rolls sat unattended in front of the pub.

Now what? She saw neither Peter nor the Land Rover.

Just as she was ordering herself not to get excited, Mutt's long face poked out the ladies' room window.

"Oy!" he called. He withdrew his head.

Tires shelling gravel, the Land Rover pulled up beside her. Peter leaned across to open the door.

Grace hopped in. "They're coming!"

"That's the idea." He floored the accelerator and they sped onto the narrow highway as Mutt and Jeff ran out of the pub.

"That's timing it a little too close. What did you do to their car?"

"Nothing subtle. Grabbed a handful of wiring." He handed her a map. "See if you can find a shortcut through these woods."

"Where are we heading?"

"Back to Penwith Hall."

Aeneas Sweet, mouth full of lemon sponge cake, eyes bulging his dismay at their reappearance, choked out, "I thought you'd left!"

"Hello to you, too," Peter returned.

Sweet gulped like a boa constrictor caught breaking his diet. He said something thickly that Grace couldn't quite decipher.

"We came back," Peter responded.

Sweet's eyes glistened. "Then you do have it? You had it all along?"

Peter interrupted crisply, "What. Is. It?"

Sweet swallowed down the last of his cake and said, "Are you serious?"

Grace said, "Don't we look serious?"

Sweet's glance was dismissing. "You look charming, my dear." He returned his attention to Peter.

A little annoyed, Grace pressed, "Is it a manuscript?"

"Manuscript? What manuscript!" Sweet's bloodshot eyes nearly popped out of his massive head.

"Is it bigger than a bread box?" Peter inquired.

The fire crackled and hissed behind the brass screen.

"Then you really don't know? You really don't have it?" He seemed to deflate suddenly, a very old, very small man. He reached for his pewter mug with a shaking hand. "It was a gift. To his daughter. A set of cameos."

"Cameos," Peter repeated slowly.

"Which daughter? Allegra?" Grace questioned.

Sweet snapped back into shape. "There's no reason to believe he had any fondness for *that* child, the product of that unfortunate alliance with that slut, Jane Clairmont." He turned to Peter. "She *forced* herself on him, you know. Byron was bored and embarrassed." Heaving himself up off the couch, he limped across the room and unlocked the tall glass cabinet containing the miniatures.

He offered a locket to Grace. She took the gold oval with careful fingers and contemplated the painted face. A rosy-cheeked child with dark curls smiled primly into history.

"Byron had only one legitimate heir."

Grace handed the locket to Peter. "So which daughter?" he asked. "The math wiz? Was there another?"

"Was there—?" Sweet turned to Grace and they shared one of those International Academic Moments.

"Medora Leigh," Grace explained. "Astarte's daughter."

"All these women," Peter complained, setting the miniature on the table.

"Funny how life imitates art," Grace drawled in a fair imitation of Peter. And then before Peter could respond to this, "If Byron and his half sister Augusta Leigh had an affair it would have been in 1813. They spent a lot of that year together, even planning a trip to Europe. The trip never happened, but then, the following year Augusta gave birth to a daughter, Medora. Medora, by the way, is the name of the heroine of "The Corsair," one of Byron's most popular poems. Not that that necessarily proves anything, because Augusta might simply have liked the name. Anyway, although he never acknowledged her as his or showed her any special favor, many scholars hold Medora to be Byron's illegitimate child. Of course, the only way to prove that would be DNA testing."

"DNA testing!" the two men echoed in horrified tones.

"That would be the only way of conclusively proving—"

"Is nothing sacred?" the old man demanded of the portrait on the wall. Byron's pale face was unperturbed.

Grace blushed. "Well, sure. It's just that it would solve one of the great literary mysteries of all time."

"She's American, of course," Peter remarked to no one in particular.

"Young lady," Aeneas Sweet said severely. "There are certain things not meant to be known."

Owned but not known?

"I wasn't suggesting digging anyone up. Anyway, Medora herself believed she was Byron's daughter."

"Tell us about these cameos," Peter said. "Where did they come from?"

Sweet raked his hair out of his eyes. "The legend is Byron purchased the last of the collection shortly before his death. He died in Missolonghi during the Greek war for independence, you know."

"Yes, of a fever," Peter replied. "He never saw any actual military service. I suppose the cameos vanished after his death?"

"Yes. The story is that Trelawny—you'll naturally have read his journal and his account of taking charge of Byron's effects after his death—mistakenly handed them over to Teresa, Countess Guiccioli, who hung on to them for many years. After that . . . no one knows."

"John Trelawny's journal, *Records of Shelley, Byron and the Author* was recently republished," Grace supplied. "In fact, not too long ago there was a book about Trelawny himself, called *Lord Byron's Jackal*. He's a fascinating figure in his own right, although historians question his credi—"

Peter interrupted, "And who was this Countess Guiccioli when she was at home?"

Grace filled in the blanks. "She was an Italian noblewoman Byron took as his mistress in 1822. It was a huge scandal because he was living as a guest in the home of the countess and her elderly husband. She wrote a memoir called *My Recollections of Lord Byron and Those of Eye Witnesses of His Life*."

"Tripe!" exclaimed Sweet. "Whitewash! Antiseptic! Hogwash!"

Grace clarified, "She was about sixty when she wrote her account and she was trying to clean up her reputation and Byron's."

Peter put a hand to his head, as though it hurt. "What makes you think these gewgaws are genuine?"

"They're genuine all right." The old man glared at him. "I thought you knew about antiques."

"A little."

"Then you must know that even without the Byron connection a collection like this would be worth a fortune."

Grace stared at Peter. She couldn't tell anything by his expression.

"Possibly. How many pieces?"

"Nine or ten. Ten, I think. I only saw them once for a few moments."

"When?"

"When that man Dylan came here like a thief in the middle of the night."

"Who? Oh, Delon. He *was* a thief. Do you know how he came by the set?"

"He refused to say." Sweet added, "I'm not a rich man, but whatever that woman has offered, I can better. Maybe not by much, but I can top her."

"I think this is our cue," Peter told Grace.

"Think about it!" Sweet commanded as they headed for the door. "Whatever that woman offers you, I'll double it!"

"Cameos?" Grace said. "That's it? Cameos?" How disappointing after her dreams of a long-lost master-piece!

"What do you know about cameos?"

She shrugged. "Not much. I know that genuine cameos are reliefs carved out of shell. Or is it coral? I know they've been popular since the fifteenth century. Oh, and I know that a profile cameo is called an intaglio."

Peter's strong tanned hand operated the stick shift. "That's more than most people know."

For a moment Grace was distracted by the sheer male competency he exuded. There was something to be said for that brand of unconscious assurance. Was it uniquely male or simply unique to certain males? She was willing to bet Byron had possessed it as well.

Realizing that she had not fully answered, she

said, "My parents gave me an antique cameo locket when I earned my teaching credential. It had a little card explaining the history of the cameo."

"Yes. Well, that's all true. Cameos—genuine cameos—can be quite valuable. Depending on the size and condition, a cameo from the 1920s might be worth anywhere from two to four hundred pounds."

"What about something like Sweet described? Ten pieces?"

Peter slowed and turned off onto a still narrower lane. His eyes went to the rearview, but he and Grace had been free of pursuit since losing Mutt and Jeff. "I'm not sure. In the eighteenth century, English tourists visiting European souvenir shops used to purchase cameos in themed sets. But typically those cameos were made of pressed white chalk or red sealing wax. They were fastened in wooden trays and fit into specially designed cabinets or leather-bound books destined for some toff's private library. None of that sounds like an appropriate gift for a small girl."

"Byron wasn't exactly an ordinary parent."

"True."

Grace mulled this over. "I suppose these cameos would be valuable because of their fragility; chalk and wax don't tend to hold up through the ages."

"Right. But most of those sets are larger than Sweet described. Say, sixty pieces in various sizes. On the gilt-paper edge of each piece would be written a number in India ink to match a master sheet identifying which icon it represented, for example, the Greek goddess Athena or the Roman philosopher Cicero. That kind of thing."

"How valuable would something like that be?"

"Given the Byron connection?" He shook his head. "A hundred thousand pounds is probably a conservative estimate. Especially if it went up for auction."

"Yes, but they can't really auction stolen antiquities."

"A private auction then. There are plenty of collectors who don't ask questions. Do you think Lady Vee would be troubled by a piece's murky history?"

Grace mulled this over.

"What if the cameos in this collection aren't made of wax? What if they're genuine?"

Peter's answer seemed guarded. "It would depend on a number of factors. Some of the earliest cameos were made of Mediterranean stones like sardonyx, carnelian and agate."

"Semiprecious stones."

"Right. Usually you'll find gold ribbon wrapped around the cameo and then embellished with strings of pearls, double-wire braids or even diamond settings. A single piece could be worth thousands of pounds—even without the Byron connection."

"Supposing a collection existed of ten genuine cameos each handpicked by Lord Byron for his previously unacknowledged daughter on the occasion of her tenth birthday?"

"Would she have been ten at the time of Byron's death?"

"The very month. April."

Peter's eyes slanted toward her. "Let's put it this way: murders have been committed for less. A hell of a lot less."

✣ 1 0 ✣

*I*t was late.

Grace was sleeping when they reached Rogue's Gallery. Her neat little head rested comfortably against his shoulder.

Peter parked and glanced down. She was the tidiest girl he'd ever met; that gorgeous riot of auburn hair always coiled or braided or tied back. Sensible little shoes on her well-grounded feet. Cute little spectacles on her prim little nose. Small, stubborn chin at odds with that cupid's bow mouth; she looked a bit like a cameo herself.

Which was all beside the point, the point being . . . well, he wasn't sure what the point was. He kept remembering her in that black dress. He kept remembering the feel of her body lying against his, her scent. She was, to quote her dead poets, something of a help and something of a hindrance. Now that he knew what Delon had been hawking, he didn't need her. In fact, better for her to get clear and stay clear.

Not that she would be easy to shake. On the topic of The Great Romantics, Miss Hollister herself was a little bit of a fanatic.

Peter shrugged his shoulder and Grace mumbled protestingly.

"Rise and shine, Esmerelda."

She rubbed her face against his arm, sat up and yawned—covering it with a polite hand.

"Where are we?"

"H—back at Craddock House."

"That was fast." She leaned forward staring out the windshield. "Hey, something's wrong!"

Peter followed her gaze. Distracted by—well, who knows by what—he had merely glanced at the shop, seeing what he had expected to see. Now he noticed, despite the darkness and the overhanging trees obscuring the view, that the shop window appeared to be boarded up.

"Bloody hell!" He got out of the Rover and Grace got out with him. "Stay here," he ordered.

"Whatever happened, it's over and done," Grace pointed out, "if someone's got around to patching the place up."

She was right—which was one more aggravation he didn't need.

Peter strode up the walk. The night was cold and heavy with the scent of flowers. Dew sparkled on the grass and limned the leaves in silver moonlight.

As they reached the shop they could see the bow window was boarded but the front door was intact. Yellow police tape indicated a crime scene.

Peter unlocked the door, switched on the light. Behind him, Grace gasped.

"Oh no!"

"Oh no," was putting it mildly. It looked like the proverbial bull had been let loose in a china shop. Legs kicking the air, the merry-go-round horse lay on its back in a bed of smashed pottery and broken masks. Shelves had been knocked over—along with about everything else in the place.

Hundreds, no thousands of pounds worth of damage. He felt light-headed for a moment. It wasn't so much the money as the wanton destruction of all these beautiful fragile things.

Books had been tossed over the balcony above; they lay with pages spread wide like shot birds.

"Oh Peter," whispered Grace. Her eyes looked huge and green. *Like light dissolved in star-showers thrown . . .* She put her hand on his arm and he had the craziest desire to turn to her for comfort.

Instead he pulled away, stepped over a smashed Prince of Wales chair and made his way to the stockroom.

To his relief the shelf guarding the passageway was still standing, the hidden door, still sealed. His intruder must have been stopped before he made it this far.

"It can't have been the same person who killed Danny Delon," Grace said. "He didn't know about the passage."

Or he had gone in through the front door of the flat. Peter turned and nearly knocked Grace over.

Steadying her, he moved her aside, headed for the stairs, taking them two at a time.

"The intruder must have triggered the alarm when he broke in," Grace said from downstairs. "The police must have grabbed him before he could—"

Before he could break into the flat.

The door was still standing, still locked tight. The relief was overwhelming. Sanctuary was still his. For a moment Peter stood there, his hand resting against the lacquered door.

Then he unlocked the door, pushed it wide. Everything was as he had left it.

"Oh, Peter, I'm so sorry," Grace's voice drifted up to him. She kept saying that. Oddly, it didn't bother him. It was almost a relief to have someone else there to share this disaster.

He went through the rooms and everything was as they had left it the day before. Grace's spectacles still lay on the curio table. Her green jumper hung on the back of a chair—and that seemed right, too.

He went into the kitchen and pressed play on the answering machine. Grace joined him, putting the kettle on.

"Your insurance will cover this, right?" she asked.

A tinny unfamiliar female voice interrupted.

"Grace? It's me, Monica. Who's this Peter Fox? Where the heck is Innisdale? Grace, I've got some news. You're not going to believe it. I don't know if I believe it. But I want to tell you, not a machine. I'll call back."

Click.

At his shoulder, Grace groaned. "*Why* can she *never* leave a number?"

The machine beeped again and Chief Constable Heron's voice filled the silence.

"Mr. Fox, this is Chief Constable Heron. We've been unable to reach you regarding the damage to your property. Please contact us when you get in." He looked over at the clock.

"It's too late tonight," Grace interjected. "The morning is soon enough to deal with this mess. There must be something I can do. Can I make you something to eat?"

There was something vaguely funny about that but he couldn't think what.

"I need a drink." He went into the other room, poured a stiff one.

When he returned to the kitchen Grace had out a tin of Belgian chocolate and was heating cocoa.

"You should eat something," she told him. She was mothering him. He couldn't remember that ever happening before. His dear old mum had certainly not thought he needed mothering.

"I'm fine."

She cut a slice of fruitcake, rich with nuts and rum and set it before him.

"Who do you think it was?" she asked, sitting down across from him.

"Not Mutt and Jeff."

"Our friends the kidnappers?"

"I've got to call the insurance company." Peter swallowed a mouthful of whisky. He welcomed the burn. "Sid," he said abruptly. "Sid something. Hall maybe. I knew I'd seen him before."

"Seen who? Who's Sid Hall?"

"A little hoodlum with big ideas. The bloke you call the Queen Mother." Absently he picked up his fork.

"Sid." Mentally she matched the name with the little brute she so well remembered. "I remember overhearing him say something about crossing 'The Man,' " Grace said, carving herself a wedge of cake. "Do you think they could be working for Sweet?"

"It would explain what they were doing crawling around inside the walls of Penwith Hall." He rubbed his forehead wearily.

"Do you think they found it?" Grace asked tentatively. "The set of cameos?"

He shook his head. "I've no idea."

She covered his hand with hers. A small, soft and unexpectedly strong hand. "It'll be better in the morning," she said.

The heavy-lidded eyes studied her for a long moment, as though he were seeing her for the first time.

"You could be right," he said.

• • •

"Ram Singh!"

Grace watched Peter over the rim of her coffee cup.

He was on the phone chatting with the Innisdale police. So far his end of the conversation had consisted of one-word comments like "What?" and "I—" Now at last things were getting interesting.

Although, if she were honest, things were already interesting. Peter was wearing only Levis. Feet and torso were bare and while he spoke to the local authorities he absently scratched his smoothly muscled chest. For some reason Grace found this fascinating—as though she'd never seen well-developed biceps before. Fine gold was sprinkled between pectorals to his navel. Grace's thoughts were interrupted as Peter hung up the phone.

"Ram Singh," she asserted, so that he would know her mind had been on his conversation and not his pecs. "They're holding Ram Singh?"

"They caught him red-handed the night before last. The odd thing is they received an anonymous phone call about a prowler even before the alarm went off."

"That's weird. And they've no idea who called? Whether it was a man or a woman?"

"I didn't ask," Peter admitted.

Grace swirled the dregs of tea in her mug as though trying to divine an answer. "Sweet must have sent Ram Singh right after we claimed we didn't bring the gewgaws. Did they find the cameos on him?"

"They didn't say. I've got to go down there."

"It could be a trap," Grace said. "I'll go, too."

"That might not be a good idea. We don't know what he's revealed to the cops."

"He's mute."

Peter's expression was chiding. "Be serious."

"I'm always serious." Once that would have been almost true. "Ram Singh won't have told them about Sweet. He doesn't appear to have anyway. Sweet didn't seem to know he was gone—although that was probably an act."

"I don't know if it was an act. He probably forgot he'd sent him. He's nuttier than that cake we ate last night."

Peter headed for his bedroom.

"Now that I've got money again, I'll buy my hat," Grace called after him. "That way, if they arrest you, I'm right there ready to bail you out. And dressed for the occasion." She was kidding—at least she hoped she was, but he didn't seem to be listening. Hurriedly she changed into jeans and a plush, oversize mocha sweatshirt, catching up to him as he walked around to the garage.

As they drove, flashing in and out of sunlight and shade, she studied Peter's profile.

"Are you all right?"

He gave her a haughty look. "Why wouldn't I be?"

"I just notice that the police make you nervous."

He was silent. She supposed he was offended, but to her surprise he said, "I have a dislike of confined spaces."

"Well, lots of people do."

"An intense dislike."

"Like claustrophobia?"

"Let's just say I'll do my damnedest to stay out of anything resembling a cell. Or a closet. Or a hatbox. They all feel about the same size."

"Is that from being in pri—what happened to you in Turkey?"

"Got it in one."

Grace digested this silently. She would have liked to ask him why he had been imprisoned, but didn't have the nerve.

And then Peter changed the subject. "You might try the library when you've finished buying your hat. Our librarian is one of your lot."

"My lot?"

"Barmy about the Cumbrian literary heritage."

"Sounds like a man of discerning taste and refinement."

Peter grinned at that but made no comment.

They were crossing the little stone bridge and opportunity for further discussion was lost.

"I'll meet you back here in one hour," Peter said, letting her off in Daffodil Street.

"Meet me at the library," Grace suggested.

"Will do." His eyes looked preoccupied.

She hesitated. "Good luck."

"Yes. Thanks."

She watched him drive down the street and park, then turned and went into the milliner's shop.

The dream hat was still there and amazingly enough it was as lovely as she remembered.

"It looks as though it were made for you," a shop girl with purple hair and a ring in her nose said as Grace modeled for the mirror. "The leaves are just the color of your eyes."

"If only it was made for my pocketbook."

The girl shrugged. "You only live once."

Taking a deep breath, Grace paid the two hundred pounds and arranged to have the hat shipped back to the States. It was the last of her vacation "mad money." But then this whole vacation had been a little mad.

Leaving the shop she began walking toward the library. All up and down the crowded streets the little shops were open and doing brisk business as the tourist season wrapped up. Grace lingered outside the sweet shop for calorie-laden moments, but reason prevailed. She couldn't afford to keep a "fat" and "thin" wardrobe while vacationing in a foreign country.

Her gaze wandered to the big blue hand raised above a small white shop. The palm of the hand read: FORTUNES. There were matching blue plastic flowers in the window boxes, and a blue lacquered door. On impulse, Grace decided to check it out. If nothing else it would make a good story to tell Peter.

A bell chimed musically as she stepped inside the blue door. Décor by the Purple People Eaters, she decided, blinking at the plum-colored carpet and gauzy lilac draperies. The lavender walls were adorned with gold-framed pictures of Jesus and a giant astrological chart. What sign was Jesus, Grace wondered?

Grace cleared her throat. The scent of passion-flower incense was almost overpowering. No one seemed to be around but she could hear a radio from behind more gauzy draperies, these spangled with purple sequins.

"Here now, Charlie," a woman's voice said. "You're taking a hell of a risk coming back here. Suppose someone recognizes you?"

"No one's going to recognize me. Not after all these years." Grace had opened her mouth to call hello, but she knew that voice, the man's voice.

"Don't lose your nerve, Anna."

For a moment she stood motionless, unbelieving. The man in the dog mask. Sid's partner.

It was a small world after all. And getting increasingly smaller.

The bells rang again. Grace turned.

" 'Ello, 'ello," said Sid. He reached up and turned out the lights.

"You can't leave her here!"

"It's just for a few hours. We'll get the van—"

"And suppose she wakes up and starts yelling her head off?"

"She's out cold."

"Well, she'll wake up, won't she? He hasn't killed her, has he? And then what?"

"Just leave it to Sid."

• • •

Grace opened her eyes.

Even that little movement hurt. She closed them again.

A while later—time seemed to have lost meaning—she tried again. She seemed to be lying in a dungeon. Cobwebs drifted gently over her head. She was lying on something very hard. Hard as stone. And cold. The floor.

Now why would that be?

Vaguely she recalled a long feverish dream about a fortune-teller who was wearing the most beautiful hat with jade green leaves edged in silver, and then a tower had fallen on her . . .

Grace groaned.

The sound alarmed her. It also alarmed something in the darkness with her. She heard it scampering away. A mouse perhaps. Or something bigger. A rat.

Best not to think about that.

She had to be quiet. She couldn't let them know . . .

Why? And what was it they couldn't know?

It was all fuzzy.

She remembered then. She had walked into the fortune-teller's shop. A blue lacquered door . . . Then Sid Hall had hit her with a lead pipe. Mr. Hall in the shop with the lead pipe. Like *Clue*.

Grace drifted.

Sid was coming back.

Grace's eyes flew open. Things were coming back into focus. She had to get out of here. Wherever "here" was. She had to get out before Sid came back with the van.

Slowly, cautiously, she sat up. Her head hurt . . . indescribably. Her neck and shoulders hurt, too. The room did a wide spin and Grace hung on to the floor to keep her balance.

When it stopped spinning, Grace got up and staggered over to the nearest thing she could lean on. That was the wall. She leaned on it for a while and then, her eyes picking out shape in the gloom, zigzagged to the door.

Leaning against the door, she listened intently. Though she couldn't hear anything, she could see a thin band of light shining beneath the door. That made sense. They wouldn't leave her alone in the shop.

Resisting the temptation to lie down on the floor again, she felt around for a light switch. There was one by the door and she turned it on. Wincing at the too-bright light, she looked around. She saw that there was another door, probably a garden entrance. There was some kind of a pet door set in the door.

She wove her way to the second door. It was locked of course. She squatted down and checked out the pet door.

It had been nailed shut.

That seemed to be that. Grace sat the rest of the way down and leaned against the door and closed her eyes. It was better that way. She could think. While she was thinking it occurred to her that a basement probably had tools. That was reasonable, right? She pried her eyes open and looked around the hellishly bright room.

There was a workbench at the other end of the basement. Why did these things always have to be on the other side of the room? She pushed off from the wall and staggered to the workbench. Rummaging through the drawers she found more nails, rivets, measuring tape, glue—and then noticed the hammer was hanging on the wall.

She ran back, sliding into place beside the door like a baseball player sliding onto home plate, aches and pains momentarily forgotten in the panic to escape. Desperately, she pried at the nails with the hammer. It wasn't easy. She dug and gouged at the wood, tearing her fingernails in the process. But at last she had the nails out.

The pet door swung free.

And Grace wondered what the hell she had been thinking because there was no way on earth she could fit through that opening.

She tried though. She tried long and hard, fitting one leg and then withdrawing and trying to go arm first. Then head first.

At last she conceded defeat. She rested her aching head on her knees and tried to think. Her peek out the pet door had informed her that it was night. Late. The village of Innisdale was sleeping peacefully. She wished she were. She wished it were all a dream.

Grace raised her head and inspected her prison

once more. She could try to start a fire but the odds were she would die of smoke inhalation before she could get free.

That's when she noticed the saw that was hanging right next to where the hammer had been. There really seemed to be something the matter with her head tonight.

Rising, she lurched over to the wall, played tug-of-war with the saw, tottered back to the door and began sawing at the pet door, trying to make it wider.

She sawed and hacked and sliced and trimmed.

She began to laugh hysterically. How could her captors not hear this racket?

Grace bit her lip and sawed some more and at last had splintered and carved the wood enough that she thought she could kick through.

She kicked hard and her legs were out. Wriggling on through, her braid caught in the jagged wood. As Grace reached up to free herself, the basement door flew open.

"Charlie!" shrieked a woman. "She's getting away!"

Encouraged by this overstatement of the situation, Grace yanked her hair free and shoved the rest of the way out the broken door.

She found herself in a little yard with a high fence. Too high to jump.

Her captors were slamming against the locked back door.

"Go round, Charlie!" yelled the woman.

Grace dragged a chaise lounge over to the fence,

climbed onto it, pulled herself up clumsily. She balanced briefly on top of the fence and then jumped down into the alley. As her feet touched ground a now familiar black van pulled up.

Grace froze, caught in the van's headlights. Then the van accelerated forward. Grace whirled and ran.

The van breathed hotly down her neck as she fled. He was going to mow her down, it seemed. Desperately, she looked for something to dodge behind, a doorway, another alley, something, anything.

She ducked around the first corner, and before her lay an empty field.

Beyond the fields was a stream, shining in the moonlight, and beyond the stream stretched the woods.

Grace made for the woods. Running across the open field left her exposed, but the boulders and ditches would be difficult to drive across. She heard the slam of a van door and knew Sid was coming after her on foot.

Reaching the embankment, Grace half fell, half slid her way down the slope to the water's edge. Looking up through the reeds and brush she could see Sid prowling along the embankment searching for her.

She lay very still, not daring to move, afraid to breathe. Her head was pounding, she was sweating, she felt like throwing up. With my luck I have a concussion, she reflected dimly. Or maybe she was having a heart attack after all that exertion and her recent diet. If Sid and Charlie found her, it would all be over anyway.

Sid would have run her down. She had no doubt about that. Grace wondered if he would hear her teeth chattering from where he stood. He seemed to be taking a long time.

As she watched, he turned.

"Bring the van around. Tell Anna to watch the field. She may try to cut back to the village."

"Do you see her?"

"No, but she's down there."

Grace considered her options. She was cut off from the safety of the village and she couldn't get across the streambed without being seen. Her only chance was to scoot along the bank until she reached the bridge several yards down. The bridge would offer enough concealment for her to cross into the woods—that was her theory anyway.

Of course this was the wrong direction from the one she needed to go. She ought to be heading for phones and people. Craddock House lay on the other side of the woods, but it was at least ten miles away. She didn't think she was in any shape to run ten miles. Or even crawl ten miles.

Although she did seem to be crawling now . . . slowly and painfully.

Grace looked up and Sid was farther down the stream. He was expecting her to do the rational thing and head for the road, but since she couldn't get to the road without being spotted, she would continue to make like an inchworm for the bridge.

It took at least an hour. It felt like it took half her life—and at one point she realized she had dozed off. She woke chilled and alarmed and began crawling toward the bridge again.

At last she reached the bridge. This was the tricky part—all things being relative. Cautiously Grace waded out. The water was only up to her shins and the current was not strong. She splashed across to the other side as quietly as was possible.

She hadn't seen or heard Sid and Company for some time. That didn't mean they weren't out there.

Reaching the other side of the stream, she scrambled up the hillside, climbed over a stone wall and crept into the woods. Collapsing in the dead leaves and pine needles, she rested for a bit. After an indeterminate time she rolled over and spat out the moldering bark. Through the lacework of leaves she could see a black night void of stars.

It was torture to have to keep moving, but Grace pushed up and began to creep through the undergrowth.

She thought she was going in the right direction, but she wasn't sure. Nothing looked familiar from this side of the road. The road itself was empty and silent. She walked on, no longer bothering to be quiet. She'd lost them somehow. Perhaps they were still waiting for her on the other side of the bridge.

At last a car came along, headlights sweeping the deserted road.

Grace stumbled out of the brush and into the road, waving her arms wildly.

The MG swerved widely and braked. The driver's window rolled down.

She couldn't see the driver's face but a familiar voice called out, "Miss Hollister? Is that you?"

Grace stumbled up to the Honorable Al's car and leaned against it. It was a small car. A toy car. A fashion accessory of a car. Grace grabbed at her straying wits. "Can you help me? Can you give me a ride to Peter's?"

"Yes, of course." Al's face was unreadable in the gloom. "I can do better than that. I'll take you to Auntie's."

"Peter's will be fine."

Al reached across and opened the door. Grace came round and half fell into the car.

The hot air jetted out of the heater. It felt wonderful.

"Peter's gone," Al informed her. "Didn't you know?" Her features looked sharp and greenish in the glow of the dash lights.

"Gone?" Grace couldn't seem to take it in. "Gone where?" She tried to focus on Al's fuzzy features.

Al shrugged. "I don't know. I stopped by there this evening but he was gone. The shop is boarded up." She said sympathetically, "You do look a fright. There are twigs in your hair. What in the world has been happening?"

The shop was boarded up? Foggily, Grace knew there was something about this that she needed to explain to Allegra. It was so hard to think. She dropped her head back on the seat and mumbled, "It's . . . complicated."

"So many things are, aren't they? Let me take you to Auntie's and we'll call the police, shall we?"

Grace considered this from an increasing distance. "I feel . . . bloody." She informed Al.

"Oh dear," Al murmured.

When Grace opened her eyes she found herself in a strange bed in a moonlit room. Tall bed posts loomed over her, casting their shadows across the brocade duvet.

As her eyes adjusted to the darkness she sort of remembered Allegra saying she would drive her to Lady Vee's. Grace sat up and felt her way across the carpeted floor to a door.

Tentatively, she turned the handle.

The door was locked.

A uniformed chambermaid brought breakfast. She seemed to find nothing queer about having to unlock the bedroom door. Smiling politely, she deposited the tray over Grace's legs and then opened the drapes, letting in the sunlight.

At least they weren't planning to starve her. The tray was laden with enough food for an entire country house: porridge and cream in a primrose china bowl, deviled kidney, bacon and eggs, hot rolls and marmalade, and a gallon of hot coffee to wash it down with.

Grace was just finishing up her deviled kidney and eggs when Allegra strolled in.

"No wire hangers, no starch," she said cheerfully, draping Grace's things over the rocker. "Feeling better?"

"Loads," said Grace. "Thanks for . . . everything. I must have passed out."

"Rather."

"You didn't . . ." it was all a little awkward in the face of Allegra's blank courtesy, "think we should call the police?"

"The police?" Allegra's delicate brows arched. "Maybe you'd better speak to Auntie Vee first." She glanced at the ormolu clock on the fireplace mantel. "Say in about an hour? I know you must be longing for a nice hot bath."

Grace had her nice hot bath, dressed and made her way downstairs. As she reached the front hall she made a detour toward the door, but a small gnomish man seemed to pop out of the wallpaper. He moved to intercept her, although his face remained impassively courteous.

"This way, miss." He beckoned toward the drawing room.

"Oh, sure!" Grace offered a feeble smile. "It's such a big house, isn't it?"

Jeff's smile was equally meaningless. He ushered her toward the drawing room where Lady Venetia and Allegra waited.

"Oh there you are, my *deah*," Lady Vee greeted her, speaking around the ivory cigarette holder. "What a relief to see you looking so well after your misadventures."

Lady Vee looked well, too. Today's ensemble was a white tea-length frock and three ropes of pearls down to her navel. Her blue-black hair shone glossily in the light streaming through the tall windows. Hair that shiny had to be a wig, Grace decided.

"Thank you," Grace said. "And thank you for your kindness last night. I can't help feeling that we should have called the police though."

"My *deah*, it is our pleasure to help Petah's little friend." Lady Vee's purple shadowed eyelids dropped briefly like a sleepy snake's.

Allegra stared out the window, her arms folded. Wearing riding breeches and a hacking jacket she could have stepped from an old episode of *The Avengers*.

Lady Vee glanced at her niece and then returned her attention to Grace. She smiled still more widely. Between the parchment skin and that glossy black bob, she reminded Grace of an Egyptian mummy. Grace smiled back.

"May I use the phone?"

"Of all the exasperating things, my deah! It's out of order."

"You're joking," Grace said.

"No, my dear. Allegra, what is the news about the phone?"

"I have no idea."

"Is there a phone in the stables or the garage?" Grace tried again.

"Why, my dear?"

It was like trying to converse in a foreign language. "To begin with, to call the police."

"The police!" Lady Venetia tittered as though someone had made a rude joke. "Well of course you *may*, but perhaps you had better hear my little proposition first."

"Peter won't appreciate the police being called in," Al put in suddenly. "The entire county is gossiping about him now. Gossiping about the body in his garden."

"Where is Peter?" Grace questioned, looking from one to the other of them.

Lady Vee wafted the cigarette holder. "My deah, how should we know? You must have some arrangement for getting in touch with him."

"Has something happened to him?"

Allegra laughed bitterly. She kept her gaze fastened out the window as though the answer to all her problems were on the horizon.

Lady Vee soothed, "Don't be ridiculous, child. Peter Fox is more than capable of taking care of himself."

Grace was silent. It began to seem like a good idea to hear what her hostess had to say.

"Now, I am still prepared to be quite generous, although I must say I am monstrously disappointed in Peter—"

"We don't have it," Grace interrupted, forgetting all about being quiet and listening to what Venetia had to say.

Lady Vee shook her head. Her raven hair swung against her wrinkled cheeks. "My *deah* . . ." she protested.

"It's true. We've never had it. Danny Delon was murdered before he could tell Peter where he hid the cameos."

"Murdered!"

"You must think we're pretty stupid," Allegra sneered, at last turning to face the room.

Grace avoided the obvious answer. "It's the truth," she repeated. "We didn't even know what we were looking for until a couple of days ago. Delon's is the body the police found in the lake. Someone murdered him and tried to kill Peter when he was in Kentmere. He was on a buying trip."

Allegra and her aunt exchanged a certain look.

"That maniac!" exclaimed Lady Venetia.

"Peter?" Grace inquired.

"Ram Dam or whatever his name is. Sweet's serving man."

Grace put the pieces together fast. "Ram Singh murdered Danny Delon?"

"But of course. Ram Singh attacked Peter. Bartleby saw him do it."

"B-Bartleby?" Grace faltered.

Lady Vee tapped cigarette ashes into a brass ashtray and shook her head regretfully. "My deah, you would be so much safer dealing with me than those dreadful people Aeneas Sweet employs. Sweet cannot be trusted. He is *unbalanced.*"

"Fine," Grace said. "We'll deal with you. It doesn't matter to me who—just let me talk to Peter. Let me call him."

"She's lying," Allegra said.

"Of course she is," Lady Vee agreed.

"She's going to try and pull something."

"Naturally."

No empty seats at the Mad Hatter's table.

"Now," Lady Venetia said briskly, "As I said, I'm quite prepared to be generous, but we must come to some agreement. I'm afraid that you, my dear, are our bargaining chip."

Grace stared. "Let me get this straight: you're planning to hold me hostage?"

Lady Venetia looked pained. "What a thing to suggest. We simply wish to ensure Peter's attention."

"But you don't know where he is."

"He's looking for you, my dear. Where else would he be? We'll let him look for a while and then he'll be very glad to make a deal."

"Maybe he'll make another deal in the meantime."

"Then he would have to unmake it." Lady Vee shrugged her skeletal shoulders. "Anyway, you underestimate yourself."

"Not really," Grace sighed.

Détente ended there. Grace was marched back upstairs and locked in the bedroom with its gilt fixtures and blue brocade wallpaper.

For a few minutes she sat there considering her options. Then she checked out the windows. She had had great luck with windows lately, but not today. The guest room was three stories off the ground and there wasn't a tree branch in sight.

She paced up and down the black Oriental carpet and then wandered over to the dressing table. Like any well-equipped dressing table it had various items including hairpins, hair comb and a nail file. She tested the point of the nail file against her fingertip and went to examine the door.

Of course picking locks looked so easy on TV. Grace stared at the knob and suddenly an idea occurred, almost startling in its simplicity. Using the nail file, she unscrewed the doorknob, removed it and opened the door. A quick glance up and down the hall assured her the coast was clear. Sneaking into the room next door, she spotted a phone. A dial tone greeted her ears. Grace dialed Peter's number.

The phone rang and rang and then . . .

Peter's answering machine came on.

"It's me," she said, keeping her voice down. "Pick up. If you're there, pick up."

Nothing.

Please, please, she prayed.

Nothing.

Grace spoke hurriedly into the mouthpiece. "I'm at Lady Venetia's. They're holding me here to try and force you to bargain with them."

From down the hall she could hear a vacuum. Replacing the phone, she poked her head out the door. In the hall she spied a vacuum cleaner and a hose leading into a bedroom. Presumably the maid was at the other end of the hose. Grace ducked into the hall, tiptoeing along to her room and letting herself back inside. She replaced the knob, which hung lopsidedly if anyone was noticing. She hoped no one would. If Lady Vee suspected Grace had contacted

Peter who knew what she might do—have Grace moved to another "safe house?"

Luncheon consisted of orange-rosemary chicken, chilled vegetables and summer pudding. Grace succumbed to her tendency to eat when she was nervous, and had two helpings of pudding, which consisted of bread and fruit and clotted cream. In short, a calorie fest.

In between bites, Grace asked Lady Vee about the history of the cameos. She was treated to the tale of Byron's last days.

"Of course he was the only one with the least idea of organization. The Greek Army was a joke! B. spent nearly all his own fortune as well as all the money collected by the English supporters of the Greek Revolution, trying to make soldiers out of peasants. But it was a noble cause and one dear to his heart."

Grace made some polite acknowledgment. It seemed to her that Byron would have done better to stay home and keep writing.

"And the darling boy's health was never good. *How* he suffered, if we are to believe Trelawny's report of his examination of Byron's embalmed body!"

Not exactly mealtime conversation, but Grace couldn't refrain from arguing, "But didn't Trelawny later recant his story that both Byron's feet were clubbed? From what I've read it seems that most historians believe Trelawny took all kinds of liberties with the facts."

Lady Vee waved this off as of no importance. "And

then of course there was the epileptic seizure Byron suffered in February. So difficult to know what may have triggered it, and while it was not the cause of his death, it certainly must have contributed. How ironic that one so gallant, so vital should in the end die as a result of catching a chill."

"But didn't Byron actually die of the treatment he received?"

Lady Vee's face suffused with color. "Yes! I see that you do know your Byron. The poor darling suffered a relapse of the malaria he had contracted in 1811. Those so-called doctors and that *fool* valet killed him with their purges and their leeches! B. actually said they were assassinating him . . ."

Lady Vee fell silent. Following her gaze, both Grace and Al glanced around. Through the French doors they watched a white Land Rover enter the stately gates and drive slowly along the circular drive before vanishing out of their sight.

"He's here," Allegra said unnecessarily.

Lady Venetia allowed herself a tiny smile, and took a bite of summer pudding. "Naturally." She beckoned to one of the servants to lay another place setting.

Thirty seconds later a bell chimed musically throughout the house.

Lady Venetia met Grace's doubtful gaze. "Have another pudding, child," she invited, with the cool confidence of a woman holding all the cards.

Thirty seconds after *that* there came a sound like someone throwing someone else into a table.

And then a sound like someone threw someone into a wall.

The pictures on the dining room wall slid back and forth like pendulums. The double doors to the dining room banged open.

To borrow the vernacular of Grace's students, Peter looked . . . awesome. Cuban boots, slim-fitting Levis, a vest of crushed teal velvet and a white poet's shirt. In fact, he looked like a very hip poet. What he said was prosaic enough. "I really don't have time for this." He glanced Grace's way. "Grace—"

Grace was already on her feet.

"So nice to see you again," she couldn't resist saying in passing.

Allegra sat like a stone. Lady Venetia was on her feet, hands braced on the table. "What do you think you're doing?" she shrieked. "You can't just walk in here and—and *take* her."

A little nastily Peter said, "Really? Why's that?"

"We have to—to talk. We have to decide—"

Grace heard Peter say, "Actually we don't."

"But-but—" The old woman looked about for her conspicuously absent minions.

They went out through the main hall, and Bartleby and Jeff—or perhaps it was Mutt and Bartleby—were lying on the floor. They did not actually have stars or songbirds orbiting their heads but they gave the general impression that they were through for the day.

"My hero," Grace said.

"I bet you say that to all the boys." On the porch

Peter kissed Grace once, hard. Then grinned. "Hello again."

"Miss me?" Grace inquired.

"A little."

They got into the Land Rover and Grace watched the white house in the side mirror grow smaller and smaller in the distance till it was the size of a dollhouse.

"If they had brains," Peter remarked, "they'd be dangerous."

As the Land Rover zipped along the hilly road, Grace related her adventures.

"When I left the police station, I looked for you," Peter said grimly. "When you didn't show at the library, I tracked you to the milliner's and then . . . you vanished. I tried the sweet shop."

Grace huffed, "Well, I went to the tarot reader."

"The tarot reader!" For once he seemed floored.

"It was just . . . for fun."

He made a polite sound. "I admit I didn't think of checking there."

Grace repeated the bit of conversation she had overheard.

"Charlie Ames," Peter said thoughtfully. "Now why's that familiar?"

"Wasn't Ames the name of the old woman who used to own the farmhouse where the Que—I mean, Sid and Charlie took me? Or no, it was the name of the housekeeper, wasn't it?"

Peter directed an approving look her way. "I think

you're right. That explains how they knew about a handy and isolated place to stow kidnap victims. As I recollect there was something about a Charlie Ames who was sent up for B and E." For Grace's benefit he clarified, "Breaking and entering. Nothing necessarily violent."

Grace felt her still tender skull. "His friends aren't so particular. And by the way, Lady Vee confirms that Sid and Charlie are working for Sweet."

"Did we need confirmation?"

"Certainty is nice," Grace said.

An unfamiliar blue Mustang was parked outside Craddock House. Beside it stood a brawny silver-haired man. A small blonde woman sat on the hood. They were kissing.

"Ah hell," muttered Peter.

"It's Monica!" gasped Grace. They exchanged glances.

Peter pulled up beside the Mustang and Grace practically fell out of the Land Rover.

"Monica? What are you doing here?" She couldn't help the accusatory note that crept into her voice. "*Where* have you been?"

Monica, the large silver-haired man in tow, went to hug Grace. "Surprise, surprise! Congratulate me. We just got married!"

Grace froze midhug. "You're . . . kidding me."

"Nope."

The silver-haired man nodded sheepishly at Peter. Peter nodded back.

"Calum Bell?" Grace said doubtfully. She moved to shake hands but was swept into a bear hug.

"Of course it's Calum," Monica laughed. "Who else would it be?"

Tom? Grace thought, feeling stunned by Monica's revelation. More, she felt . . . unsettled, as though Monica's jumping the rails had some implication for herself.

"So this is wee Grrrrace." Calum spoke with a charming Scottish burr. He was about fifty and very handsome. He wore jeans and a Harris Tweed sweater and did not look like anyone's college professor.

"But . . . congratulations!" Grace said helplessly.

"You can't believe it, can you?" Monica chuckled. Grace studied her friend as though they had just met. In a way, it seemed as though they had. Monica was about forty, petite with short blond hair and a laugh like a jolly little boy.

Grace gathered her wits. "It's just . . . I'm surprised." She turned to Peter, introducing him.

Seeming to pick up on her mixed emotions, Peter came to the rescue. "Let's go inside," he invited. "I'll open a bottle and we can celebrate."

He led the way up the cobbled walk. Linking her arm with Grace's, Monica whispered, "Oooh! He's delicious."

"I've never seen a man carry velvet off before," Monica observed, toying with the cork from the wine bottle.

"Monica, what about Tom?" Grace interrupted. She and Monica were preparing a tea tray in the kitchen while Peter gave Calum a tour of the house. Not the complete tour, Grace was willing to bet.

Monica sighed. "Oh, Grace, Tom was just a . . . a convenience. Like Chaz."

"Chaz isn't a convenience!" exclaimed Grace. "I don't even know what that means." She felt defensive although she couldn't explain why.

"Sure you do. A convenience is an otherwise eligible man who fills in while you're waiting for the real thing."

"Why couldn't the convenience be the real thing?"

"True love, Grace, that's what I'm talking about. Surely you've heard of it?"

"Once or twice."

"I'll bet Shelley and old Byron and—" Grace rolled her eyes and Monica changed tack. "So tell me about Peter Fox."

"Uh-oh, I don't like that meaningful tone. Peter is just a friend. I don't even know if he's really a friend. He's sort of my . . ."

"Accomplice?"

Grace had already briefly filled Monica in on some of the events of the past few days. It was a highly abridged account, reading more or less like the back cover blurb of a gothic romance: ruthless crooks searching for lost jewels that they believed had fallen into Peter's possession. Grace left out the Byron connection and Peter's less-than-savory past. She knew that Monica, with her passion for old crime and mystery movies, would swallow this up without question. Or at least without too many questions. Monica would believe it because Monica would hope it was true.

Monica tossed the cork and caught it, one-handed. "He's beautiful. You should marry him."

"*Marry* him? Because he's beautiful? Besides, he's not the marrying kind."

Monica grinned. "He's smart. He could learn."

Grace stared at this stranger in Monica's skin. "Seriously though, Monica. What about your job? What about your life?"

Monica said cheerfully, "I'm starting a new life. It feels wonderful."

"Since we're here we may as well help you put this place back together," Calum offered after they had toasted the newlyweds a couple of times.

Peter hedged politely.

The shop looked better than it had when Grace and Peter returned from Penwith Hall. Somehow, between the time when Grace went missing and his rescue of her, Peter had managed to shovel out most of the broken glass and smashed furniture, although Rogue's Gallery was still a mess.

"And we can help you hunt," Monica put in eagerly.

"A grrrand notion," Calum agreed.

"Oh, well . . ." Grace began, knowing what Peter's expression meant.

At the same time, Peter started, "Very kind, but—"

"But you're not sure the jewels are here?" Monica concluded.

"The jewels? No." Peter seemed to be about to clarify and then answered, "Delon may not have had them on him." He added a little irritably, "I've no notion why he came back here. I told him I didn't want any part of it." The real surprise to Grace was that he answered Monica's question candidly.

"He probably had them on his perrrrson," Calum said cheerfully, rolling his "Rs." "He wouldn't trust leaving them anywhere, right?"

"Anyway," Monica said, "Four heads are better than two."

An odd thought flitted into Grace's head. What did they really know about Calum Bell? It had been how many years since Monica had last met him? Wasn't it a huge coincidence that she had bumped into him when she had?

But then reason reasserted itself. Monica had drifted off with Calum before Grace had ever met Peter, before she ever pulled him out of that Kentmere stream. No one could have planned for that. Mentally, Grace shook her head at her own paranoia. Paranoia was Peter's department; she waited for him to go all secretive and peculiar, but he said wearily, in answer to Monica's proposal, "Why not? The more the merrier."

While Peter and Calum took the main floor of the shop, Grace and Monica were awarded the task of bringing order to the library. They spent the next hour or so restacking books on the shelves, climbing up and down the ladder, checking the hollowed books. It was companionable work, punctuated by Monica chattering about Calum and Scotland.

"This could take years." Monica sighed after a time, handing Grace a leather-bound volume. "Give you a good reason for staying on."

Grace shot her friend an evil look, but Monica merely chuckled. "Admit it, Grace. You're having the time of your life. I've never seen you so . . . alive."

"I'm sure you mean that as a compliment." Grace levered another book onto the shelf above her head. She couldn't see Peter, but from her perch on the ladder she watched Calum on the ground floor going through the drawers of a walnut highboy.

She said slowly, "Doesn't it seem like a huge coincidence that you would run into Calum? It's been, what? Twenty years?"

Monica shrugged. "Life is made up of coincidences. Haven't you noticed?"

"Not really." Or at least, not until recently. She inquired casually, "So, what does he teach? I mean, what's his field? They don't really even have 'dons' anymore, do they?"

"He's a Younger Fellow and a Tutor in Creative Writing at Balliol."

"Balliol? Why is that familiar?"

"Lord Peter Wimsey's old alma mater," Monica said. "Calum's a writer."

"What does he write?"

Monica looked vague. "You wouldn't have read any of his work."

Grace filed that evasion away to examine later. "And he's never been married?"

"Of course he's been married." Monica seemed amused at the notion. "He's divorced with one child. A son. Sixteen years old. He lives in Scotland with his mother. The son, I mean. I'm not sure if Calum's mother is still living." She cocked her head, handing Grace another oversize edition. "Are you really as shocked as you seem, Grace?"

"It's just that this all happened so fast. How well can you know each other?" *What do you know about him?* That was what she really wanted to ask.

"I know what I need to know," Monica said. "Calum makes me happy."

There didn't seem to be an answer to that. Grace was happy for her friend, of course, but she felt uneasy as well. Perhaps it was simply that Monica's rejection of her life—a life so similar to Grace's—forced Grace to examine her own situation.

After another two hours they had cleared—and searched—only a few feet of landing. The empty shelves towered above them while the walkway still appeared to be knee-deep in books. Not even the highest shelves had been ignored. It was as though Ram Singh had deliberately swept every book off the shelves. Was there a reason for that? Was it sheer destructiveness or had there been some method to this apparent madness? Did Ram Singh know something about where the cameos had been hidden?

No, more likely he had come across the stack of hollowed books while he was trashing the rest of the shop. The same thought would have occurred to him that occurred to Grace: the hollowed-out books would make a dandy hiding place. Probably this same thought would have occurred to Danny Delon, too, if he had come across the stack of hollow books, but there was no way of knowing if he had or had not.

How much time had Danny had before his killer found him? Was he aware that he was being pursued? Did he stash the cameos in the first available hiding place or had he opportunity to look around and find a suitable niche?

There seemed to be miles yet to cover when Grace excused herself and retired from the field to start dinner. By then the men had joined Monica on the landing and were helping her restock the shelves.

Peter Fox's kitchen was beginning to feel as familiar to her as her own, Grace realized as she browned garlic and crushed pepper in olive oil. She could hear Monica and Calum's laughter drifting along the hallway, followed by Peter's lazy voice. Feeling herself smiling, she shook her head. Yes, she was growing way too comfortable here.

She added anchovy fillets to the pan. She couldn't hope to compete with Peter's culinary feats, but she did have a trick or two up her sleeve, and Spaghetti Puttanesca was her secret weapon.

While the tomatoes simmered in their liquid, she settled on the sofa and pulled out a sheet of paper to jot down notes. Sometimes seeing a thing written out made more sense. Besides, she wanted to distance herself from Monica's well-meant but unsettling insinuations.

Chewing the end of her pen, Grace told herself that at least now they knew what the item was that they were looking for, so progress *had* been made. Even if it didn't feel like it.

So far they knew for sure that they had two buyers for Byron's gewgaws: Aeneas Sweet and Venetia Brougham. Could anyone else be involved? There was no way of knowing who Danny Delon might have contacted.

Allegra was involved, but she seemed to be working with her aunt. Grace wondered about that. The Hon. Al seemed so . . . inherently indifferent, it was hard to picture her aiding and abetting the lunatic fringe. Perhaps she had been drawn in because of Peter's connection?

Ferdy—er—Philip Sweet might also be involved, and he would make a great Least Likely Suspect, but it was obvious Sweet was keeping his nephew in the dark—and why feign otherwise? The animosity between Ferdy and his uncle made it highly unlikely they would partner in anything.

There were other players of course, but they seemed to be taking the role of henchmen. Mutt and Jeff were definitely in the employ of Lady Venetia.

Charlie and Sid were working for Aeneas Sweet; but this was according to Lady Vee, who might be mistaken. Charlie and Sid might be working for themselves.

Grace tapped the pen against her chin, thinking. But no, they had said something about "The Man." Grace wished she could remember exactly what had been said. So much had happened during the past week, her memories were no longer crisp. She should have written her thoughts down long ago, but she had not expected sleuthing to become a full-time occupation.

Could Charlie and Sid be planning to cut "The Man" out? Something they had said had given her that impression. If only she could remember their exact words.

Last but not least, there was also Ram Singh who was most certainly working for Aeneas Sweet.

That completed the cast of characters. Who, of that motley crew, was the someone who had tried to kill Peter? According to Lady Vee's henchmen it was Ram Singh. That would put Ram Singh and Mutt and Jeff all in Kentmere at the time Danny Delon had been murdered.

But Lady Vee had also accused Ram Singh of murdering Delon; he couldn't have if he had been in Kentmere.

Which meant that Sid and Charlie must have killed Danny Delon.

Except, Charlie had also been in Kentmere. Charlie

had said he had seen Grace giving Peter "the kiss of life." So that gave Charlie a sort of alibi, too.

Violence was certainly in Sid's repertoire, but judging by the farmhouse Grace had been dragged to, the plan had been to kidnap Peter, not kill him.

Who, then, had killed Danny Delon? It was hard to picture octogenarians racing around committing homicide with battle-axes, but perhaps that was ageism rather than logic. What was it Sherlock Holmes said about eliminating possibilities? *When you have eliminated the impossible, whatever remains, however improbable, must be the truth.*

Grace doodled on her notepad and contemplated the possible impossibles.

Could there be another buyer?

Both Sweet and Lady Vee seemed to regard each other as their sole threat. But could there be a third party unbeknownst to them?

Ferdy?

If they were on the trail of Lord Byron's long-lost oyster plates, Grace might buy it.

Allegra?

She was probably familiar with the history of Craddock House; she had grown up in this district. She might know about the secret passages. She was clearly in her aunt's confidence—what was to keep her from running her own side operation?

Grace stared into the curio table without registering its contents. All those little fascinating odds and ends of bygone eras. She nibbled on the end of the pen.

Charlie and Sid introduced a troubling element—a professional element. Ram Singh, Mutt and Jeff were clearly amateurs working for nuts. But Sid and Charlie were career criminals.

Could they be working for Allegra?

Peter had been convinced he wrestled with Sid at Penwith Hall. Of course, Peter could be *wrong*. It had been dark, after all—and Mutt and Jeff had been later proven to be on the premises. Or at least around the premises. On the other hand, Peter had made short work of Mutt and Jeff this afternoon.

The question remained: could Sid and Charlie be working for Allegra?

But no, because they had mentioned "The Man."

Not only that, even if it had been Sid and Charlie that Peter tangled with, someone had to have guided them through the secret passages at Penwith Hall. That *had* to indicate Sweet. Or Ferdy. But Ferdy would have to be a heck of an actor.

And what about the night Allegra had come snooping around the shop? What if she had been checking on her handiwork rather than Peter's love life? Was Allegra capable of murder?

Grace caught movement out of the corner of her eye. She turned toward the grandfather clock in Peter's living room. The door in the large wooden case was slowly opening. . . .

12

For a moment Grace wondered if the wind had— but no. There was no wind. Even as that thought formed and was instantly discarded, a huge, hairy hand pushed open the secret door of the clock.

Grace stood up, dropping pen and pad.

"Uh, Peter," she called. "You guys!" Due to the sudden lack of air in her lungs, it didn't come out as forcefully as she wished.

She could see the face of the man trying to wedge himself through the narrow opening of the clock case, and it was not reassuring. He looked like a pirate. Long, curly black hair, a dark hawkish face, and unbelievably, an eye patch. Her gasp sounded clearly in the silent room.

"Oh, hell," the intruder rasped, his scowling gaze falling upon Grace. And then, "Wait!"

Grace was already edging to the hall door and her

friends, who were maddeningly chattering away at the top of their lungs.

The man lunged out of the clock case and Grace bolted into the hall. The others broke off whatever they were doing and stared at her, as for a split second Grace mimed her plight. At last her paralyzed vocal chords recovered and she cried, "There's a man inside the flat!"

Monica and Calum gaped at her. Peter, who was on the ladder, leaped down as lightly as a cat and sprinted toward her.

Without pausing to ask questions, he went right past Grace, who followed him inside only to find the room . . . empty.

The secret door stood open and footsteps could be heard scuffling and scrambling down the stone steps of the passage.

"He's getting away," Grace exclaimed.

"What's going on? What's happening?" Monica and Calum joined them.

"Someone broke in," Grace tried to explain. And then, "You're not going down there after him?" This was directed to Peter's retreating back as he knelt and maneuvered his wide shoulders through the narrow doorway.

"Someone came in through your *clock?*" Monica was saying.

"A secret passage!" Calum sounded ecstatic.

Grace heard all this as a kind of background music. Her attention was pinned on Peter, and she very nearly grabbed his retreating boots to try and keep him from disappearing down the passage. "But we can head him off!" She ducked her head into the aperture and heard Peter's answer though it took her a moment to process it.

"There's an outside entrance."

An outside entrance?

"Is that really a secret passage?" Monica squatted down beside Grace. "Should we call the police?"

"No, no police."

"Here, let me through." Calum knelt down and Monica and Grace shifted out of the way. Calum tried to crawl through the opening, but his wide shoulders, wider even than Peter's, thwarted him.

Grace didn't wait to see whether he worked out the physical geometry or not. Scrambling to her feet, she flew downstairs, making for the stockroom with its entrance to the passageway.

This is reactive behavior, not proactive. Even as she hurried, she was lecturing herself, as though she stood before a roomful of freshman girls. *This is not the way to*—but here her critical mind balked, possibly unable to put a coherent spin on what was an utterly unreasonable situation.

Before she reached the door to the stockroom, Grace realized she might need a weapon of some kind—if her goal really was to keep the intruder from escaping out this part of the secret passage. She turned around and headed back for the stairs and the display of impressive weaponry hanging there.

She tried to grab a sword off the hooks, but discovered it was wired at the hilt. It took a few precious moments to work it loose.

"Grace, what in the world?" Monica was at the head of the stairs calling down to her. "What's the matter with you two? Why can't you call the police?"

"It's a long story."

"What?"

"No police!" Grace gasped out, freeing the sword at last. She sprinted on to the stockroom, the sword inconveniently banging into furniture and shelves as she went.

In the stockroom, Grace paused.

The secret door was still firmly in place. That was a good thing, she decided. That meant the intruder was still within the walls of Craddock House.

Come to think of it, *was* that a good thing?

After all, Peter was inside these walls, too.

Peter paused, listening.

In the darkness he could hear the intruder a flight or two below, breathing softly, and trying no doubt, to conceal that telltale sound. The man was likely disoriented. The passage was confusing, even when you knew where all the ways of egress lay.

For a moment the darkness seemed to press in on him. Reason struggled with panic. The dark was simply an absence of light; it had no texture, no weight. He could breathe as easily at night as in the daylight.

He hated these old passageways. They were useful,

of course, but the walls were so close, built to last for-ever of thick cold stone. You could yell your bloody head off inside here and no one would ever hear . . .

Impatiently, he shook off these thoughts. He couldn't afford to get careless. He had already been careless in trusting that no one else knew of the out-side entrance. Criminally careless. He must be getting old.

So which of them was it, skulking there in the shadows beneath him? Sid Hall or Charlie Ames? Or Mutt and Jeff? Was it only one of them or some combination? But Grace had said "a man," which seemed to indicate she hadn't recognized their in-truder. Was that because she hadn't seen him clearly or because she didn't know him? Was there another player? Were they about to meet "The Man?"

Peter heard the furtive scrape of shoe on stone at the bottom of this flight of stairs. That was good. That gave him something else to think about besides the narrow confines of the passageway. He could focus again.

The intruder was taking the turn toward the stock-room entrance. Peter was good at judging sounds in darkness. He could risk jumping the bloke, but caution stayed him. Sid or Charlie would be armed and Peter didn't want to risk a gunshot in these close quarters.

And then from above came the sound of charging rhinoceroses. Peter wheeled but the herd was upon him. He went down hard against the wall, but caught himself, twisting his knee in the process. The herd went on over the precipice. Only it turned out to be just one rhino, Monica's don, the bonnie Scotsman, taking a header down the staircase.

Peter's hand shot out, locking in Calum's thick sweater, yanking him back. Calum's roar cut off mid-bellow and he landed awkwardly on his hands and knees. Some colorful and erudite language followed in decibels that rang off the rock, but Peter didn't stay to listen. He could hear his quarry, the rasp of leather soles on stone, fast withdrawing.

As Peter vaulted over Calum's fallen form his knee twinged painfully, but he ignored it and sped on. He knew this passage well, but was careful even in his haste.

A flashlight flicked on ahead of him, a little circle of light bouncing down the stairs. The intruder was abandoning stealth for speed. The light searched out the treacherous accordion of steps winding down to the ground floor of Rogue's Gallery.

Peter's interest was piqued. Did the intruder know the trick to opening the secret door from the inside? Or had he taken this route by accident?

They were nearly to the bottom of the passage now. Peter slowed and then stopped, watching the circle of light slide along the walls of the hidden chamber. Yes, the other was searching for the catch. Peter could just make out the bulky form, blacker than the surrounding murk. A big man, tall and heavy.

The flashlight beam swung back his way, and Peter stepped aside lightly. But the other man had to sense Peter's presence as easily as Peter had felt his. The intruder moved more frantically in the gloom. Apparently he didn't know where the catch was, but he knew where it should be. Interesting . . .

Sure enough, a moment later the door to the stockroom slid open.

And there stood Grace, emblazoned in the outside light like some prim Valkyrie, sensible shoes planted firmly on the ground, a two-handed Viking sword upraised over her head.

"Oh no you don't," she said grimly. She made a motion like a housewife about to squash a bug with a broom. The weight of the sword nearly overbalanced her.

Peter wasn't surprised when the intruder turned to collide into him. Peter didn't like fighting, so he did his best to keep these kinds of encounters to a minimum. He used his right leg to sweep the other's own right leg out from under him, and at the same time Peter whammed the guy across the throat with his arm. The man went down like a shot bear, a snarling heavy thud.

The overhead light blazed on. Grace stood there with her hand on the switch, sword in hand.

Peter spared her a quick, "You couldn't find anything smaller?" The sword was nearly as tall as she. He dropped to his good knee and pulled the intruder's left arm back at a painful angle. "Stow it, mate." The intruder, who was dressed from head to toe in black leather, stopped flailing.

Grace stared down at the fallen man. "Who's he?"

The man lifted a pain-seamed face. It was not the most comely of faces at the best of times, but it was a face known to Peter.

"Meet Roy Blade, the village librarian," Peter said.

"Maybe we can strike a deal," Roy Blade was saying.

"I'm all ears." Peter sounded mildly interested.

They were gathered in the shop. Roy sat on the floor with his hands tied behind him. Monica and Grace were seated on a wrought-iron garden bench, like Victorian ladies enjoying the botanical gardens. The iron bench had survived the recent break-in without a scratch, which was more than one could say for Roy Blade. His good eye was puffy and his nose bore traces of its recent encounter with the stone floor of the passageway. Calum and Peter stood poised over him, prepared for action. And Grace didn't blame them. Even seated and battered, Blade made an imposing figure in his black leather and eye patch. When standing, he had to be well over six foot, taller even than Calum, and certainly broader.

"I'll be the first to admit things got out of hand," Blade added.

The thing that didn't fit was his surprisingly educated accent. "Barmy for Byron," Peter had said, referring to Blade a day or so ago (was it only the day before?). He sounded more like an Oxford don than Calum. Was he some sort of renegade scholar?

"That was your bike in the woods at Penwith Hall," Grace guessed.

The onyx-black eye turned her way. "That's right."

"But it wasn't you I tangled with," Peter said slowly.

"We've never tangled," Blade said. "Not until a few minutes ago and that was . . . er . . . unavoidable." His eye flicked back to Grace. "I was just doing a bit of surveillance that other time."

"And the day in these woods?"

Blade's face grew wary. "Which day in which woods?"

"Our woods. I mean, the Innisdale woods. I saw you watching the police," Grace said.

Blade shrugged. "Like I said, a bit of surveillance, that's all."

"How did you get in here?" Peter interrupted. "How did you find out about the outside entrance to the passageway?"

"I did my homework," Blade said. Something about the way he said it caused Grace to wonder what he was hiding. Probably a great deal. Blade added, unconvincingly, "A lot of local people know the history of this house. And I've access to certain resources through the library."

It made sense but somehow it didn't ring true, and if it didn't ring true, Grace surmised, it was because Blade was hiding something. Obviously he was hiding how he got the information about the secret passage. But this seemed puzzling because, all things being relative, this was a fairly innocuous piece of information. The fact that Blade was concealing his source meant that his source must be involved in the rest of this mess. And that he felt compelled to protect him. Or her.

"Anyway, look," Blade said, "What I'm trying to tell you is this is all one big misunderstanding. I was under a—er—misapprehension."

"Now this is interrresting," Calum put in. "And a coincidence, seeing that you have been apprrrrehended."

Blade, beginning to sweat in his black leather, said, "I'll tell you what I know, although it isn't much, if you'll let me go. See, I'm out of it now anyway."

"That you are, laddie."

Peter, eyes narrowed, said, "What misapprehension?"

"I thought you might be on to something that I might, well, might have an interest in. It was merely an academic interest, you understand."

"Like what?"

Uncomfortably, Blade said, "I thought there might be the possibility that you were on the trail of a lost manuscript. One of *his*."

"One of whose?" Monica questioned. She was asking Calum and of course he had no notion.

"Why should you think that?" Peter inquired.

Blade shrugged. "Word gets around."

"I think you'd better start at the beginning."

"That would be helpful," Monica chimed in.

Grace studied Blade. His hands, tied efficiently behind him, were big and nail bitten. The edges of inky and ornate tattoos peeped out from beneath his leather cuffs and scrolled across the back of his hands. No wedding ring. Did biker dudes wear wedding rings?

"Are you married?" she asked.

"Huh?" said Peter and Blade in unison.

"An interesting development," Monica remarked to no one.

"No," Blade said, and then intriguingly, blushed.

Noting this, Monica said to Grace, "I think you may be on to something."

Grace turned to Peter, "You and I were the only people who thought we might be looking for a manuscript rather than the . . . gewgaws. Everyone else involved knew what we were hunting for. Right?"

"Right."

"But you and I suggested to Lady Vee that we might be looking for a long-lost masterpiece."

Peter's gaze seemed to turn inward, rerunning some telling memory. His mouth quirked slightly. "I recall."

"And the first time I noticed Blade was after we went to Lady Vee's and suggested that we were looking for a manuscript."

"But Lady Vee knew what we were looking for, even before we did."

"Sure, but . . ." Grace hesitated, still working it out in her own head. "Suppose it was to her advantage to let someone else believe that a lost Byronic masterpiece was at stake."

"A lost Byronic masterpiece!" Monica and Calum echoed.

"It's a little more complicated than we led you to believe," Grace confessed to Monica. "I'll explain later." Calum's eyes were incandescent; Grace recognized the symptoms.

"You're on the wrong track," Blade said shortly. "I've barely ever spoken to the old bat. Certainly not about this."

"Not Lady Vee," Grace agreed, warming to her theory. "Allegra. Lady Vee would have told her niece everything we said, and Allegra must have thought the lure of a lost manuscript would be what she needed to recruit some help. They need help, that's for sure."

Blade folded his lips stubbornly but his face was very red.

Peter said wryly, "Al's been observing the Byron mania for enough years to know how to trigger it in one of the afflicted."

"You're daft," Blade said. "Leave her out of it."

"And Al's family has lived here for how many generations?" Grace added. "You said that a number of people were familiar with the stories about Craddock House."

Peter turned to Roy Blade. "How about it, Blade? What did she offer you?"

"Go to hell. I told you I'm out of it."

"Maybe. When did she bring you in on it?"

Blade didn't answer. Peter prodded, "Before or after Delon was murdered?"

Blade's mouth dropped, displaying white and amazingly beautiful teeth. "Who? What are you—I had nothing to do with murder! I'm not into wet work."

Grace felt the hair on the back of her neck rise at this ugly term. She could see the revulsion on Monica and Calum's faces, but Peter looked stone cold.

"No? What are you into?"

"I *told* you. A missing manuscript, well that would have been right up my lane, but this stuff. Jewels!" Blade snorted. "They're in over their heads, and that's what I plan on telling them." He lifted his arms. "Now either untie me or call the cops, because I'm tired of sitting on this bloody floor."

"Don't let him go," Calum cautioned. "I don't trust him."

"Listen, mate," Blade said to Peter, "you owe me. I'm the one who called the coppers when that bloody wog started trashing your pad."

"But you followed us to Penwith Hall," Grace objected.

"I drove down after the cops nicked Gunga Din. I know he's Sweet's man."

"Don't trust him," Calum repeated.

"I don't," said Peter, "but I tend to believe him, as far as his story goes." He spoke to Blade, "So if you're out of it, why were you skulking around here today?"

Blade said bitterly, "It wasn't until today that I found out what it was all about." His good eye rested on Grace for an instant. "I had my suspicions but then this afternoon I heard her explaining to the other bird about stolen jewels. I knew that was a crock, but there was enough truth in it to—"

"You were listening to us?" Grace exclaimed.

"My God, that's creepy," Monica said. She shivered.

A little maliciously, Blade said, "Too right I was. This place is riddled with peepholes and listening stations."

"I thought you said it was as safe as a fortress!" Grace accused Peter.

"It depends on the fortress," Blade said. "Maybe he meant one of those old Roman ruins."

"Do keep out of it," Peter said.

"It's a little late for that," Grace said.

Blade laughed.

"I can't believe you just let him go," Monica said for the third time.

They were having supper in Peter's kitchen. Though Grace's Spaghetti Puttanesca was on the blackened side, it was still edible, and the pasta was helped a good deal by several excellent bottles of red wine.

"We can't keep him prisoner." Peter said a little testily. "He told us what he knew, for what that's worth."

"The police could keep him prisoner; that's what they do," Monica pointed out.

Peter ignored her.

"Suppose he goes back to Allegra and Lady Vee?" Grace asked.

"We can only hope. What can he tell them except to confirm that we don't know where the stuff is either?"

"So we're ruling out this Allegra and her loony auntie, is that right?" This was Monica again. Over dinner Grace had filled in the parts of her story that she had left out before. While Monica had asked a number of questions and proposed countless theories, Calum had sat mostly in silence. Grace wondered if he suspected her and Peter of making the whole thing up—or perhaps of being genuinely demented.

"Although, it seems to me that this Allegra is your best candidate for murderess. She clearly knows all about the hidey holes and secret passages of this house, and she isn't above kidnapping and theft."

"She's not the type," Peter said slowly.

"Okay, I'm convinced," Grace said promptly as Monica groaned. The two women shook their heads at each other over the heartbreaking gullibility of the male of the species.

"The man's right," Calum suddenly came back to life. "From what I've heard, this Allegra exhibits none of the classic signs of the homicidal psyche."

"Which are?" Grace was curious.

"Don't ask," Monica told her. "According to Calum, I exhibit at least four of the classic signs."

Calum gave her an admonishing but indulgent glance. Grace felt a little twinge of envy. It would be lovely to be so *adored* by a man. Except for the times that it would be utterly inconvenient—which were probably frequent.

"The fact remains," Calum said, "since each and every one of these villains is convinced these artifacts are secreted here, one is forced to conclude that they must *be* here."

"That's not reasoning, that's peer pressure," Monica protested.

"Nonetheless, I think he's right," Peter said.

"I know what we're doing this evening," Grace informed Monica. "And it doesn't include looking at wedding pictures."

She was feeling less jolly about it after four hours of lugging stacks of books over to Peter who was scaling the ladder to restock the tallest shelves. The hall library was slowly resuming something like its old order, but it was time-consuming and increasingly hard on the lower back and knees. They had even quit discussing "the case." Bed began to sound like heaven. Balancing yet another armload of books, Grace thought longingly of stretching out on clean sheets and resting her weary head on a soft pillow. A look at Monica, who had been yawning for the last hour, confirmed her feeling that it was about time to call it a night. Her head was beginning to ache again. She remembered, a little bit aggrieved, that she had been knocked unconscious a mere twenty-four hours earlier, and that no one had seen fit to coddle her at all.

Peter was still doggedly shoving books back on

shelves, and Grace reflected that for him, tonight's labors had as much to do with reopening for business as quickly as possible, as treasure hunting.

She glanced at Calum. He was browsing the lower bookshelves, momentarily distracted by several gilt-stamped green book spines.

"I'm bushed," Monica announced, dropping down to sit cross-legged on the floor. "My back is killing me."

"Great gods, the tragedy of it!" roared Calum, scaring them all into momentary standstill. He turned to face them, a calf-bound book in hand. "I've searched my entire adult life for this collection, and now that I find it, a volume is missing."

"What collection, sweetheart?" Monica picked herself off the floor and joined him, staring down at the title he held.

"*Sherlock Holmes, The Complete Collection.*" Calum groaned it out as though he were lying spread-eagled on the rack. "Published between 1893 and 1930. It's the complete collection of all the Holmes stories in book form with the original illustrations." He held the book out toward Monica. "Look. *Adventures of Sherlock Holmes,* 1909." His accent sounded thicker with emotion.

"How do you know it's not complete? The volumes aren't labeled." Monica studied the bookshelf behind Calum.

"I know! I know everything about this collection. There are nine volumes in total, and there are only eight here. Eight! And six of them first editions." He gazed up at Peter who was frowning down from the ladder. "I tell you I'd pay anything for this set if it were complete!"

"It is complete," Peter said. "There are nine volumes."

Monica was counting. "Nope," she reported. "I count seven and then Calum's holding one. Eight."

"The ninth must have been put on the wrong shelf."

Calum turned eagerly back to the shelf. "Yes, perhaps that's it. Perhaps it's been misplaced." He and Monica began to scour the shelves.

Grace picked up the book, which Calum had set ever so carefully aside. She stared at the gilt-top edge, the half-calf front board. There was something awfully familiar about that book.

Feeling a sort of dreamlike detachment, she turned on heel and headed for Peter's living quarters. It seemed a mile across the expanse of polished wood floor and Oriental carpet. She knelt down beside the curio table.

There it was, sure enough. Lying between the child's silver spyglass and an old compass: one gilt-edged and somewhat battered book with a familiar silhouette on the front cover. She could just make out the title. *Study in Scarlet.*

Grace slid open the cabinet doors and reached in, feeling around the shells and toys. Her fingers grazed the smooth leather and anticipation feathered down her spine. Gently, she lifted the book out. It felt oddly light, and something slid inside it; she could feel the motion from outside the book board.

Swallowing hard, Grace opened the book to see . . . a fragile yellowed title page. It took her a moment to realize what must have happened, and she turned the first few pages. And there was the answer. Someone had carved out a big chunk of the center pages of the book so that a cavity was created. And in that cavity something sparkled. Grace's eyes focused on a little carved face peeking up at her. A white carved profile against a sardonyx background. Some venerable goddess. Artemis. Or Aphrodite. Or Athena.

Or . . . Astarte?

Grace reached for the piece with trembling fingers. The carved eye stared back, unmoved.

It made sense, she thought. Poor Danny, in fear of his life, panicking, had looked for some place to conceal the goods. He would have seen the hollowed books in the hall outside, and with that memory in mind, he must have hit on the notion of creating his own hollowed book. What had he done with the pages he ripped out? Wedged them beneath the logs in the hearth perhaps? Flushed them down the toilet? Tossed them out the back window?

Wedged beneath the first oval was another cameo, a bit larger. Framed in silver, a famous intaglio profile rose out of a deep blue backing. Grace took it out and reached for the next. One by one, she picked them out of their hiding place.

Then, unbelieving, she examined the row of carved faces lined on the table top: ten exquisite antique cameos of various shapes and sizes and colors. Lord George Gordon Noel Byron's final birthday gift to a ten-year-old girl named Medora Leigh. His daughter.

13

"*I* understand about *them*," Peter said, pointing to Grace and Monica. "What's your excuse?"

Calum looked up from the tray of cameos and waved a ham-sized hand. "Och, you've no sense of adventure."

"I love it when he says 'Och,' " Monica said. "Are there any more of these raspberry tarts?"

It was late. Very late now, and the evening had moved off to a surreal distance from Grace. The initial jubilation over her find had now died down to what felt more and more like nervous babble—or maybe Grace was projecting. She sort of wished everyone would stop talking at once and that she could be alone with Peter to . . . well, just be alone with Peter.

She turned to look at Peter. He looked as tired as

she felt. His eyes met hers briefly and she felt warmed. *We did it,* she thought. Or sort of, anyway. Now that they had found the loot, what exactly did they do with it? That had been the topic of conversation for the past thirty minutes.

"It's very simple," said Calum. "We'll do a . . . a sting."

This snapped Grace out of her lethargy. She protested, "But that never works. Not even in books!"

"Och, sting's the wrong word. We'll set them up. Something simple. We'll contact this Sweet, tell him we have the cameos and are ready to strike a bargain. Then we'll tape-record him confessing to the murder of . . . what was his name?"

"Danny Delon," reluctantly supplied Grace.

"Delon," mused Monica. "Now why does that name sound familiar?"

Peter stared at the professor for a long moment.

"And suppose he doesn't confess?"

"But he will! That's the psychology of the murderer. They can't help themselves. They want to talk."

Peter's brows drew together. He said testily, "Sweet is an elderly man in poor health. It's highly unlikely he killed anyone."

"That could be an act," Monica pointed out.

Peter seemed to struggle to find a civil response. As none was forthcoming, he didn't answer, though Monica waited politely for his reply.

Calum waved this exchange away, "Not the man himself, then, but his hired thugs. It's the same thing for our purposes. We merely need the confession—or his accusation of these others."

To cut off what she felt sure would be a sarcastic comment, Grace interjected, "We shouldn't risk the cameos. They should be in a museum. If anything happened to them—" She stared at Peter.

Gazing down at the ten exquisite pieces on the table before them, she wondered why she didn't consider Peter, given his larcenous history, as one of the threats to the cameos. She recalled the delicate way he had picked each one up in his slim fingers, a touch so light and caressing she had seemed to feel it in her bones even as she watched him. Both Monica and Calum had been afraid to touch the gems. Even Grace was hesitant to touch them again, as though they might disintegrate into mystery and legend. But they had looked right in Peter's hands; they had looked as though they belonged there.

Each cameo was unique and no doubt of significance to the man who had collected them. Besides the cameos of Byron and Astarte, there was a child's profile on coral, a relief of the Three Muses on green jasper, a lyre, a Greek warrior, a young girl writing, a dog, another unknown young woman, and another image of Byron.

Would the child Medora Leigh have understood the message of these silent stones? Could anyone now?

"Grace is right," Monica said, smothering a yawn that seemed to have taken her by surprise. "The cameos are irreplaceable. And after all, we don't need them. It's enough to say we have them."

Not need them? Grace wondered at that. Of course they must go to a museum, they must go into safekeeping where they could be preserved so that others might enjoy them, too, but it would be wonderful to keep them for a while, to study them. To copy them perhaps? She reached for her teacup, although it would take more than caffeine to keep her from sleep for much longer.

"Now there you're wrong," Calum said. "Of course we must bring them with us. Sweet will ask to see them first thing. And when he has them in his hands, that's when he'll forget to guard his tongue."

"I suppose this is more of the psychology of the criminal?" Peter asked skeptically. "Is this the kind of thing you write?"

"Och no!"

"Calum writes hardboiled detective fiction," Monica said proudly, waking up a little. He's the creator of the Mikey Tong series."

"I thought he was an Oxford fellow?"

"That's just his day job. The reading public here is slow to catch on. But Calum's series is hugely popular in Canada."

"Canada?"

Monica enthused, "Mikey Tong is an Asian-American PI. The series is set in the 1930s. It's like Charlie Chan with ba—"

Peter swallowed his tea the wrong way and went

into a coughing fit. Calum slammed him on the back a couple of times.

"He's very sensitive, isn't he?" Monica whispered to Grace. "It really is a different culture."

"I need sleep," Grace said to no one in particular. "I'm starting to hallucinate."

When Peter could breathe again he said hoarsely, "We all need sleep. We can't do anything more tonight."

"Nonsense!" Calum said. "We can't afford to lose any more time. Who knows what these rotters might be plotting right now?" The destruction of the Sherlock Holmes volume seemed to have affected him more strongly than the recounting of all Grace's perils.

"Calm yourself," Peter drawled. "I'm not going to be rushed into acting before I have a plan." He and Calum sized each other up with equal parts annoyance.

"Calum, we all need sleep," Monica put in. "Grace looks half dead."

"Too kind," murmured Grace.

Monica coaxed Calum to his feet. "How far back is it to the village?" she asked.

"You won't be able to find rooms at this hour." Peter seemed to be sizing them up, perhaps considering their fitness to drive. "Look, you can stay here tonight," he finally said grudgingly. "The chesterfield makes into a bed. We've extra bedding."

This unexpected hospitality surprised Grace. She

cornered Peter when he went to get the bed linens, while Monica and Calum were busy clearing away the remains of their midnight supper.

The scent of crisp linen and dried lavender nearly made her swoon with exhaustion as Peter pulled out immaculate folded sheets. "What's up?" she whispered.

Peter gave her a crooked grin, albeit a weary one. "Safety in numbers?"

She studied him. "Seriously? Or is it that you think they might be a target?"

Evasively, Peter said, "Let's just say I prefer to be able to keep an eye on them." He kissed the bridge of her nose lightly. "Sweet dreams."

Grace had no idea whether her dreams were sweet or not, she was out as soon as her head hit the pillow, sinking into a deep, goose-down darkness that seemed to dissolve into bright sunshine about five minutes later.

"Rise and shine!" Monica's voice fluted. "The game's afoot."

Grace rolled over and scowled at Monica in the bedroom doorway. "Aren't you supposed to be on your honeymoon or something?"

Dressed in jeans and a Fair Isle sweater, Monica chuckled. "Why do you think I'm in such a hurry to get this thing cleared up? Come on, the boys are having a council of war. There's a pot of hot coffee with your name on it."

A quick shower later, Grace took her place at the

kitchen table. Her partners in crime had apparently been up for a couple of hours. The sofa bed had been stowed away and the others were finishing up what looked to have been a traditional California breakfast: spinach and mushroom omelets, wheat toast and coffee. Grace detected Monica's expert hand.

"We saved you some," Monica assured Grace, handing a plate off the back of the stove to Peter.

Peter handed Grace her plate. "Sleep well?" His eyes held hers for just an instant longer than strict courtesy demanded.

"Like the dead." She settled down beside him, their knees companionably bumping. Inwardly, Grace shook her head at herself. Talk about behaving like a schoolgirl! She reached for her coffee cup.

"Yikes," said Monica. "I'm not crazy about your choice of words. Especially when you learn what these two have cooked up."

"These two?" Peter sounded supercilious. "I'm merely humoring Calum by hearing him out."

Calum frowned. He was not used to having his plans "gang aft a-gley." "You've a better plan, I suppose?"

"No." Peter sounded untroubled. "And, in your favor, there is the fact that we can't take the cameos to the authorities without putting ourselves in jeopardy."

"Now that's intriguing," Monica remarked.

"Peter is . . . known to the police," Grace confessed. "That's why they suspect him of killing Danny Delon."

The newlyweds stared at him with renewed interest. Peter raised his teacup in a little toast.

"Wow." Monica said.

"Nothing was ever proven in this country," Grace defended.

"Oh dear. So, like, how much more of the entire story are you concealing from us?"

"That's pretty much it," Grace said. "Sorry. It's just kind of awkward."

"Uh, *ye-ah*," Monica said, slipping unconsciously into Valley Girl Speak.

"Murder?" Calum inquired gravely of Peter.

"Theft. Stealing jewels. Diamonds mostly."

Calum's hazel eyes lit. "You could be of grrreat help to me in my research."

"That's a comfort."

"Well, you're straight now. What's the problem?"

"The coppers don't believe I'm straight." He handed Grace the pot of crab apple jam.

Grace chimed in, "The local police received an anonymous phone call telling them Peter was involved in Danny Delon's death. They've questioned him twice. If we show up with these cameos they'll be sure he's guilty."

"I don't know that that follows," Monica objected.

"It's not something I want to take a chance on," Peter told her.

"That's why we need a confession," Calum said triumphantly. "It's the only way to clear Pete's name."

"It's too dangerous. For Peter, I mean," Grace

protested. She heard herself and reddened. She sounded like his mother. A sideways glance showed Peter silently laughing at her. It was funny that she already knew him well enough to know when he was laughing inside.

Calum nearly knocked the toast rack over in his enthusiasm. "But it's not! This Ali Baba or whatever his name is, is locked up. The other two are on the run. We can handle one old drunken sot."

"But you're just assuming that Aeneas Sweet is behind it all. After all, it could be Lady Vee. It could be—"

"It could be that Hell's Angel librarian," Monica agreed. "That guy gives me the willies."

"The—?" Calum looked highly amused and for a wee moment distracted. Monica giggled and the two of them kissed over the creamer.

"Actually, I think Blade belongs to Satan's Slaves," Peter's eyes met Grace's. He made an exaggerated V of his eyebrows at Calum and Monica's breakfast smooch, and Grace had to bite back a laugh. "I think we can rule him out."

"*Why?*" That was Monica, unembarrassed and focused once more.

"Because his story makes sense. It matches up with what we already know. "Lady Vee isn't physically capable of killing someone with an ax and Al isn't the type. They aren't murderers. Or murderesses."

"That's what everyone always says about murderers," Monica said exasperatedly. " 'He was such a sweet man!' How many times have you heard that one?"

"It's the psychology, dearrr heart," Calum told her. "The psychology is wrong. Now here's what we do. We call up this Sweet—"

Grace interrupted, "Who says Sweet even has a phone? We never saw one."

"He has a phone," Peter said. "He called twice while you were being held by Lady Vee. He wanted to make a deal."

"But he knew we didn't have the cameos."

Peter's smile was wry. "But we did have them, and it appears that Sweet knew it."

Grace absorbed this silently.

"Ladies and gentlemen, it appears we have lift off." Monica popped the last bite of toast into her mouth.

"What do you think this collection is worth?" Grace nodded at the metal briefcase on the floor of the Rover. It felt heavy against the toe of her boot.

"It's priceless." Peter sounded grim. "The Astarte piece is probably tenth century. The Byron likeness alone . . ." He didn't finish it. He didn't have to.

Grace stared out the windshield. The moonlit road scrolling before them was colorless as parchment, the twisted shadows cast by the tall trees seemed to manifest themselves in mysterious Greek letters. Once more they were en route to Penwith Hall.

"Do you know what Byron's last words were? Before he slipped into that final coma."

"I've had better days?"

She bit her lip. "No. He said, 'Now I shall go to sleep.' "

"Seems a little anticlimactic."

"He'd gone riding in the rain, taken a chill and fallen into a fever. The doctors had bled him till, and I quote, 'His blood ran clear.' They literally drained the life out of him."

"You're starting to depress me," Peter said. "Do you know what Oscar Wilde's famous last words were?"

"No."

"Either this wallpaper goes, or I do."

Grace chuckled, surprising herself.

Monica and Calum had taken the "back road." Grace still hadn't worked out exactly why. Calum had mumbled something about the element of surprise. The plan, such as it was, was that they would all meet up at Penwith Hall before the witching hour.

She didn't like the idea of a midnight rendezvous, but it had taken half the day to get in touch with Aeneas Sweet, and once they had reached him he had insisted that they connect that very day. Now there was nothing left to do but ride it out to the end.

She stretched her legs, she had been sitting a long time, and her foot once more nudged the metal case. Along with the boots, Grace wore black jeans and one of Peter's black turtlenecks; he seemed to have an unlimited supply—perhaps left over from his former career. He, too, wore black jeans and black turtleneck.

"What the well-dressed commandos are wearing this season," Grace joked, plucking at the material of her shirt and glancing his way.

"We could use a couple of commandos," Peter replied, shifting gears as the road wound through the trees.

"Well, we have Monica and Calum." At least they would, if Monica and Calum didn't get sidetracked along the way. They seemed easily distracted. Especially by each other.

Peter retorted, "Exactly. We could use commandos to protect us from Monica and Calum."

She said slowly, "Do you not trust them?"

Peter said grandly, "I suspect everyone. And no one."

Grace chuckled. "Oh Monica's all right. *He's* not what I expected. Especially when you figure Monica's period is the Victorians. Robert Browning was always her ideal man."

"And instead she married the nutty professor?"

Grace chuckled but Monica's emotional detour did bother her on some (granted) irrational level. The changes Monica had made in her life and her future meant changes in Grace's own life. She would miss Monica when she returned to St. Anne's without her. Tom and Chaz would miss her, too. Tuesday night bridge would never be the same.

"I've been thinking about the cameos," she said, to distract herself from that line of thought. "I think each one was intended to represent something significant to Byron. Even the dog. Byron loved animals, especially dogs. He built a monument to his favorite dog, Boatswain, on the grounds of Newstead Abbey."

"You think the cameos would have been his tacit acknowledgment that Medora was his daughter?"

"I don't know. He never singled her out in any other way, never showed her any special attention, but if you take into account what each of those cameos seems to represent individually, especially the Astarte one, and then put them all together . . ."

"Not so tacit an acknowledgment after all," Peter concurred.

"Those cameos are as irreplaceable for what they symbolize—for what they represent to Byronic scholars—as they are in intrinsic value," Grace said.

Peter's eyes left the road and met hers for a long moment.

It was quite late by the time they reached the Penwith estate. Peter parked in the woods and cut the car engine. They could see lights from the tower rooms winking through the trees.

Peter glanced at his watch. "Right on schedule."

"Should we wait for Monica and Calum?" Grace shivered. It wasn't that cold in the Rover, so it had to be nerves catching up with her. The night was alive with the sound of crickets, the whisper of leaves.

Normal friendly sounds that somehow emphasized how alone they were.

"Look to your left."

She looked. Several yards away, deep within a stand of trees, a car's headlights flashed once, twice, and then all was black.

"Do you think it's a trap?" Grace whispered as Peter reached for his door handle. He paused.

"Gee, a midnight meeting in a tomb in the middle of the woods? I don't know," he whispered back. For some reason his smart-aleck response cheered her up.

Together they walked across the cleared area to the blue Mustang parked in the trees. Monica and Calum were waiting beside their car.

Monica gave Grace the thumbs-up. Calum offered Peter a drink from his flask, which Peter declined. Monica took a swallow instead. It didn't appear to be the first time the flask had made the go-round. Grace could feel Peter's exasperation, but he controlled it as he reminded everyone of his and her various roles in "The Plan."

Grace thought that "plan" was an exaggeration, but they had come too far to turn back now.

At the appointed hour they separated once more, Monica and Calum tip-toeing off amid the crunch of autumn leaves.

Peter sighed and then glanced down at Grace.

"Ready?"

"As I'll ever be."

He hesitated. Grace put a hand on his arm. "I know," she said.

His smile in the starlight seemed twisted. "Then you're way ahead of me, Esmerelda. I've no idea what I'd say to you even if we had time to say it. Just keep your head down, will you?"

"I've had a lifetime of practice."

In white relief above the square entrance, Grecian women wept into hankies. At least they looked like hankies. Grace supposed the ancients had another word for them.

She glanced at Peter, wondering if he would have trouble entering the confines of the crypt. She remembered his reluctance the morning of their first visit to Penwith Hall. He looked cool enough now, though stern. Meeting her gaze he gave her a crooked grin.

"Scared?"

Grace shrugged. "I'm getting used to it."

"One way or another it will all be over tonight."

"That's not as reassuring as you may think." Her eyes scanned the darkness looking for a sign that Calum and Monica were providing backup as planned.

Ahead of them, the door to the crypt stood open. Open but not inviting. There was no light inside, no sound of voices or movement. Could they be first to arrive?

"Ladies first," Peter said.

"Very funny."

He slipped through the black mouth and Grace followed cautiously. Inside it smelled of cold and damp, old moldering leaves and something sharp and metallic that raised the hair on the back of Grace's neck.

Peter's flashlight beam played over cobwebs and stone sarcophagi, lighting at last on a body lying facedown in a pool of blood.

Grace sucked in her breath to scream. Peter's stillness, his lack of surprise, held her silent.

"It's Aeneas Sweet," she breathed at last, taking in the disheveled mane of white hair, the giant frame now soft and boneless.

Peter knelt, rolling Aeneas over onto his back. His head lolled. Grace closed her eyes.

"Bugger all," she heard Peter mutter.

That was all the confirmation she needed. She moved, backing toward the door.

"Not so fast," a familiar voice said. A hard hand in the middle of her back shoved her forward. "You've got something that belongs to us."

As Grace stumbled forward, Peter steadied her.

"Well, well," Sid said, stepping into the spotlight of Peter's torch. "The gang's all here." Grace could only see the round black eye of the gun barrel staring at her in the flashlight's glare. To Charlie, hovering behind him, Sid ordered, "See if they're carrying."

"Carrying?" Grace glimpsed Peter's grim profile.

"Packing. Armed."

Charlie, his face just as dour without the dog mask, moved toward Peter.

"That'll do, laddie!" Calum's voice came sharply. He filled the doorway behind Sid, his genial face looking surprisingly tough. Grace went weak with relief. "Get their weapons," Calum instructed Monica.

"Don't step in front of the gun," Peter warned as Monica squeezed between Calum and the door frame.

"What? Oh." Monica edged over to Grace. "Do you believe this?" she said under her voice, and then gingerly took Sid's gun from his unresisting hand. Both Sid and Charlie seemed dumbfounded at this turn of events.

A new voice cried shrilly, "Cancel that! Cancel that, I say!"

It should have been funny. There was a kind of surreptitious exchange of group glances. Otherwise, no one moved, although there was motion behind Calum's bulk.

"Drop that gun. Put your hands up!" The voice persisted.

Calum started and dropped the gun. His hands went up.

I know that voice, Grace thought, but it seemed too farcical to be true.

"Get in there!"

Calum crowded into the room, past Sid. Ferdy

wriggled through the doorway and squinted into the flashlight's rays. He pointed his gun at the light. "Lower it."

The flashlight beam dropped down. Tonight's bow tie was black. It seemed appropriate, coordinating as it did with the funereal gleam of the small gun Sweet's nephew held.

In books and movies bad guys whip out guns and good guys unhesitatingly tackle them. In real life it wasn't like that. Everyone had gone stiffer than the wall frescoes. It was so quiet they could hear the crickets outside. Aeneas Sweet's body was a vivid illustration of what guns could do.

"And just who the hell are you?" Calum demanded, as Sid plucked his gun out of Monica's grasp.

Ferdy's gun swung toward Calum.

"Easy," Peter said. "Let's think this through."

The gun veered back to Peter. "I've thought it through," Ferdy said. His voice wavered. "You came here to rob my uncle. The old fool struggled with you and you shot him."

He didn't look dangerous, Grace thought numbly. Even now he seemed more like someone out of a Wodehouse novel than Raymond Chandler. An evil Bertie Wooster? And yet, as innocuous as Ferdy appeared, something mean and cornered in his eyes did not bode well for them.

Peter still reasoned with him in that calm, slightly ironic tone. "In the family crypt?"

"Why not?"

"It's a bit unlikely, don't you think?"

Ferdy waved the gun impatiently and his accomplices, eyes on the barrel, shifted uneasily. "We'll clean this up and move him into the house naturally."

Peter's eyes never left the gun. "And what about the other four bodies? How do you plan on hiding a massacre?"

"Shut up!"

"Actually, I'd rather discuss it now, while I'm still breathing."

Ferdy looked to his henchmen for guidance. Sid said staunchly, "What's the problem? We'll leave 'em here in the crypt and lock the door. No one comes here, right? None of the regulars is going to object, eh? They could be here for years and who's the wiser?"

"Are you crazy?" demanded Monica. Perhaps it was rhetorical; no one answered her.

Grace, shaking off the horror that had gripped her from the moment she had spotted Sweet's body, spoke at last.

"So it's all about money? You killed him for money?" Her voice cracked.

Ferdy snapped back, "What else would it be? Who the hell cares about bloody Byron or his buttons? I've got a Japanese buyer who can pay three million pounds for these trinkets." Ferdy nodded at the metal case Peter held.

"He's daft," Peter said to Sid. "You know how it works."

"Sure, I know," Sid drawled. The look he cast Ferdy did not promise a long working relationship.

Ferdy burst out, "For *years* I've listened to this . . . *twaddle!* Byron's lost manuscript, Byron's jewels, Byron's—"

"*Manuscript?*" Grace, Monica and Calum echoed.

"Oh for Christ's sake!" Ferdy fired at the ceiling. Something whined past Grace's ear and, beside her, Charlie keeled over.

One glance at his face told her all she needed to know. One glance was all she had time for. Monica screamed, her voice joining the reverberations of the bullet, rolling around the stone confines of the tomb. Peter swung the metal briefcase and clobbered Sid, who crashed into Ferdy. They went down like dominoes.

"Go!" Peter pushed Grace out the door.

"But—"

"Run!"

She ran. Her feet pounded across the wet grass. A glance over her shoulder showed a light flitting like a firefly in the crypt. The sound of pandemonium echoed through the woods. More shots rang out.

Oh God, Grace prayed. *Please don't let anyone else be killed.*

She faced forward in time to avoid plowing into a tree. She had no idea where she was going—or what she would do when she got there.

She thought she was headed in the right direction, but before long she slowed, then stopped. She was lost. She had no idea where the cars were. And Peter still had the keys.

Intently, she listened to the night sounds. To her left she could see the tower lights still flickering through the trees. She could try to call the police from the Hall, perhaps. She didn't have many options at this point.

Then she heard it.

Something—someone—was moving toward her. Grace recognized the crackle of leaves, the snap of twigs. She turned and banged into another body.

Hands fastened on her shoulders.

"Where are they?" Ferdy shrieked into her face. In the glimmering light his face looked pale and inhuman. His breath was hot on her skin.

"In the case!" Uselessly, she tried to twist away.

"They're not! I looked!"

Where was Peter? Where were Calum and Monica? What had those other shots meant? How had Ferdy had time to check the case?

"I dropped them!" Even as she said it, Grace realized she should never have admitted to carrying the cameos, but reason didn't seem to be something Ferdy would listen to.

"Where?" Ferdy's fingers bit into her shoulder muscles. He was stronger than he looked. "Show me."

"I don't know where. Back there. They're gone, that's all!" But she was stumbling forward, urged on by Ferdy's grip. He was a small man, but he was enraged and scared and apparently believed he had nothing to lose. All in all, a bad combination— made worse by the gun he was jamming in her side.

"Where's Peter?" she asked dully. She was afraid to ask.

"Sid's taking care of Mr. Fox," Ferdy said, his breath coming in little gasps that sounded close to childish sobs. Apparently he was in worse physical shape than she was. Or a lot more upset.

"Did you kill Danny Delon?" In books they always kept the murderer talking to give the cavalry time to show up. Was any of the cavalry left in one piece? Grace had no idea.

"Who?" Ferdy's foot slipped on the grass and the gun jammed harder against Grace's side. She cringed away, terrified his finger would slip on the trigger. He kept his grip on her, using her to steady himself. "Oh, that creature. I spotted him for what he was when he came here to meet with the old man. It wasn't hard to figure out their stupid little scheme."

"What scheme? He was just going to buy the cameos from Danny Delon, wasn't he?"

"With *my* inheritance!" Ferdy's voice shook with outrage. "Do you know what it's been like watching him squander it all away, year after year? And he wouldn't have sold the bloody things. Oh no, he'd have locked them up in his cabinet to gloat over while the place fell to rack and ruin around him."

"So you killed him. And you killed Danny Delon."

Ferdy concentrated on his footing for a moment before saying off-handedly, "*That* was an accident. He should have just handed the damn things over to me. I explained the situation to him. Instead he tried to double-cross me. He went straight to Fox. I followed him. I watched him break in, and I followed him inside."

An accident? With a battle-ax? Who, besides Vikings, had accidents like that?

"Then why didn't you find the cameos? You knew about the secret passage." Grace's questions were motivated by genuine curiosity as much as the conviction that she needed to keep this unbalanced twerp talking.

"There wasn't time!" Ferdy sounded irate, whether from Grace's lack of understanding or the situation itself. "The phone kept ringing and then that stupid girl showed up. Alley Oop or whatever her name is. The old hag's niece. She kept snooping around, and cars kept driving past to see if the shop was open. It was *intolerable!*"

"So who wrote Astarte in . . ." Grace swallowed hard, "blood."

"Me, naturally." Ferdy was smug for a moment. "And a very nice touch it was, too. A nice little warning to hand over the jewels."

Except that no one had understood his message,

which is the downside of cryptic messages in blood. And also the downside of trying to deal with psychopaths.

"This is where they fell," Grace said, stopping in her tracks. She pretended to search the grass. "There! What's that shining by the tree root?"

Ferdy peered at the ground. Grace shoved against him with all her might, and he toppled forward, letting go of her.

She whirled and ran, zigzagging through the trees, boots stamping the damp earth. Every moment she expected to hear a shot ring out. Her legs were shaking, making it hard to run; her heart thundered against her ribs. She gulped the damp night air in great gusts that burned in her lungs.

Why didn't he shoot? Why didn't she hear him? Not that she could hear anything above the blood pounding in her temples. She ran on, narrowly avoiding tripping over a tree root. A low branch slapped her in the face.

Where was she? Where were the others?

And then abruptly, Grace knew where she was, pulling back in time to save herself from falling over the ledge above the sunken garden. She had managed to double back. That meant the crypt stood behind that copse of trees, and that Penwith Hall was only a few yards away if she could make it without bumping into Ferdy or his cohorts.

But that was what Ferdy and his pals would

expect her to do. They would be waiting for her to try to reach the Hall and its relative safety.

Grace paused at the head of the steps, panting. She remembered Peter clowning by the poolside just a few days before.

"In mossy skulls that nest and lie, ever singing, 'Die, oh! Die.' "

She pulled out the handkerchief in her jacket pocket. It chinked as she dropped it into the tall stone urn at the head of the stone staircase.

Softly she crept down the stairs into the overgrown garden. The brackish water lay like black oil in the shifting moonlight. The waist-high weeds swayed gently in the night breeze. They wouldn't look for her here; she could take a few minutes to catch her breath. She needed time to think, to figure out her next move. Peter, Monica, and Calum's lives might all be depending on her.

Sticking close to the long stone wall, Grace moved down the length of the garden. At the sound of a foot scraping the stairs above, she froze. She flattened herself against the rough surface.

She could see him, silhouetted against the moon. An incongruously sinister figure in a bow tie. Slowly, he came down the steps.

Grace held her breath.

She could see him scanning the bramble-choked yard. She knew the moment he spotted her, by the way his body relaxed.

"Come out, come out wherever you are."

Grace turned and ran for the pool. It was instinct, but it was not a good instinct. She splashed into the water, slipped on the slimy bottom and went down on her knees. It wasn't deep—certainly not deep enough to hide in—where had she got the idea it would be?

Ferdy laughed and pointed the gun at her.

"Get out. Now."

She crouched there a moment, shivering, trying to think. Nothing came immediately to mind.

Movement on the ledge above caught Grace's eye. A black figure launched itself from the precipice onto Ferdy who pitched from the stairs with a squeal and hit the ground like a thunderbolt had struck him.

Peter, landing on top, reached for the nearest weapon. It turned out to be the half-shattered stone head of the Grecian statue still resting beside the mossy pool. He brought it down hard on Ferdy's head and the other man went limp.

"I thought—I was afraid—I didn't know—" Grace heard herself and quit babbling. Bad enough to feel this way without dribbling it all over Peter Fox.

Peter got to his feet, breathing hard. He reached a hand down to Grace, drawing her out of the pool. She squelched onto the bank. Full circle, she thought.

"Why, it's the Lady of the Lake," said Peter.

• • •

Calum was sitting on the doorstep of the crypt. Monica hovered over him while above their heads, the ladies in the stone relief wept into their hankies. The big man was holding his head and keening—or swearing.

"He knocked himself out running into the marble cornice," Monica explained wryly.

"Ouch," Grace sympathized. There didn't seem to be much blood, though it was difficult to tell from the way Calum carried on.

"He's very upset at missing all the action."

"The bigger they are, the harder they fall," Peter remarked. He opened the ball of linen-wrapped cameos that they had retrieved from the stone urn. The stones twinkled in the moonlight like tiny fallen stars.

Staring up at them, Calum swore more loudly. "D'you mean to tell me she had them all the time?"

"A precaution," Grace said apologetically.

Peter handed the jewels her way with such alacrity that Grace wondered if he was tempted to keep them. He grinned a little, meeting her gaze.

"Wow," Monica said. "I don't know if I'm relieved you had them safe or hurt that you apparently didn't trust us."

"It was kind of a last-minute impulse," Grace explained.

"I know something about those."

Grace's eyes fell on Sid's sprawled form, which

was artistically draped at Calum's feet. "Is he . . . dead?" The Penwith estate seemed littered with dead or unconscious bodies.

"Not that I can tell," Monica said. She held up her cell phone. "The cops are on the way."

"That's the first time I recall thinking that was good news," Peter remarked.

Epilogue

*T*he sun was rising over the lush green hills, gilding the hanging apple boughs and vines in glancing golden light as the Land Rover pulled up before Craddock House.

Parking beneath the spreading hazel trees, Peter turned off the engine. He turned to Grace. He looked tired—and very dear to her. The bruise on his forehead was now turning woodland verdigris, there was a gleam of gold down on his cheekbone, and laugh lines fanned out from his impossibly blue eyes. Her gaze rested on the mocking tilt of his sensitive mouth. She would miss him. More than she had ever missed anyone in her life.

The last miles of their drive had passed in a silence more weary than companionable. There was so much she would have liked to say, but . . .

Instead Grace said, trying to postpone the inevitable, "Do you know that a fragment—fourteen stanzas—of 'Don Juan' was found in Byron's quarters in Missolonghi? They were published in 1903."

"Yes?"

"The story about the cameos was true. Maybe there *is* a missing manuscript?"

"I suppose it's possible." Peter glanced at Craddock House. He seemed to find something fascinating in the arrangement of its chimneys.

Silence. The surrounding woods were already turning autumn gold and brown. A few red leaves drifted gently down. One settled on the windshield.

"Well," Grace said brightly, "It was quite an adventure."

"Rather."

"What do you suppose will happen to the cameos once the police are finished with them?"

"A museum, I imagine. Although Byron's heirs might lay claim, I suppose." He didn't sound terribly interested in the fate of the cameos. Or in anything, really.

He glanced at his watch.

That was her cue. Grace reached for the door handle. "Oh. Well, I suppose I should be packing. I've got a plane to catch." She scooted over. "There shouldn't be any problem now in getting the consulate to re—"

Peter's hand prevented her exit. "About that plane," he said.

"Yes?" There was something in his eyes, something that gave her pause, that started her heart beating fast.

Peter cleared his throat. With unaccustomed diffidence he said, "Perhaps . . . we could talk about that over breakfast?"